Married by Christmas

featuring

New York Times bestselling author
DIANA PALMER,
Catherine George & Louise Allen

Praise for Diana Palmer:

"Nobody does it better."
—*New York Times* bestselling author Linda Howard

Praise for Catherine George:

"*The Millionaire's Convenient Bride* contains an
intriguing mystery that never interferes with the
developing relationship – which simmers with
restrained passion that eventually explodes."
—*Romantic Times BOOKreviews*

Praise for Louise Allen:

"Louise Allen is one of Mills & Boon Historical
romance's brightest stars… *The Viscount's Betrothal*
is sheer reading delight from beginning to end!
Witty, romantic and gripping!"
—*Cataromance*

Married by Christmas

NEW YORK TIMES BESTSELLING AUTHOR

DIANA PALMER

CATHERINE GEORGE
LOUISE ALLEN

Harlequin
Mills & Boon

First Published 2008
First Australian Paperback Edition 2008
ISBN 978 0 733 58967 6

MARRIED BY CHRISTMAS © 2008 by Harlequin Books S.A.

The publisher acknowledged the copyright holders of the individual works as follows:
SILENT NIGHT MAN © 2008 by Diana Palmer
CHRISTMAS REUNION © 2008 by Catherine George
A MISTLETOE MASQUERADE © 2008 by Louise Allen
Philippine Copyright 2008
Australian Copyright 2008
New Zealand Copyright 2008

Published by
Harlequin Mills & Boon®
Level 5
15 Help Street
CHATSWOOD NSW 2067
AUSTRALIA

® and ™ are trademarks owned by Harlequin Enterprises Limited or its corporate
affiliates and used by others under licence. Trademarks marked with an ® are
registered in Australia and in other countries. Contact admin_legal@Harlequin.ca for
details.

Printed and bound in Australia by
McPherson's Printing Group

Silent Night Man
DIANA PALMER

Dear Reader,

When I was invited to contribute a story to The *Married by Christmas* collection, I was very thrilled and immediately thought of including a character from my Desire™ book, *The Iron Cowboy*. This was Tony Danzetta, better known as Tony the Dancer.

He is mysterious and he has a history with a young librarian who worshipped him, but a rival fed him lies about her and kept them apart. Now the rival, his best friend, is dead, and Tony blames Millie for his suicide. When Millie's life is threatened, it is up to Tony to keep her alive. But she 'hates' Tony and doesn't want to be around him.

I do love these warring backgrounds. They do make lovely romances, especially for Christmas, which is a time of setting aside differences and learning to get along.

I hope you enjoy *The Silent Night Man*. I did so enjoy writing it for you!

Love,

Diana Palmer

CHAPTER ONE

At the funeral home the friend of the deceased was a big, richly dressed man who looked like a professional wrestler. He was wearing expensive clothing and a cashmere coat. He had olive skin, black eyes and wavy black hair that he wore in a long ponytail. He stood over the casket without saying a word. He looked aloof. He looked dangerous. He hadn't spoken to anyone since he entered the building.

Tony Danzetta stared down at John Hamilton's casket with an expression like stone, although he was raging inside. It was hard to look at the remains of a man he'd known and loved since high school. His best friend was dead. Dead, because of a woman.

Tony's friend, Frank Mariott, had phoned him at the home of the man he was working for temporarily in Jacobsville, Texas. Tony had planned to stay around for a little longer, take a few weeks off from work before he went back to his real job. But the news about John had sent him rushing home to San Antonio.

Of the three of them, John had been the weak link. The other two were always forced to save him from himself. He fantasized about people and places that he considered were part of his life. Often the people were shocked to learn that he was telling his friends that he was on close terms with them.

Tony and Frank thought that John was harmless. He just wanted to be somebody. He was the son of people who worked for a local clothing manufacturing company. When the company moved outside the United States, they went to work at retail stores. Neither of them finished high school, and John often made up stories to tell classmates about his famous rich parents who had a yacht and their own airplane. Tony and Frank knew better, but they let him spin his yarns. They understood him.

But now John was dead, and that…woman was responsible! He could still see her face from the past, red with embarrassment when she'd asked him about one of their assignments at the adjunct college class they were both taking in criminal justice. That had been six years ago. She couldn't even talk to a man without stammering and shaking. Millie Evans had mousy-brown hair and green eyes. She wore glasses. She was thin and unremarkable. But Tony's adopted foster mother, who had been an archivist at the local library, was Millicent Evans's superior and she liked Millie. She was always talking about her to Tony, pushing her at him, right up until the day she died.

Tony couldn't have told his foster mother, but he

knew too much about the girl to be interested in her. John had become fixated on her a couple of years ago and during one of Tony's rare visits home, had told him about her alter ego. In private, he said, Millie was hot. Give her a couple of beers and she'd do anything a man wanted her to do. That prim, nervous pose was just that—a pose. She wasn't shy and retiring. She was a party girl. She'd even done a threesome with him and their friend Frank, he'd told Tony in confidence. Don't mention that to Frank, though, he'd added, because Frank was still embarrassed about it.

What Tony had learned about Millie Evans had turned him right off her. Not that he'd found her attractive before that. She was another in a long line of dull, staid spinsters who'd do anything to get a man. Poor John. He'd felt sorry for his friend, because John was obsessed with Millicent Evans. To John, Millie was the queen of Sheba, the ultimate female. Sometimes she loved him, John moaned, but other times she treated him like a complete stranger. Other times, she complained that he was stalking her. Ridiculous, John had told Tony. As if he had to stalk her, when she was often waiting for him at his apartment, when he got off from work as a night watchman, wearing nothing at all!

John's description of the spinster was incomprehensible to Tony, who'd had beautiful, intelligent, wealthy women after him. He'd never had to chase a woman. Millicent Evans had no looks, no personality and she seemed rather dull witted. He never had been able to understand what John saw in her.

Now John was dead. Millicent Evans had driven him to suicide. Tony stared at the pale, lifeless face and rage built inside him. What sort of woman used a man like that, abused his love to the extent that she caused him to take his own life?

The funeral director had a phone call, which forced him to approach the silent man in the viewing room. He paused beside him. "Would you be Mr. Danzetta?" the man asked respectfully. The caller had identified him as tall and unconventional looking. That was an understatement. Up close, the man was enormous, and those black eyes cut like a diamond.

"I'm Tony Danzetta," he replied in a deep, gravelly voice.

"Your friend Mr. Mariott just phoned to tell us to expect you. He said you had a special request about the burial?"

"Yes," Tony told him. In his cashmere coat, that reached down to his ankles, he looked elegant. "I have two plots in a perpetual care cemetery just outside San Antonio, a short distance from where my foster mother is buried. I'd like you to put John in one of them." He was remembering a hill in Cherokee, North Carolina, where his mother was buried and a cemetery in Atlanta that held the remains of his father and his younger sister. He'd been in San Antonio since junior high school, with his foster mother. He described the plots, one of which he intended for John. "I have a plat of the location in my safe-deposit box. If I could drop it by in the morning?"

"Today would be better," the man replied apologetically. "We have to get our people to open the grave and prepare it for the service on the day after tomorrow, you understand."

He was juggling appointments, one of which was with his banker about a transfer of funds. But he smiled, as if it was of no consequence. He could get the plat out of the box while he was doing business at the bank. "No problem. I'll drop it by on my way to the hotel tonight."

"Thank you. That will save us a bit of bother."

Tony looked down at John. "You did a good job," he said quietly. "He looks…the way he used to look."

The man smiled broadly.

Tony looked at his watch. "I have to go. I'll be back when I've finished my business in town."

"Yes, sir."

"If Frank shows up before I get back, tell him that, will you? And tell him not to go out for food. I'll take him out to eat tonight."

"I will."

"Thanks."

The funeral director walked out of the viewing room, pausing to speak to someone. Tony, his eyes resting sadly on his friend's face, only half noticed the conversation.

He heard soft footsteps come toward the casket and pause beside him. He turned his head. And there she was. The culprit herself. She'd be twenty-six now, he judged, and she was no more attractive than she'd been all those years ago. She dressed better. She was wearing a neat gray suit with a pink blouse and a thick dark coat. Her dark brown hair was in a bun. She was wearing contacts in her green eyes, he imagined, because his foster mother had often mentioned how nearsighted she was. The lack of glasses didn't help her to look any prettier. She had a nice mouth and good skin, but she held no attraction for Tony. Especially after she'd been responsible for his best friend's death.

"I'm very sorry," she said quietly. She looked at John with no visible sign of emotion. "I never meant it to end like this."

"Didn't you?" He turned, his hands in the pockets of his coat, as he glared down at her with piercing dark eyes. "Teasing him for years, playing hard to get, then calling the police to have him arrested as a stalker? And you didn't mean it to end like this?"

She felt cold all over. She knew he'd worked in construction years ago, but there had been rumors about him since, whispers. Dark whispers. John had intimated that Tony was into illegal operations, that he'd killed men. Looking into his black eyes now, she could believe it. He wasn't the man she'd known. What had he said about her teasing John?

"Don't bother to lie," he said icily, cutting off her question even before it got out of her mouth. "John told me all about you."

Her eyebrows arched. What was there to tell, except

that his friend John had almost destroyed her life? She drew herself up straighter. "Yes, he was quite good at telling people about me," she began.

"I never could understand what he saw in you," he continued, his voice as pleasant as his eyes were homicidal. "You're nothing to look at. I wouldn't give you a second look if you were dripping diamonds."

That hurt. She tried not to let it show, but it did. God knew what John had told him.

"I…have to go," she stammered. She was no good at confrontations. This big man was looking for a fight. Millie had no weapons against him. Long ago, the spirit had been beaten out of her.

"What, no urge to linger and gloat over your triumph?" He laughed coldly. "The man is dead. You drove him to suicide!"

She turned, her heart breaking, and met the tall man's eyes. "You and Frank could never see it," she replied. "You wouldn't see it. Other men have infatuations. John had obsessions. He was arrested other times for stalking women—"

"I imagine you put the women up to reporting him," he interrupted. "John said you'd accuse him of stalking and then be waiting for him at his apartment, wearing no clothes at all."

She didn't seem surprised at the comment. He couldn't know that she was used to John's accusations. Much too used to them for comfort.

She moved one shoulder helplessly. "I tried to make

him get help. When I finally had him arrested, I spoke to the district attorney myself and requested that they give him a psychiatric evaluation. John refused it."

"Of course he refused it. There was nothing wrong with his mind!" he shot back. "Unless you could call being infatuated with you a psychiatric problem." He raised both eyebrows. "Hell, I'd call it one!"

"Call it whatever you like," she said wearily. She glanced once more at John and turned away from the casket.

"Don't bother coming to the funeral," he said coldly. "You won't be welcome."

"Don't worry, I hadn't planned to," she replied.

He took a quick step toward her, infuriated by her lukewarm attitude, his dark eyes blazing with fury.

She gasped, dropped her purse and jumped back away from him. Her face was white.

Surprised, he stopped in his tracks.

She bent and scrambled for her purse, turned and ran out of the room.

There were murmurs outside the room. He glanced back at John, torn between anger and grief. "God, I'm sorry," he said softly to his friend. "I'm so sorry!"

He forced himself to leave. The funeral director was standing at the front door, looking worried.

"The young lady was very upset," he said uneasily. "White as a sheet and crying."

"I'm sure she was grieving for John," Tony said nonchalantly. "They knew each other a long time."

"Oh. That would explain it, then."

Tony walked to his car and felt better. At least he'd dragged some emotion out of her on behalf of his friend. He got behind the wheel of his expensive sports car and revved it out of the funeral home parking lot, his mind already on his appointment with the bank.

Millie Evans sat at the wheel of her little black VW Beetle and watched Tony drive away, out of her life. She was still crying. His coldness, his fury, had hurt her. She'd had to deal with John's histrionics and threats for two years, watching her life and career go down the drain while he told lies about her to anyone gullible enough to listen. He'd persecuted her, tormented her, made a hell of her daily life. Now he was dead, and Tony wanted to make her pay for driving his poor, helpless friend to suicide.

She wiped at her eyes with a handkerchief. Poor friend, the devil! Perhaps if he and Frank had realized that John was mentally ill years ago, they might have made him get help. He might have straightened out his life and gone on.

Millie was secretly relieved that John hadn't carried out on his last, furious threat to end her life. He'd told her that she wouldn't get away with rejecting him. He had friends, he told her, who wouldn't hesitate to kill her for the right amount of money. He had savings, he'd raged; he'd use it all. He'd make sure she didn't live to gloat about pushing him out of her life!

She'd worried about that threat. The news was full

of people who'd gone off the deep end and killed others they blamed for their problems, before killing themselves. It was, sadly, a fact of modern life. But she'd never dreamed that she—plain, prim little Millie Evans—would ever have something like that happen to her. Most people never even noticed her.

She'd wanted to be noticed by Tony. She'd loved him forever, it seemed. While his foster mother was alive, she'd coaxed the older woman into talking about her adoptive son. Tony had come a long way from North Carolina. He and his sister, both Cherokee, had lived with their mother and her abusive husband—but not their biological father—in Atlanta just briefly, but the man drank to excess and was brutal to the children. Tony and his sister went into foster homes in Georgia. After his sister, also in foster care, died, Tony's nurturing foster mother moved him to San Antonio, where she had family, to get him away from the grief. She worked as an archivist at the public library in San Antonio, where Tony was a frequent patron; and where Millie worked after school and between classes while she went through college.

Millie had loved hearing stories of Tony as a boy, as a teenager, as a soldier. Sometimes his foster mother would bring letters to the library and show them to Millie, because they were like living history. Tony had a gift for putting episodes in his life down on paper. He made the countries where he was stationed come alive, and not only for his parent.

Millie had hoped that Tony might spend some time at the library when he came home on leave. But there were always pretty girls to take on dates. Frank Mariott worked as a bouncer in a nightclub and he knew cocktail waitresses and showgirls. He introduced them to Tony, who always had a night free for fun.

A library, Millie supposed, wasn't a good place to pick up girls. She looked in her rearview mirror and laughed. She saw a plain, sad-faced woman there, with no hopes of ever attracting a man who'd want to treasure her for the rest of her life. It was a good thing, she told herself, that she'd stockpiled so many romance novels to keep her nights occupied. If she couldn't experience love, at least she could read about it.

She wiped her eyes, closed up her purse and drove herself back to work. She'd forced herself to go and see John, out of guilt and shame. All she'd accomplished was to find a new enemy and hear more insults about herself. She knew that she'd never meet up with Tony again after this. Perhaps it was just as well. She'd spent enough time eating her heart out over a man who couldn't even see her.

Tony made his funds transfer, got the plat from the safe-deposit box, had the bank copy it for him and replaced the original before he went back to the funeral home.

All the way, in the back of his mind, he kept seeing the fear in Millie's face when he'd moved toward her.

That reaction was odd. She might have been surprised by the speed of his movement—a lot of people had been, over the years. But she'd expected him to hit her. It was in her eyes, her face, her whole posture. He wondered what had happened to her in the past that made her so afraid.

Then he chided himself for that ridiculous compassion, when she'd caused John's death. At least he'd made sure that she wouldn't come to the funeral. That would have been the last straw.

He pulled up at the funeral home and locked his car. It was getting colder. Strange weather, he thought. First it was like summer then, in a matter of days, winter arrived. It was normal weather for Texas in late November, he mused.

As he walked into the funeral home, he saw some of John's family gathered, talking among themselves. Frank spotted Tony and came out into the hall. They shook hands.

"I just have to drop this off," he told Frank, lifting up the copy of the plat. "Then we'll spend a minute talking to John's people before we go out to eat."

The funeral director spotted them and came forward. He took the copy of the plat, smiled at Frank and went back to his office.

"You may get a shock," Frank murmured as they walked into the viewing room.

"What do you mean?" Tony asked, surprised.

John didn't have much family. His parents were

long dead. He did have a sister, Ida. She was there, dry-eyed and irritable. She glanced at the doorway and put on a big smile.

"Tony! How nice to see you again!" She ran up to him and hugged him. "You look great!"

"Sorry we have to meet like this," Tony began.

"Yes, the idiot, what a stupid thing to do!" Ida muttered. "He had a life insurance policy worth fifty thousand dollars. I paid the premiums for him, me and Jack, and look what he does! Suicide! We won't get a penny!"

Tony looked as if he'd been hit in the eye.

"Oh, there's Merle. Sorry, honey, I have to talk to her about the flowers. She's giving me a good deal on a wreath…"

John's cousin Ben came forward to shake hands.

"What a mess," he told the two men. He shook his head. "I bailed him out of jail. He didn't exactly skip bond, but I'll forfeit what I put up," he added heavily. "Two thousand dollars," he grumbled. "He swore he'd pay me back." He wandered off, still shaking his head.

An elderly woman with dyed blond hair and wearing a hideous black dress, peered at Tony. She grinned up at him. "You must be that rich friend of Johnny's," she said. "He said you owned several islands out in the Atlantic and that you were going to give him one and a yacht, too, so he could get to and from this country."

"That's right, Blanche," Frank said, smiling. "Now, you'll have to excuse us, we've got an appointment. We'll see you at the funeral."

"I sure would like to see that yacht," Blanche added.

Frank took Tony by the arm and propelled him out into the lobby.

They were sitting in a good Italian restaurant fifteen minutes later, having given in their order.

"I can't believe it," Tony said furiously. "His own family! Not one of them seems to be sad that he's dead!"

"He was nothing but trouble to them," Frank replied. "He didn't work, you know," he added, shocking Tony, who'd already had a few shocks. "He told the government people that he had a bad back and he fed liquor to two vagrants who signed sworn statements that they'd seen the accident that crippled him. He convinced his doctor and got a statement from him, too, and talked a lawyer into getting him onto partial disability." He shook his head. "But it was barely enough to live on. He pestered his relatives for handouts. When he got arrested for stalking, this last time, he talked Ben into posting his bond. I warned Ben, but he said John had promised that his rich friend would pay Ben back."

"I've known John since high school," he told Frank. "You've known him since junior high. He was a good man."

Frank paused while the waiter served them appetizers and ice water.

"He changed," Frank said quietly. "More than you know. You only saw him on holidays, while your foster mother was still alive, and hardly at all in the past couple of years. I saw him constantly."

"You're trying to say something," Tony murmured, eyeing the other man.

Frank toyed with his salad. "He made friends with some members of a gang a few months ago," he said. "It really thrilled him, that he could kick around with people who weren't afraid of the law. He hated cops, you know," he added. "Ever since the arrest for stalking, when he went after—"

"Yes," Tony interrupted him. "That Millie creature!"

"Creature!" Frank sat back, shocked.

Tony was beginning to feel uncomfortable. "She caused John to kill himself, remember?"

"Who told you that?"

"John did. He sent me a letter. Left me a letter." He pulled it out of his pocket. It had arrived the day he got the news that John was dead, obviously having been mailed in advance of the suicide. "He said she tormented him…hell, read it for yourself." He pushed it across the table.

"I can imagine what's in it," Frank said. He ignored the letter and finished chewing a bite of salad. "He accused women of teasing him when they were only trying to get him to leave them alone. Millie was more kindhearted than most—she kept forgiving him. Then when she refused dates, he started telling tales on her to her co-workers." He glanced at Tony, sitting stiffly, still unbelieving. "You've seen Millie. Now, you tell me, does she really look like the sort of woman who'd lie in wait at John's apartment wearing a French maid's costume with a bottle of champagne in one hand and a champagne flute in the other?"

"It would be tough to imagine," Tony had to admit. "Still, mild-looking women have done crazier things."

"Yes, but Millie's not like that." Frank's face softened. "She sat with your foster mother when she was dying in the hospital, before you could get home. She was there every night after work."

"Sure, you'd defend her, when you did a threesome with her and John!" he snapped.

Frank gaped at him. "I beg your pardon?"

The other man's reaction made Tony even more uncomfortable. He fiddled with his water glass. "John told me about it."

"Oh, for God's sake!" Frank burst out. "I've never done a threesome in my life, much less with Millie!"

"Maybe he made a mistake with the name," Tony mumbled.

"Maybe he made a mistake telling you lies about me," Frank shot back. "I'd give anything to have Millie notice me! Don't you think I know how little I have to give to a woman with her brains? She has a degree in library science. I barely got out of high school. I'm a bouncer," he added heavily. "A nobody."

"Stop that!" Tony said immediately. "You're not just a bouncer. It's a rough job. It takes a hell of a man to do it."

"I'm sure there are guys in New York City who place

ads hoping to get hired as bouncers in bars," Frank said sarcastically. "Here in San Antonio, it's not exactly the dream job of most men."

"You're sweet on Millie Evans, so you're defending her."

"I'm sweet on her, all right. If the competition wasn't so stiff, I might even try my luck. That's what made John crazy. He couldn't stand the competition, either. He knew he'd never replace that other guy Millie's been in love with for six years."

"What other guy?" Tony asked carelessly.

"You."

It was as if time stopped and everything went around in slow motion. Tony put his fork down and looked across at Frank as if he'd gone mad. "Excuse me?"

"Do you think Millie needed courses in criminal justice to be a librarian?" Frank asked drolly. "She took those courses because your foster mother had told her you were taking them, in addition to your regular college classes, so you could get your degree faster. It was an excuse to be around you."

Now, horribly, it made sense. He hadn't even questioned her presence in the classes.

"Great," Tony muttered. "The murderer of my best friend thinks I'm hot!"

"She didn't kill him. But no jury would have convicted her if she had," Frank persisted. "He got her fired, Tony. He went to her boss and told her that Millie was hanging out in bars to have sex with men for an audience. He told that to three of the library's richest patrons, one of whom sat on the board of directors for the library. They demanded that she be fired."

Tony watched the other man warily. "And how do you know it wasn't true?"

"Because I went to a friend of mine at the local precinct and got John's rap sheet and showed it to them."

Tony was feeling ill. "Rap sheet? John had a rap sheet?"

"Yes. For fraud, defamation of character, petty theft, three charges of stalking and a half dozen other charges. I got a statement from the last woman he'd stalked, a receptionist for one of the dentists John went to. She swore in court that John had threatened her life. He convinced a lawyer that she was lying and produced a witness who heard her bragging that she'd get John arrested."

Tony waited for the rest.

"The gang members testified in his favor and got the case thrown out of court. A couple of weeks later, the receptionist was raped. Nobody was ever caught or charged."

Tony leaned forward. "Don't tell me John was mixed up in that!"

"He never admitted it," Frank replied heavily. "But I knew he was. A few months later, one of the gang members was pulled in on a rape charge and he bragged to the arresting officer that he could get away with it any time he liked. He had witnesses, he said. Turned out they were also members of his gang. Sadly for him, on the second rape case, the new gang member he bragged to was wearing a wire. He's doing hard time now."

"But John wasn't like that," Tony protested. "He was a good man!"

"He was sick," Frank said flatly. "He utterly destroyed Millie's life because she didn't want him. Even his relatives apologized to her for what he'd done. There are still people who go to that library who are convinced that Millie has orgies down in the basement, because John told them she did."

"I can't believe it," Tony said to himself.

"Obviously. You didn't know the adult John became. You still saw the kid who played sandlot baseball with you in ninth grade."

"He had a rap sheet. I never knew."

"He was a troubled man. There's something else, too. My friend at the precinct said that when they searched John's room, they found an open bank book on the coffee table. It showed a withdrawal of five thousand dollars in cash—John had apparently sold everything of value that he had. The pawn slips were there, too, neatly arranged. There was a note, addressed to Millie, with only a threat: 'You'll be sorry.' The police haven't told her yet, and they warned me not to say anything. But I'm afraid for her."

"What do you think John did with the money?" Tony asked.

"I don't know."

Tony was frowning. "Any of those gang members ever been suspected of murdering anybody?"

"Yes," came the curt reply. "John had a vindictive

nature. It wouldn't surprise me if he didn't put out a contract on Millie."

The John whom Tony knew as a teen wouldn't have been capable of such actions. The man he was only now coming to know might well have done it. He could hardly get his mind to function. He'd come home with clear-cut ideas of the good guy and the bad woman, and now his theories were worthless. He was remembering Millie's tragic expression when he accused her of murdering his friend. He was remembering, too, what Frank had just told him, that Millie had cared about him. It was a good bet that she didn't anymore, he thought cynically.

Frank checked his watch. "I have to get back to the funeral home. Millie said she was coming over to see John. I tried to talk her out of it, but she said that it was something she had to do, that she felt responsible. Even after all Tony had done to her, she still felt sorry for him."

Tony closed his eyes and groaned. He didn't know how to tell his friend that Millie had already come to see John, and that Tony had treated her like dirt and made her run out of the building in fear of him. It wasn't a revelation he was looking forward to.

CHAPTER TWO

FRANK actually winced when Tony told him how he'd treated Millie when he'd seen her at the funeral home earlier.

"Good God," Frank said heavily. "That poor woman. How could you, Tony?" he asked accusingly.

Tony grimaced. "I didn't know any better," he defended himself. "All I had to go on was the letter John sent me and the memory of those visits I made home, when he'd cry on my shoulder about how bad she was treating him. I was sure that she'd killed my friend with her heartless behavior."

Frank sighed heavily. "I wish she hadn't gone to the funeral home early."

"Yeah. Me, too," Tony replied. He was never going to be able to forget Millie's mad dash out the door. It would haunt him. "Look, that friend of yours at the precinct," he said. "Could you get him to ask around and see if there's any word on the street about a potential hit?"

"I could do that," Frank said, and brightened a little.

"Maybe John just left a lot of money to an animal shelter and made the threat to scare her," Tony said.

Frank gave him a sour look.

Tony held up both hands. "Sorry."

"It won't matter what he finds out," Frank said. "There's no budget for protective custody on supposition, no matter how educated. They won't be able to assign anybody to protect her."

"I'm off until the new year," Tony said. "I can handle that."

Frank blinked. "I'm sure she'll welcome having you around, after the warm reception you gave her at the funeral home."

Tony flinched. "Yeah. Well, I'll have to apologize, I suppose."

Frank didn't say anything to that. Privately he thought Tony was going to find it difficult to bend enough to convince Millie that he was sorry. His friend had spent most of his life in violent surroundings. His social skills were a bit rusty, especially around women like Millie. Tony's taste was the brassy, forward sort of females he could find in bars. Millie was both refined and reserved. It would be a tough combination to crack for a hard nut like Tony.

The next morning, a penitent Tony joined Frank at the funeral home for John's last rites. There was a very small group of people there, mostly family. A couple of rough-looking men were sitting in the back, looking around constantly. Tony wondered if they might be John's gang friends.

After the brief service, Tony drove Frank and himself to the cemetery for the graveside service. It was equally brief.

Tony noted that the rough-looking men had also come to the cemetery. One of them was intent on Tony and Frank, as if he found their presence suspicious.

"We're being watched," Tony told his friend as they walked back toward Tony's sports car.

"I noticed," Frank replied. Working as a bouncer had given him a sixth sense about trouble. Tony, in his line of work, also had developed it. They pretended to talk casually, without making it obvious that they saw the two men.

When they got to the car, and were seated and ready to travel, Tony looked in the rearview mirror and noted that one of the men was unobtrusively writing down his license plate number. He started laughing as he pulled the car around two of the family's vehicles and exited the cemetery road.

"What's funny?" Frank asked.

"They're cops," he said.

"What?"

"They're cops," Tony repeated. "Gang members wouldn't give a hoot in hell about my plate number. They want to know who I am, and what my connection is to John." He glanced at his friend. "How about asking your contact in the police department what they want to know about me? I'll phone him with the details."

Frank chuckled. "Fair enough. I'll call him when I get home."

Tony grinned. It amused him to be viewed with suspicion. He mostly was these days. He kept a low profile and never talked about his job.

He dropped Frank off at his apartment, and promised to meet him the following day for lunch. Then he went back to his hotel.

He noted that he was being followed again. He gave his car keys to the valet who handled the parking, walked into the lobby and slowed his pace as he went toward the elevator. He felt eyes on his back. Someone was following him. This was amusing.

He got into the elevator and pretended to be disinterested in his surroundings. A man whom he recognized as one of the two strangers at the funeral got in with him and stood apart, also pretending unconcern.

When Tony got off, on the wrong floor, he noted that the man remained behind but jotted down a number.

He took the staircase down, and was waiting in the lobby when the man following him got off the elevator. He looked up into Tony's black eyes and actually jumped.

Tony gave him a worldly look. "If you want to know who I am and why I went to John's funeral, come on in the bar and I'll buy you a drink and give you the lowdown."

The man raised his eyebrows, and then started laughing.

"How did you figure it out?" he asked, when they were seated at the bar.

"I've worked with cops before," Tony told him, "in between jobs overseas."

"What sort of jobs overseas?"

Tony chuckled, reached into his pocket for his wallet, flipped it open and displayed his credentials.

The man whistled softly. "I thought about going with them, once, but after six months of being called, inter-rogated, lie-detected, background-checked and other-wise investigated to death, I gave up and joined the police force. The pay's lousy, but I've only been involved in one shoot-out in ten years." He grinned. "I'll bet you can't say that."

"You'd be right," Tony had to admit. "I'm carrying enough lead in me to fill a revolver. They can't take some of the slugs out because of where they lodged."

"You knew the deceased, I gather."

He nodded. "He was my best friend since high school." He grimaced. "But it turns out I didn't know him at all. He was stalking a woman we both knew and I thought she was lying about it."

The man pulled out a notepad. "That would be Miss Millicent Evans."

"Yes."

"She wasn't lying," the police detective told him. "She called us in on a 10-16 domestic, physical," he added, using the ten code for a domestic disturbance call. "He'd knocked her around pretty badly."

Tony felt two inches high as he remembered Millie's unexpected reaction when he'd moved so abruptly in the funeral home. He couldn't speak.

"But when it was time to press charges, she wouldn't," the detective said flatly. "We were disappointed. We don't like women beaters. She said he was drinking heavily and had apologized, and it was the first time he'd hit her."

"Was it only the one time?" Tony had to know.

"I think so. She isn't the sort to take that kind of abuse on a routine basis. About a week later, he killed himself." He leaned closer. "We got word that a local gang boss took money to have her killed. That's why we were at the funeral. You got a friend named Frank?"

"Yes."

"He and my lieutenant are best friends," the man told him. "He's got us looking for people who might fit the description of a hit man."

Tony laughed. "And I fit the description."

"I've seen mob hit men who look just like you." He cocked his head. "You Italian?"

Tony grinned. "Cherokee," he said. "My mother's husband adopted me, but he wasn't my father."

"Goes to show," the detective said, "that you can't tell who people are by looking."

"Absolutely."

Tony went by the library the next morning, hoping to apologize to Millie and go from there. But the minute she spotted him in the lobby, she went through a door that had the sign Employees Only and vanished. He asked for her at the desk, as if he hadn't noticed. The clerk on duty went back through the door and reappeared a minute later, red faced and stuttering.

"I'm sorry, I…couldn't find her," she finished.

Tony smiled sadly. He didn't blame Millie for hating his guts. "It's okay," he said. "Thanks."

He left. Apparently protecting her was going to be done at a distance, unless he could think of a way to get her to listen to him.

He tried calling her at the library when he got back to his hotel. The minute she heard his voice, she hung up. He sighed and called Frank.

"She ran the other way," he told his friend. "I expected it. But I can't convince her that she needs protection if I can't get within speaking distance of her. Any ideas?"

"Yeah," Frank said. "I'll go by her apartment and speak to her."

"Thanks. Tell her I'm sorry. It won't do much good, but I really mean it."

"I know you do."

"I bought one of our tails a drink," Tony told him. "He said they were looking for guys who fit the profile of a hit man. He thinks I do."

Frank burst out laughing. "If the shoe fits…"

"Thanks a lot," he muttered.

"I'll get back to you when I've seen Millie," he promised.

"Okay. I'll be here."

* * *

Frank called him the next morning. "She'll talk to you," he told Tony. "But it took a lot of persuading. And she won't believe that John would do anything so drastic as to hire someone to kill her. You're going to have a hard time selling her on the idea of protection," he added.

"Well, I'll work on my people skills," Tony replied.

There was a pause. "I heard a comedian say that you can get a lot more with a smile and a gun than you can with a smile. That about sums up your people skills."

Tony burst out laughing. "You do have a point," he conceded. "I'll try to mellow before I go to see her. Any news from your detective friend?"

"Not yet. He anticipated me, it seems." He chuckled. "He already had his men working on the gang angle, to see if anybody hired a shooter. Maybe he'll turn up something."

"Meanwhile, I'll do what I can to safeguard Millie," Tony replied. "See you."

"Yeah."

Tony dressed casually for the visit to the library, hoping he wouldn't attract too much attention if anyone was watching Millie. He wore jeans and a cotton shirt under a leather jacket. He looked outdoorsy, like a cowboy, but he refused to put on a wide-brimmed hat. He'd never liked to cover his black wavy hair, and he still wore it in a ponytail. He wasn't going to be conservative, no matter what the job called for. He was too much of a renegade.

He walked to the desk and asked for Millie, smiling

at the clerk. She smiled back, obviously interested in him. She picked up the phone, pushed a button and told Millie she had a visitor out front.

As she spoke, she was sorting mail. "Oh, and you got a package," she added, still talking to Millie on the phone, her hand reaching toward a flat but lumpy-looking brown envelope with spiky writing on the front.

"Don't touch that," Tony said at once, whipping out his phone. He dialed the emergency services number and requested a squad car and the bomb squad.

The clerk looked at him as if she thought he'd gone nuts.

"Get everybody out of the building," he told her in a tone bristling with authority. "Don't waste time," he said when she hesitated. "There's enough explosive in there to blow up a city block. Hurry!"

She rushed into the back as Millie came out front. She stopped at the desk, where Tony was still arguing with the dispatcher about the bomb squad.

"Listen, I work for the government," he said in a deep, steady tone. "I've seen letter bombs before. I know what I'm talking about. Do you want to read in the newspapers tomorrow morning that a library blew up because you didn't take the threat seriously? They'll even spell your name right…yes, that's what I said, the bomb squad. And hurry!"

He glanced at Millie, his face hard, his eyes glittering. "We have to get out of here," he told her.

"Out? I've got a package there…"

He caught her hand as she reached for it. "If you like

having two hands and a head, you'll do what I tell you. Come on!" he called to the clerk, who was hurrying several patrons and a couple of employees out the front door.

"You are out of your mind," Millie said primly. "I'm not leaving…!"

"Sorry," he said as he whipped her up in his arms and carried her right out the front door, which a grinning patron held open for him. "I don't have time to argue."

A squad car rolled up along with the bomb squad. Tony went to talk to the sergeant in charge.

"It's a letter bomb, on the counter in there," he told the man. "I worked a case in Nairobi with one that looked just like it, but I couldn't get anybody to listen to me. It killed two foreign workers when it went off."

The sergeant sighed. "Okay. We'll check it out. But if you're wrong, you're in a lot of trouble."

"I'm not wrong," Tony told him, and showed his credentials. The sergeant didn't say another word. He went straight to work.

The librarians were skeptical; so were Millie and the patrons. But they all stood patiently in the cold while the bomb squad went hesitantly into the building and looked for the brown envelope Tony had described.

The sergeant came back out, grim-faced. "I'm not completely convinced," he told Tony, "but we'll go by the book. It does look suspicious."

They had a robot with a gripping arm. They sent it into

the building to retrieve the package. It took a long time, and many spectators gathered, kept back by two more units of police who arrived to help with crowd control.

There was a camera crew from a local television station on the scene now, and people with camera phones were snapping images to send to the media as well. Some of them were laughing. One man, a grumpy library patron, said he was going to catch cold while the police wasted their time on a bomb threat that would turn out to be a package of photographs or something equally stupid.

As he was speaking, the robot reached the containment bin in which the bomb squad collected suspicious packages. No sooner had it gone in than there was a terrific explosion which knocked the robot onto its back and had spectators screaming and running away.

Tony glanced at the bomb squad sergeant who grimaced. He turned to Millie. She was white-faced and sick at her stomach. If Tony hadn't come in when he did, if she'd opened that package…

He caught her as she slumped to the pavement.

When she came to, she was lying in the back seat of Tony's rented car. He was holding a cold soft drink at her lips, supporting her with one big arm.

"Come on. Take a sip. It will help," he said quietly.

She managed to swallow some of the fizzy liquid. She coughed. "I fainted. I never faint."

"If somebody sent me a bomb, I'd probably faint,

too," he replied with a grin. "You're okay. So is everybody else."

She looked up at him quietly. "Why?"

The grin faded. "Some men take possession to the grave with them. John couldn't have you. He wanted to make sure that nobody else ever did. He paid somebody a lot of money to do this. And he almost pulled it off. Now we have to keep you alive while they find out who he hired."

She sat up, breathing heavily. "Surely they won't try again? They'll know that the police are watching now."

"The police don't have the sort of budget they'd need to give you round-the-clock protection. The bomber will know that. Of course he'll try again."

"He's already got the money," she faltered.

"I wouldn't bet on that. More than likely, John set it up so that he can't get it until you're dead and the bomber has proof that you're dead," he told her flatly. "If a gang leader is holding the money, it will be a point of honor with him. Don't look like that, they do have honor among themselves, of a sort. Especially if the leader was John's friend and felt an obligation to him for some reason."

"You knew it was a bomb without touching it," she recalled. "How?"

"It isn't my first bomb," he replied. "I don't do ordinance, but I know guys who do. I learned a lot by watching, the rest by experience."

She frowned. "In the Army? Or working on construction gangs?" she asked.

He hesitated. "I work for the government, in between freelance jobs," he said. "I'm an independent contractor."

"A what?"

"I'm a professional soldier," he told her. "I specialize in counterterrorism."

She was very still. Her pale eyes searched his dark ones. "Did your foster mother ever know?"

He shook his head. "She wouldn't have approved."

"I see."

His eyes narrowed on her averted face. "You don't approve, either, do you?"

She couldn't meet his eyes. She rubbed her cold arms. "My opinion wouldn't mean anything to you."

She climbed out of the car, still a little rocky on her feet. He steadied her.

"You need to get your coat and your purse and come with me," he told her. "We have things to talk about."

"But—" she began.

"Don't argue, Millie," he interrupted. "If you stay in there, you're endangering your co-workers."

That hadn't occurred to her. She looked horrified. "But I have to work," she protested. "I have bills to pay…!"

"You can ask for a leave of absence, can't you?" he persisted. "A few days off won't put you on the streets."

He was making sense, and she knew he was right, but she was afraid that if she asked for time off, she'd lose her job. She'd been at the library all her working life, and she loved what she did. Her superior still hadn't gotten over the gossip John had caused by insinuating that Millie had a wild lifestyle. God knew what she'd say when she heard about the bomb.

"I may not have a job when my boss finds out what happened here today. She's out of town until next Monday," she added sadly.

"Come on. I'll go in with you."

He escorted her back into the building and insisted on seeing her supervisor with her. He explained the situation matter-of-factly, adding that he was certain her colleagues wouldn't like to risk another such incident by insisting that she stay on the job until the culprit was apprehended.

"Certainly not," Barry Hinson said at once. "Millie, we can manage without you for a few days. I'm sure Mrs. Anderson would agree."

Millie sighed. "I don't suppose I have a choice. I'm very sorry," she began.

"It isn't your fault," Barry said firmly. "None of us ever blamed you for what that man did. He should have been locked up," he added, unaware that Tony had been John's friend.

Millie flushed. She didn't look at Tony. "Well, I'll get my things and leave. I'll be back next week."

Barry smiled. "Of course." He glanced warily at Tony. "You won't let anything happen to her?" he asked, assuming that the big man worked for law enforcement.

"No," Tony assured him. "I won't."

Millie didn't want to feel that enveloping warmth that his words caused. She'd risked her heart on this man once before and had been crushed by his rejection. If only, she thought, you could banish feelings and make them leave you alone forever. She went to get her purse and coat and explain to the clerk what she'd been working on before the bomb disrupted their day.

"Now, what?" Millie asked as she paused by her little black VW in the parking lot. It was used, but clean and well looked after.

"Now, we go somewhere and talk and make decisions."

"There's a cafeteria down the street, where I usually have lunch," she said, naming it.

"I'll meet you there."

She nodded meekly and got into her car.

Ten minutes later, they were having sandwiches and coffee, a late lunch because disposing of the bomb had been a protracted business. Millie ate and drank automatically, but she didn't taste much. It was disconcerting to realize that John actually meant to kill her.

"Stop brooding," Tony said as he sipped coffee. "It won't help."

"I never thought John would want to kill me," she said.

His eyes narrowed. "He beat you up."

She gasped. "How did you know that?"

"Frank."

Her lips made a thin line. "He'd been drinking. He said it was all my fault that his life was falling apart, because I wouldn't marry him. I tried, for the twentieth time, to explain that I didn't love him in that way, but he wouldn't listen. He lost his temper and the next thing I knew, he was slamming me into a wall. Even when it happened, I could hardly believe it. I screamed and screamed, and when he let go of me, I locked myself in the bedroom and called the police."

"You didn't press charges," he muttered.

"He was in tears by the time the police got there. He swore it was the alcohol, that he didn't realize how much he'd had. He said he loved me, he couldn't believe he'd done such a thing. He begged me not to press charges." She shook her head. "I should have. But I felt sorry for him. I always felt sorry for him. He had mental issues, but he wouldn't face that, and he wouldn't get help. I thought I could do something for him."

"You can't fix a broken mind," Tony said heavily. "He was obsessed with you."

His tone intimated that he didn't understand why. She knew what Tony thought of her, because John had told her, time and again. Tony thought she was the most boring woman on earth, and he'd need to be drunk to want to touch her. Looking at his expression now, she was certain that John had been telling the truth. She was plain and prim and unexciting. It was a fact she'd faced long ago.

She pushed back her coffee cup. "After that night, it got to the point that I couldn't walk out of my apartment without running into John. He said he was going to make sure that I didn't have any other man in my life, and he was going to watch me night and day. When he told those lies about me, and then started spending the day in the library, it began jeopardizing my job. I finally decided that I had no other choice than to file stalking charges against him." She ran a hand over the tight bun she kept her long brown hair in. "It was what pushed him over the edge. I even knew that it would—it's why I waited so long to do anything about the problem. He swore he'd get even, no matter what it took." She looked tired, drained of life. "When I knew that he was dead, I was so ashamed, but all I could feel was a sense of relief. I was finally free of him."

"But you came to the funeral home," he commented.

Her face tautened as she recalled Tony's attitude when he'd met her there. "Yes. It was the guilt. I had to see him. I thought it might make amends, somehow."

"And you found me, instead," he replied, grimacing at her expression. "You have to understand, all I had to go on was what John told me. And he told me a lot. He left me a letter, blaming you for his death. I had no reason to doubt him, at the time. Not until Frank told me the truth."

Of course he'd believed his friend, she thought. It wouldn't have occurred to him that Millie wasn't a wild girl. He didn't know Millie. He didn't want to know her. It hurt, realizing that.

"I'm sorry for the way I reacted," he said stiffly. "I didn't know."

She shook her head. "Nobody knew. I was harassed, blackmailed and slandered by him for years, and he made everybody think it was my own fault, that I encouraged him." Her gaze was flat, almost lifeless. "He was the most repulsive man I've ever known."

He frowned. "He was good-looking."

She glanced up at him. "You can't make people love you," she said in a subdued sort of tone. "No matter what you look like. He was coarse and crude, and ugly inside. That's where it counts, you know. The outside might have been attractive. The devil, they say, was beautiful."

"Point taken."

She finished her coffee. "Where do I go now?"

"Back to your apartment. I'm coming with you, to see what I'll need for surveillance."

She frowned. "Surveillance?"

He nodded. "I want cameras and microphones everywhere. It's the only way we can save your life."

And in that moment, she realized, for the first time, just how desperate her situation really was.

CHAPTER THREE

MILLIE'S apartment was on the third floor of a building about ten blocks from the library. She had a small balcony, on which lived many plants during the warm months. Now, the pots contained nothing except dead remnants of the autumn foliage that she'd been too busy to clean out. The past few weeks had been hectic indeed.

Her walls were full of bookcases and books. She was a great reader. Tony noted the titles ranged from history to gardening to languages to true crime. He smiled when he noticed all the romance novels, including several that had to do with professional soldiers. He'd never told her what he did for a living until today, and she hadn't guessed. But apparently she had an adventurous nature that she kept tightly contained, like her hair in that bun.

He noted that she liked pastel colors, and used them in her decorating. The apartment's contents weren't expensive, but they suited the rooms in which she lived. She had good taste for a woman on a budget.

He poked his nose into every nook and cranny of the

place, making notes in a small notebook, about entrance, exit and possible avenues of intrusion. Her balcony was a trouble spot. A man with an automatic rifle could see right into the apartment through the glass sliding doors, which had no curtains. The doors had the usual locks, but no dead bolts. The apartment was only feet away from an elevator and a staircase, which gave it easy access. There was no security for the building, and Tony had noticed two or three suspicious-looking men on his way up in the elevator.

He dug his hands into his pockets. It had seemed like a good plan at the time, but now that he'd seen where Millie lived, he knew he couldn't just move in with her and start waiting for an attack to come.

"This won't work," he said flatly.

She turned from the hall closet, where she'd been pulling out a coat and a sweater, and stared at him blankly. "What?"

"This place is a death trap," he said matter-of-factly. "Easy entrance and exit right outside the door, no dead bolts, a perfect line-of-sight aim for anybody with a high-powered rifle with a scope. Add to that a noticeable lack of security and a few shady characters who live in the building, and you've got an impossible situation. You can't stay here."

"But it's where I live," she said plaintively. "I can't just move because some crazy person is trying to kill me. Besides, wouldn't he just follow me?"

"Probably," he had to admit.

"Then what do I do, live out of my car and switch parking lots every night?" she wondered.

He burst out laughing. He hadn't credited her with a sense of humor. "You'd need a bigger car," he agreed.

She let out a long breath. "I guess I could do something illegal and get arrested," she thought aloud. "I'd be safe in jail."

"Not really," he replied. "Gangs operate in every prison in this country, and in other countries. They're like corporations now, Millie—they're international."

"You're kidding," she said, aghast.

"It's the truth. They have a hierarchy, even in prison, and some measure of control and exploitation. They can order hits inside or outside."

She sat down heavily on the arm of her sofa. "Call the U.S. Marshal's office," she said. "Tell them I qualify for the witness protection program. I can be renamed and transplanted."

"Not unless you testify against somebody really evil," he returned. "Sorry."

Her eyebrows arched. "Ouch."

He lifted a huge shoulder. "So we have to look for a different solution. I'll take you back to the hotel with me—"

She flushed and stood up. "I'm not moving in with you."

"Okay. Which one of your co-workers would you like to put into the line of fire?" he asked. "Because that's your choice right now."

She looked worried. "I don't know any of my co-workers that well, and I wouldn't ask them to risk being killed on my account even if I did."

His eyes were curious. "You've worked there for years, and you don't know any of your colleagues well?"

She bit her lower lip. "I don't mix well. I live in another world from most modern people."

"I don't understand."

She laughed. It had a hollow sound. "I go to church, pay my bills on time, obey the law and go to bed with the chickens, alone. I don't fit into a society that rewards permissiveness and degrades virtue. I don't go around with people who think cheating is the best way to get ahead, and money doesn't mean much to me, beyond having enough to get by. Making money seems to be the driving force in the world these days, regardless of what you have to do to get it."

She made him feel uncomfortable. She was describing his own world, into which he fit quite well.

She saw that and sighed. "Sorry. I told you I wasn't normal."

"I haven't said a word," he said defensively.

She searched his dark eyes. "Frank mentioned that you think women are a permissible pleasure, and that the brassier they are, the better you like them."

His jaw tautened. "What's wrong with that?" he asked. "I'm a bachelor and I don't want to settle down."

She lifted her hands. "I didn't mean it as an insult. I'm just pointing out that our views of life are very different. I'm not going to be happy staying in the room, overnight, with a man I barely know."

He could have debated her take on their relationship. They'd known each other for years, even if distantly. But he didn't pursue it. He cocked an eyebrow. "I haven't offered you half my bed," he said curtly. "And I never would. You aren't my type."

"I thought I just said that," she replied.

He made a sound deep in his throat. She made him feel small. He looked around the apartment. "I've got a suite," he said after a minute. "You'll have your own bedroom. The door has a lock." He looked straight into her eyes. "Not that you'll need it."

That was meant as an insult. She understood it. But she'd had years of practice at hiding her feelings from him. She didn't react. She didn't have much of a choice, either. Thinking of her close call at the library was still unsettling. John's criminal friends would see her dead, if they could. Tony was the only thing standing between herself and a funeral parlor, and she was arguing. She pushed back a wisp of brown hair and turned away from him. She was running out of choices.

"Well, I can't stay here," she said to herself.

"No, you can't. And local law enforcement doesn't have the sort of budget they'd need to house and feed you indefinitely. This could go on for weeks, Millie."

"Weeks?" She was staring at him with pure horror. "Surely not! The bomb…"

"…may have been a test," he interrupted, "to give

your assassin a dry run, show him how quickly local law enforcement reacts to an emergency call."

"I hadn't considered that," she confessed.

"You should. This isn't some petty criminal," he added. "He's a professional. He may not be the best— that plastic explosive he used for the bomb wasn't well concealed or particularly well made. But he knows how to get to you, and that makes him—or her—dangerous. We have to put you someplace where he doesn't have easy access, lure him in and help him make a mistake, so we can nab him."

"How do we do that?" she asked.

"You move in with me," he said simply. "We let the word get around. Then we wait for developments."

"Wait." She tugged at a lock of loose hair. "I can't wait a long time," she worried. "I have to work. I have to support myself."

"You have to be alive in order to do those things," he reminded her. "I'll call Frank. He can get his contact in the police department to help us out."

"That might be wise," she agreed. She was still debating her options, but she didn't seem to have any left. She wished she could go back in time, to a period in her life when she hadn't known Tony Danzetta. She'd eaten her heart out over him for so many years that it had become a habit. Now here he was, protecting her from danger, for reasons he still hadn't disclosed. He was honest to the point of brutality about his lack of interest in her as a woman. Was it guilt, she wondered, that drove him to help her? Perhaps she'd have the opportunity in the days ahead to learn the answer to that question.

His hotel suite was huge. Millie was fascinated by the glimpse of how the other half lived. She knew what a suite cost in this luxury hotel, and she wondered how Tony's government job made it affordable to him. Maybe, she considered, his father, the contractor, had left him a lot of money. He was obviously used to having the very best of everything.

"Hungry?" he asked when he'd put her suitcase inside what was to be her bedroom.

"Actually, I am," she said. "Could we go somewhere and get a salad?"

He pursed his lips, smiling. "What sort of salad?"

"A Caesar salad would be nice," she said.

"How about a steak to go with it, and a baked potato with real butter and chives and sour cream?"

Her eyes widened. "That sounds wonderful. Coffee, too."

He nodded. He picked up the phone, punched in a number, waited a minute and then proceeded to give an order to someone on the other end of the line. It must be room service, she thought. It fascinated her that he could just pick up the phone and order food. The only time she'd ever done that was when she ordered pizza, and small ones, at that.

"Thirty minutes," he said when he hung up.

"I've never stayed in a hotel and had room service,"

she confided. "I went on a trip for the library one time, to a conference up in Dallas and stayed in a hotel. It was small, though, and I ate at a McDonald's nearby."

He chuckled. "I couldn't live without room service. I flew in from Iraq late one night, starving to death. I ordered a steak and salad and this huge ice cream split at two o'clock in the morning."

"There's room service then?" she exclaimed.

He didn't mention that he paid a big price for having those items sent up, because room service didn't operate in the wee hours of the morning. He was also friends with the general manager of that particular hotel. "There is in New York City," he told her.

She sat down in one of the big armchairs and he took off his jacket and sprawled over the sofa.

"I guess you've been a lot of places," she said.

He closed his eyes, put his hands under his head and smiled. "A lot."

"I'd like to go to Japan," she said dreamily. "We have this nice old couple who came from Osaka. I love to hear them talk about their home country."

"Japan is beautiful." He rolled over, facing her, tugging a pillow under his head. "I spent a few days in Osaka on a case, and made time to take the bullet train over to Kyoto. There's a samurai fortress there with huge wooden gates. It was built in 1600 and something. They had nightingale floors…"

"What?"

"Nightingale floors. They put nails under the flooring

and pieces of metal that would come in contact with the nails if anyone walked on the floor. It made a sound like a nightingale, a pretty sound, but it alerted the samurai inside instantly if Ninja assassins were about to attack them. Ninjas were known for their stealth abilities, but the nightingale floors defeated them."

"That's so cool!" she exclaimed.

He studied her with new interest. When she was excited, her face flushed and her eyes shimmered. She looked radiant.

"I've read about Japan for years," he continued. "But little details like that don't usually get into travel books. You have to actually go to a place to learn about it."

"I watch those travel documentaries on TV," she confessed. "I especially like the ones where just plain people go traipsing into the back country of exotic places. I saw one where this guy lived with the Mongols and ate roasted rat."

He chuckled. "I've had my share of those. Not to mention snake and, once, a very old and tough cat."

"A cat?" she asked, horrified. "You *ate* a cat?!"

He scowled. "Now, listen, when you're starving to death, you can't be selective! We were in a jungle, hiding from insurgents, and we'd already eaten all the snakes and bugs we could find!"

"But, a cat!" she wailed.

He grimaced. "It was an old cat. It was on its last legs, honest. We used it for stew." He brightened. "We threw up because it tasted so bad!"

"Good!" she exclaimed, outraged.

He rolled onto his back. "Well, the only other thing on offer was a monkey that kept pelting us with coconuts, and I'm not eating any monkeys! Even if they do taste like chicken." He thought about that and laughed out loud.

"What's funny?" she wanted to know.

He glanced at her. "Every time somebody eats something exotic, they always say, 'It tastes just like chicken!'"

She made a face. "I'll bet the cat didn't."

"You got that right. It tasted like..." He got half the word out, flushed and backtracked. "I'd rather have had pemmican, but it's in short supply in the rest of the world. My great-grandmother used to make it. We visited her a couple of times when my stepfather was working in Atlanta and we lived with him. She lived in North Carolina, near the reservation," he recalled thoughtfully. "She was amazing. She knew how to treat all sorts of physical complaints with herbs. She went out every morning, gathering leaves and roots. I wish I'd paid more attention."

"She was Cherokee?" she asked, even though she knew the answer.

He nodded. "Full blooded," he added. His expression grew dark. "Like me. My mother married an Italian contractor. They didn't like it. He was an outsider. They disowned her, everyone except my great-grandmother. She died when I was a kid, and I haven't been back since."

"That's sad. You still have family there, don't you?"

"Yes. An uncle and a few cousins. I heard from my uncle a couple of years ago. He said I should come home and make peace with them."

"But you didn't."

"My mother had a hard life," he said. "When my sister and I went into foster care, it was like the end of the world. Especially when they separated us." His face went taut. "She killed herself."

"Your sister?" she asked, sad for him.

"Yes." He glanced at her. "Didn't my foster mother tell you any of this?"

Millie flushed. The woman had told her quite a lot about Tony, but nothing really personal. She wasn't going to admit that she'd tried to worm things out of her. She averted her eyes. "It must have been hard on you, losing your sister."

"Yeah." He stared at the ceiling. "Some boy in foster care got her pregnant and tried to force her to have an abortion. She wouldn't. She was deeply religious and she saw it as a sin if she went for a termination. She told the boy. So he made threats and she felt that she had nowhere to turn." He sighed, his eyes sad. "She would never have done that if she hadn't been half out of her mind. She thought of suicide as a sin, too. But in the end, she took the only way out she could find."

"I hope he ended up in prison," she muttered. "That boy, I mean."

He made a deep sound. "He did. And shortly afterward, he died mysteriously. Strange things happen to bad people."

She wondered if Tony had any hand in the boy's demise, but she didn't want to ask.

There was a knock at the door. Tony sprang to his feet, grinning. "Food," he guessed.

He peered out the keyhole and saw the trolley, and the waiter. He opened the door and let him in.

Lunch was delicious. Millie had never had food served on a white linen cloth, with heavy utensils and dishes under metal covers. It was a revelation. She munched her salad with obvious enjoyment and went into ecstasies about the tenderness of the steak and the delicious baked potato. Even the coffee was wonderful.

Tony found her obvious delight in the meal humbling. He took fancy food and fancy hotels for granted. He'd long since become blasé about such things. But Millie came from a poor background, and lived on a meager budget. He imagined she'd never stepped into the lobby of a luxury hotel, much less been a guest in one. He pictured taking her out for a spin in his convertible, or taking her sailing on his yacht down in the Bahamas and lying with her in the sun. She had a delightful body. He wondered how it would feel to make love to her on a sandy tropical beach. Then he wondered what the hell he was thinking of. She wasn't his sort of woman. Millie would never go to bed with a man she hadn't married, no matter what her feelings for him were.

That brought back a comment of Frank's, that Millie had once been in love with Tony. He recalled her shy presence at his foster mother's house from time to time as an invited guest, her radiance when he dropped in at the library to see his parent and Millie happened to be around. He must have been blind, he decided, not to have noticed how his presence illuminated the quiet, introverted woman across from him at the table.

Millie stopped eating and stared at him, disconcerted by his unsmiling, level stare. "Am I...doing something wrong?" she asked at once, her attention diverted to the silverware. "I don't know about fancy place settings—"

"It's just lunch, Millie," he interrupted. "I wasn't studying your eating habits. I was thinking about something, in the past."

"Oh." She was watchful, unconvinced.

He sipped coffee. "Why didn't you tell me what John was doing to you when I came home two years ago?" he asked.

She felt the question keenly. "I knew you wouldn't believe me. You've never liked me."

He frowned. "I didn't know you."

"And didn't want to, either." She laughed hollowly. "I was the invisible woman whenever you came home to visit your foster mother. She'd invite me over sometimes, because she knew I had no life to speak of. You never even noticed that I was around. You only stayed long enough to say a few words and then you were off on some hot date that Frank had fixed up for you, from the bar where he was a bouncer."

That made him feel worse. "I didn't want to get serious about anyone," he said after a minute. "Those glittery women are fine for a good time. You don't plan a future around them."

He was insinuating that they were fine for a one-night stand. The thought embarrassed her, made her uncomfortable. It was one more reminder of the distance between her world and his. She picked at her baked potato and lifted a forkful to her mouth. She wasn't really tasting it now. It was something to do.

"Why didn't you tell John to get a life and get off your back?" he asked suddenly.

She seemed to draw into herself. "It wouldn't have done any good," she told him. "I did try that, repeatedly. It just made him mad."

"Maybe it would have helped drive the point home if you'd stopped forgiving him," he continued doggedly. "Especially after he beat you up. No self-respecting woman would take that sort of behavior from a man."

Her face flushed. She put down her fork and glared at him across the table. "That's so easy for a man to say," she began in a low, angry tone. "You've never been beaten to your knees by an enraged man bent on making you pay for not loving him. I had bruises all over my body and I was terrified that he was actually going to kill me! He yelled at me and called me names and said he'd beat me to death if I didn't give in and agree to marry him." She wrapped her arms around her body, as if she felt a sudden chill. Her eyes went blank. "I believed him. I was sure that he was going to kill me. In the end, I just screamed and screamed. I expected to die. It was a miracle that I got a locked bedroom door between us in time to call for help. The sound of police car sirens was the most beautiful music I'd ever heard," she added in a soft undertone that made Tony feel even worse. "The policewoman who came in first gave John a furious look and when he started toward her, she drew her service pistol and pointed it right at his nose. I knew she'd shoot if he came any closer, and I guess he knew it, too, because he stopped. He sat down on the sofa and started crying. He said it was all my fault because I wouldn't marry him."

"Had he been drinking?"

"Yes. But not enough to make him out of control," she said bitterly. "The policewoman told me that. She asked me to press charges, but John came on his knees to beg me to forgive him. He was sobbing. I felt embarrassed and guilty and I agreed not to have him arrested. It didn't win me any points with the police," she added. "But I don't know that having him arrested again would have done any good. It certainly hadn't stopped him from stalking me, or spreading lies about me. He'd been arrested before, but he was always out in a few days, starting all over again. I got over the beating, but I would never go to his apartment again or let him in if he came to mine. I made sure there were always people around when he came to the library."

Tony felt very small. "Frank said he spread lies about you to your boss."

"Yes. And to the patrons." Her eyes closed in bitter memory. "I thought I'd lose my job forever. I would have, if Frank hadn't talked to a few people. He's been the best friend to me through all this. I don't know what I would have done without him."

"He's sweet on you," he said deliberately. "But he thinks you wouldn't give him the time of day because he works in a low class of job."

"The job wouldn't matter if I could feel that way about him. I wish I could," she added quietly. "But I can't."

The confession made him feel good. He didn't want to know why. He finished his coffee. "Want dessert?" he asked.

She laughed. "I'd have to put it in my pocket," she said. "I'm stuffed."

"So am I. They have a good kitchen staff here."

"I'll say." She finished her own coffee. "Do we push the trolley back down to the kitchen?" she asked.

"Good heavens, no," he exclaimed. "They come and get it."

She flushed. He made her feel like an idiot.

He noticed that and grimaced. "Millie, I wasn't always rich," he said gently. "I had to learn about things like proper table settings and etiquette, too."

She shrugged. "I'm just a country hick, you know,"

she said with a faint smile. "I live frugally. This—" she waved her hand around "—is like another planet to me."

"Learning new things doesn't hurt," he said. He chuckled. "The first time Jared and I ate in a five-star restaurant, we had to ask the waiter about the utensils and all the courses. Fortunately he was a nice person. He could have made us feel small, but he didn't. Jared tipped him a hundred dollars."

She gasped. That was almost a week's salary for her.

"I know. It was a lot of money to me, at the time," he said. "I'd been a soldier, and before that, a common laborer, working in a construction crew."

"How did you make so much money?" she asked, genuinely curious.

"Hiring out to governments as an independent contractor," he said simply. "Including our own. Jared and I learned counterterrorism skills and for a while, he ran a security company that I worked for. Counterterrorism skills are a valuable commodity in some circles. It's a specialized job and it pays very well."

"Do you go into combat?" she asked.

"If the job calls for it," he replied. "You can't teach in a classroom in a combat zone," he added with a smile. "We teach small forces about incursions and stealth tactics, about IEDs and organizing local militia—stuff like that."

"What's an—" she felt for the word "—IED?"

"You could answer that now." He chuckled. "It's an improvised explosive device. You had one sent to you."

The smile faded as he remembered how dangerous her introduction to the world of terror had been. The device, as clumsily built as it was, could have killed her in a heartbeat.

"You said it wasn't well made," she recalled.

"It wasn't. The good ones would pass for a small manuscript," he said. "It's a cowardly way to kill somebody."

She sighed, staring at the carpet. "I can't believe John was this desperate," she said, shaking her head. "To kill somebody, just because they couldn't love you. It's…" She searched for a word.

"Insane," he said through his teeth. "John had mental problems. I'm still shocked that Frank and I didn't see it and you did." It made him uncomfortable for another reason, too, but he wasn't telling her any secrets about his past. Not yet.

She laughed hollowly as she looked up at him. "That's because he wasn't trying to force you to marry him."

He drew in a long breath and looked at his watch. "I've got to meet a man in the lobby about a job," he said. "You stay put, okay?"

She nodded. "Thanks for lunch."

"My pleasure."

He left her sitting on the sofa and went downstairs to see a government agent from his department. There had been a string of kidnappings of rich persons along the Texas border, and Tony's skills might come in handy, they thought. He put Millie out of his mind before he exited the elevator.

She wandered around the suite while he was gone, straying into his bedroom out of curiosity. His suitcase was open on the bed. She picked up a shirt on the carpet that had been hastily discarded, probably when he changed early this morning. She held it to her nostrils and drew in the smell. She smiled, with her eyes closed. People had a personal fragrance, she thought, every one different. She'd know Tony's in a dark room. He smelled of the outdoors, of spice and fir. She loved the smell. She recalled the feeling it gave her to be carried, when he'd taken her out of the library protesting. His arms had been warm and strong and she'd never wanted to leave them. But she was going to have to move on.

She put the shirt down. After a minute she realized that he'd know it had been moved, a man as sharp as Tony. She dropped it back onto the carpet, went out of the bedroom and closed the door.

CHAPTER FOUR

It was late when Tony came back. She was watching a movie on television, curled up on the sofa in slacks and a soft yellow knit shirt, with her bare feet under her. He smiled at the picture she made. He thought of a small kitten, cuddly and sweet, and snapped that thought right out of his mind.

"Found something to watch, I gather?" he teased.

She fumbled for the remote control. "Just a movie on regular television," she said quickly, flushing.

He frowned. "You can watch pay-per-view if you want to," he said. "Listen, kid, three or four bucks for a movie isn't going to break the bank."

She flushed even more. "Thanks."

Her embarrassment made him uncomfortable. He was used to women who didn't mind ordering the most expensive items on the menu, who asked for trips to the most expensive concerts, who wanted jewelry for presents. This one was nervous because he might think she'd watched a movie on the pay channels. He felt odd.

She sat up and worked her feet back into her loafers.

"You want to take in a show or something?" he asked.

She stared at him. "A show?"

"There's a good theater company here. They have a ballet, an orchestra. Somebody's probably doing something Christmasy, even though it isn't quite the holiday season."

She would have loved to go. But she recalled that she didn't have a dress that would do to wear to something fancy. Her clothes closet was bare, except for a few mix and match outfits suitable for work. She didn't even have the sort of shoes she'd need for an evening on the town. Tony probably had a dinner jacket or even a tuxedo packed away in that hanging bag she'd seen on the door to his bathroom.

"Mmm...no," she drawled. "I don't think so. Thank you."

Unaware of her wardrobe difficulties, he took the refusal in stride, thinking she probably didn't care for highbrow entertainment.

"Do you play cards?" he asked.

She shook her head. "Sorry."

He shrugged and sighed. "It's going to be a long week," he murmured. He studied her curiously. "Okay, then. When you're home, what do you do at night?"

She looked uncomfortable. "I read books, mostly, if there's nothing interesting on the military history channel."

His eyelids flickered. "You like military history?"

"I love it," she replied, smiling.

"Which period?"

"Any period," she told him. "I've read everything I could find about Alexander the Great, Julius Caesar, Napoleon, cavalry and Native American battles of the nineteenth century, generals of the Second World War," she rattled off. "I never met a battle I didn't want to read about."

He sat down across from her. "I took my degree in criminal justice," he said. "But I minored in history. My favorite period was World War II, European theater."

She smiled. "I remember. Your foster mother said you were always outlining battle plans to her over dinner."

He chuckled. "She didn't understand a thing I talked about, but she was always patient and kind." The smile faded. He looked down at his shoes. "She convinced me that not all foster parents are bad. I went through several after we moved from the reservation in North Carolina down to Georgia."

This was an experience that had left scars in him. She'd heard his foster mother talk about it. "You said once that your mother died when you were young."

He looked up. His eyes were flat, lifeless. "That's not quite true. I haven't really talked about her in years. About him, either. My stepfather, I mean." His broad shoulders rose and fell. "I tell different stories about them to anybody who asks. I guess I've been running away from the truth all my life."

She didn't speak. She just listened. Waited. Hoped.

He noticed and smiled. "My real father was my

mother's second cousin. He lived on the Cherokee reservation in North Carolina where she grew up. But he was married. She got pregnant and she didn't have any money for a termination. So there was this big, loud Italian construction worker doing a project near the res. She started going out with him and by the time she told him she was pregnant, he thought it was his. Then she gave birth to a full-term baby in what he thought was her sixth month, and the jig was up. He hated her. But they stayed together for three more years, until my sister was born. He took a powder and left her with the kids."

"That must have been rough. Was she young?"

"She was nineteen when she had me," he said. "Not terribly young. But my sister was half Cherokee and half white, and my mother couldn't take the constant criticism from her family. When I was seven, she left the reservation and took us on a bus to Atlanta. We didn't know it, but her husband was working there. He found out from her kin where she was. He moved back in with us. She might have tried to run, but he told her that he had legal rights to take the kids if she ran away. So she stayed. And I ended up with an Italian name that has nothing to do with my ancestry." He laughed. "The only good thing about it is that it saved a few soldiers' lives when I got teased. They didn't make Indian jokes around me, because they thought I was Italian." His eyes glimmered. "I'm proud of my ancestry. Cherokees are still a proud people, even after all the hell the government put us through when they marched us out to Oklahoma in the dead of winter, walking, in 1838."

"I know about that," she said. "It was a tragic episode."

"One of many," he agreed.

She saw the pain on his face. He was talking around his childhood, trying not to remember. She wanted him to deal with it. She might be the only person alive that he'd ever really talked to about it. It would help him. "Your parents didn't have a happy marriage," she prompted.

He shook his head. He traced the back of a big fingernail absently. "My so-called father drank. A lot. And when he drank, he remembered that I wasn't his kid and made me pay for it. I was in the emergency room every few months with bruises and cuts. Once, with a broken bone."

She winced, thinking how hard it must have been for him, at that age, to be so badly treated by a man he considered to be his father. "Didn't your mother do anything to protect you?" she asked, aghast.

"She couldn't. She was a little woman. He knocked her around all the time. He was a big man. She was scared to death of him. She had no place to go. He knew it. He liked that." His face tautened. "But then he started doing things to my little sister, when she was about eight." His whole body seemed to contract. "My mother caught him at it, late one night. She was very calm. She went into the kitchen, got the biggest butcher knife she could find and hid it behind her. She went back into the living room, smiling. She said it was all right, she wouldn't make a fuss. He smirked. He knew she wouldn't do anything. He said so. I can still see her, smiling at him. She went to him like somebody sleep-walking. She stabbed that knife up to the hilt in his stomach, all the way to the heart. He never saw it coming. She was still smiling when he fell down on the floor." His eyes closed. "I never saw so much blood. She didn't move. She stood there, holding the knife, while the life drained out of him. She never stopped smiling, not even when they took her away in the police car."

Millie was horrified. No wonder he wasn't eager to get married and settle down. "What happened to her?" she asked gently.

He drew in a long breath. "They committed her. They said she was insane."

Her heart jumped. "Was she?"

He met her eyes. "I've never been sure, Millie," he said gently. His expression was tormented. "She died long before they had tests that could have backed up their theories." He shifted a little. "Our first set of foster parents told us very little, but they did mention that the psychiatrist said it was schizophrenia. There's a hereditary tendency toward it, I've read."

No wonder he wouldn't reveal his background. He was ashamed. Perhaps he was afraid, too. Maybe he thought he'd go mad himself.

She got up from the sofa and knelt down in front of him, balancing herself with a hand on one big knee. "I've read about mental illness. Some disease processes have a genetic tendency. That doesn't guarantee that anybody else in the family will ever develop the same illness," she said firmly. "You're as sane as I am," she added. "If you'd had mental deficiencies, believe me, they'd have shown up early. Very early."

He looked down at her, scowling. "You think so?" he asked.

"I know so. Did you ever torture an animal for fun? Set fires in your house? Wet the bed when you were in your teens?"

He laughed. "None of those."

"I'm no psychologist," she told him. "But I'm a great reader. Children show signs of mental illness in childhood. Since you were in the child welfare system, I'm sure the case workers paid close attention to you, considering your mother's illness. They would have put you in therapy immediately if they'd even suspected you had problems."

He cocked his head and laughed hollowly. "I can tell that you've had no contact with the system," he said with a sigh. "There are people who do their best for foster kids. The woman you knew, who brought me to San Antonio and got me through high school was certainly one of the best foster parents. But I lived with one family in Atlanta who had seven foster kids. They used the money the state gave them to gamble. They went up to Cherokee every month and blew it on the slot machines, hoping to get rich. Meanwhile, the kids went without school clothes, food, attention, you name it. No case worker ever set foot in the house. Nobody investigated when we went to school dirty. The state did finally get wise, when one of our teachers started asking questions. We were removed from that house. But, you see, there wasn't another family willing to take me and my sister together. That's when we got separated, just before I was fostered to the woman who adopted me and eventually brought me to Texas."

"I'm sorry," she said.

He drew her hands up to his mouth and kissed them. "You always did have the softest heart," he said gently, surprising her. "I remember how you loved kids. You'd tell stories in the library during summer vacation, and they'd gather around you like flies around honey." He laughed softly. "I loved watching your face when you told those stories. You lit up like a Christmas tree."

She was surprised. "When did you see me doing that?"

"Many times," he said surprisingly. The smile faded. "I thought a lot of you. I was in a dangerous profession and a long way from wanting to settle down. But I used to think that if I ever did, you'd be high on my list of prospects." His face darkened. "And then John started feeding me lies about you. And I listened."

She started to draw away, but he caught her wrists and held her there, his black eyes steady and probing.

"I wish I could take it back," he said. "But I can't. I'm really sorry for the way I treated you. Especially at the funeral home."

The feel of his big, warm hands around her wrists wasn't threatening to her. They were comforting. "You didn't know me," she said.

"I didn't want to know you." He grimaced. "Maybe I won't ever go off the deep end like my mother did. But I've got a past that's going to make it hard for any woman to live with me on a permanent basis. I make my living with guns, Millie," he added, watching her face. "I work for a government agency that sends me in when every other option fails. It's dangerous work. I can't afford any sort of distraction. That's why I don't get involved with nice girls. Girls like you."

It began to make sense. Good time girls didn't expect happy endings. They, like Tony, lived for the moment. He liked his job, had no thought of ever quitting it, and he was telling Millie to back off. In a nice way, but definitely the same message.

She forced a smile. "You're warning me off," she said, trying to sound nonchalant. "Should I be flattered?"

He let go of her wrists. "I don't want to hurt you," he said solemnly. "I could. You're not worldly."

She got to her feet and went back to the sofa and sat down. "I guess I'm not. I'm a librarian," she said philosophically. "Library work isn't Indiana Jones stuff."

"No. But if you read military history, you're an armchair adventurer, at least," he teased.

She smiled, hiding her misery. "What do you like to read?"

"The classics," he said. "But I'm partial to military history myself."

"Do you have a hobby?" she asked, fascinated with what she was learning about him.

He grinned. "I like to cook," he told her. "I can make almost anything, even French pastries."

She laughed. "So can I."

He pursed his lips. "Pity we don't have a kitchen here."

"Isn't it, just?"

He stood up and stretched, powerful muscles rippling in his chest and arms. "It's been a long day. I usually stay up late, but I'm pretty tired. Watch another movie, if you like. It won't disturb me."

She nodded, but she looked uncomfortable.

"What is it?" he asked.

She grimaced. "I was so upset that I forgot to pack anything to sleep in…"

"Now that's a problem I can solve," he told her. He went into his bedroom, rummaged in his suitcase and came back with a round-necked white T-shirt in pristine condition. "It will swallow you whole. As good as a gown, I'd say." He grinned.

She laughed and fought a blush. He really was huge. It would come down to her knees and wrap around her three times. "Thanks."

"Hey. We're bunkmates. We have to share, right?" He winked at her. "Sleep tight."

"You, too."

He went into his room and closed the door. She turned off the television and withdrew into her own room. After she'd put out the light, she lay in the darkness, loving the feel and smell of the T-shirt against her skin. She wondered if she could find some excuse for not giving it back.

She was delighted that he'd told her the true story of his background. She understood him much better. He had good reasons for wanting to stay uninvolved with women. But she wondered if he was beginning to feel the need for companionship, more than just a night's worth. And he'd mentioned watching Millie read to the kids, as if he'd cherished the memory. She felt warm all over at the idea that he'd felt something for her, until John killed it with his lies.

Her heart grew heavy. It was very well to think that she'd touched that cold heart, but he wasn't saying that he loved her or wanted to live with her. He was just looking after her, probably out of guilt because of the way he'd treated her. This wasn't a prelude to a life of happy togetherness. To Tony, it was just another job. She was a job. She'd do well to remember that and get her priorities straight. When the danger was over, she'd go back to her library and Tony would leave and never look back.

She closed her eyes and tried to sleep. It was almost morning by the time she finally managed it.

Two more days passed with no sign of any hired killer. Tony was in contact with both Frank and his detective friend. There was no gossip on the streets about the hit. That bothered Tony. He knew that the killer probably knew where Millie was, and he was biding his time until he saw an opening. This could drag on for weeks. Millie couldn't stay out of work forever, and Tony had a commitment coming up overseas. But there didn't seem to be any way to draw the hired killer out into the open.

Millie was wearing on him. He found himself watching her. She was pretty, in a way, and her figure was tantalizing. He was aroused by her. She didn't dress in a provocative manner, but she had pert little tip-tilted breasts that weren't disguised by her bra or the knit blouses she wore. He spent more and more time thinking how they might feel in his mouth.

It made him ill-tempered. He was used to women who gave out without reservations. Millie was attracted to him, too. He could see it. Frank had said that she was in love with him. He was tempted to see how far she'd let him go, but he wasn't certain about his own ability to stop in time. He hadn't had a woman in months, and he wasn't a man who could abstain for long periods of time.

Millie noticed his growing irritability and guessed that he didn't like having her cramp his style. Obviously he couldn't cavort with another woman while he was protecting her. She felt guilty. She would have liked to go home, and have him smile at her again, even if it meant giving him up to some flashy woman. She was resigned to the fact that he was never going to want her. He'd said several times that she really wasn't his type.

The next night, he paced the floor until he made her uncomfortable enough to go to bed.

"Don't rush off on my account," he said curtly. "I'm just not used to this much inactivity."

"No, I'm really sleepy," she assured him. "Good night."

"Yeah. Good night." He said it with pure sarcasm.

She put on his T-shirt and stretched out on the bed with the lights still on. She was as restless as he was, and probably just as uncomfortable. She ached for something, for kisses, for caresses, for human contact. He hadn't touched her since he'd held her wrists while he was talking about his mother. But he'd watched her. His eyes were narrow and covetous. She might be innocent, but she recognized that heat in him. It was in her, too, and she didn't know what to do about it. She'd never felt it so strongly before.

She stretched again, moaning softly as she thought how sweet it would be to lie in Tony's arms and let him kiss her until the aching stopped.

She heard the phone ring. A couple of minutes later, he rapped on her door and opened it without asking if she was decent.

He froze in the doorway, his eyes homing to the sharp peaks of her breasts and the long, uncovered length of her pretty legs. His teeth clenched. "A shark must feel like this, just before he bites," he said in a harsh tone, and he laughed.

"What?" she asked, breathless.

He closed the door behind him, tossed the cell phone he'd been using onto the dresser and made a beeline for the bed.

While she was conferring with herself about what to do next, he moved onto the bed, slid his big, warm hands under the T-shirt, and started kissing her as if he were starved. The combination of the heated, urgent kiss and his warm, enormous hands on her taut breasts was more than her prim scruples could overcome. She arched up into his hands and moaned so hungrily that he swept between her long legs without a second's hesitation, letting her feel what she already knew—that he wanted her.

It was every dream of passion she'd ever had, coming true. He smelled of rich spice and soap. His long, wavy black hair was unbound, around his shoulders. She gathered it into her hands and savored the silky feel of it, loving its length. She looked down through a heated mist at his mouth on her soft skin, completely covering one small breast. It was so erotic that she arched up off the bed to force his mouth closer. She closed her eyes, shivering with tension that built and built until she thought she might die of the ache.

The T-shirt was on the floor somewhere, along with his pajama bottoms. His mouth was all over her, on her throat, her mouth, her breasts, sliding down with expert cunning to her flat belly and lingering there while his hands teased at the edge of her briefs. He felt her trembling, heard her breathing catch. Just a few more seconds, he thought with pure lust, and she wouldn't be able to stop him. He was on fire, so far gone that his head was spinning with the sweetness of her skin under his mouth.

She felt his hand go under her briefs and when he touched her, instead of completing the arousal, it shocked her into the realization of what they were about to start. He would leave town and go back to work and never even remember what had happened. She would be left with a tarnished dream and a possible pregnancy, because she had nothing to use for birth control.

But when she pushed at his shoulders, he didn't realize she was trying to stop him. He was working the briefs off and she was almost too hungry to argue. But she had to. He'd never forgive her…

"I can't!" she burst out. "Tony, I can't! You have to stop!"

He lifted his head. His eyes were glazed. He was breathing like a distance runner. His broad, muscular, hair-covered chest was heaving with every breath. "What?" he choked.

"I…I can't!" she repeated.

The breathing didn't slow, and his hand was still moving. "Why not?"

"I'm not on the pill!" she burst out.

"Not on the pill." He blinked. "Not on the pill."

"I could get pregnant!" she insisted.

Sanity came back in a cold rush. He took slow breaths until he could control himself. That only made it worse, because he'd been totally helpless and she'd seen it. His eyes grew hot with anger, with condemnation.

With one smooth motion, he bounded away from her and rolled off the bed to his feet. He jerked on his pajama bottoms and turned to face her, still condemning as she scrambled under the bedcover.

"Well, if that doesn't beat all!" he muttered furiously. "You give me a come-hither look, open your arms to me and give it back like a professional. Then at the last minute, when I'm out of my mind, you jerk back and say I have to stop because you could get pregnant! That's just priceless! Priceless!"

"I didn't realize…!" She tried to defend herself.

"Of all the dirty, mean tricks to play on a man, that's the worst," he said in a tone that could have taken rust off. "You were getting even, weren't you? I treated you badly at John's funeral and you wanted payback?"

She flushed and dropped her gaze. She wouldn't cry. She wouldn't cry! She bit her lower lip, hard, as she fought for control. "I didn't do it to get even."

"The hell you didn't!"

"I didn't have anything to use," she protested shakily. "I've never…I haven't…I don't know…"

"You knew all that when I came in here," he said coldly. "You could have said so then."

He was right, of course. She could have. But she'd never been in Tony's arms, held close by him kissed by him, and she'd have died for the experience. It had been like paradise, for those few heated minutes before she came to her senses. She couldn't defend herself. He was probably hurting. She gritted her teeth. She didn't even know how to apologize.

He glared at the picture she made, wrapped up in the cover, only her head showing, her eyes hidden, her face white. If he hadn't been hurting so badly, he might have been less volatile in his treatment of her. But the pain was bad.

He turned and slammed out of the room, leaving the door ajar, fuming and cursing under his breath. His cell phone rang and rang. He finally realized it was on the dresser in Millie's room. She hadn't moved an inch when he scooped it up and opened it.

"Hello," he said furiously.

"Hi, stranger," came a purring, sexy tone. "I heard from Frank that you were in town. How about a little action? I don't have a thing to do tonight."

"Nothing to do?" His voice changed. The tone dropped. He sounded seductive, aware that he was still standing in the doorway of Millie's room and that she could hear every word. "We can't have that. Tell you what, baby, why don't you come over here and we'll have a couple of drinks and see what develops."

"What a nice idea!" she enthused. "Since I already know the name of the hotel, and the room number," she said, "I'll see you in about, ten minutes?"

"Ten minutes will be fine. Just enough time for me to have a shower and get into something comfortable. See you, sweetheart."

He didn't look back. He could imagine Millie's expression, and it made him feel good. She'd given him a nasty surprise, it was fair play for him to give her one. He went right into his own room, swiped up some clean clothes and walked right into the bathroom to shower without a single regret.

CHAPTER FIVE

MILLIE heard Tony's brazen invitation to the other woman with pure anguish. He didn't bother to look her way as he headed toward his own room. Maybe she'd frustrated him, maybe he was angry, but that was no excuse for bringing one of his glittery women over here to seduce her in earshot of Millie.

She might be a disappointment to him, as a woman, but she wasn't a doormat. No way was she staying in here to listen to him cavorting with his girlfriend! No way!

Furious, now, she threw on her clothes and her overcoat, fighting back tears, grabbed her purse, closed the bedroom door and walked right out of the apartment. The last thing she heard on the way was the sound of the shower running.

Tony had on slacks and a blue shirt that flattered his dark complexion. He greeted Angel with a smile and invited her in. She was wearing a sexy pair of black slacks with a lacy blouse, and her long black hair was swinging free.

Her black eyes teased him as she walked in front of him to the living room.

"Long time no see." She laughed. "You look good."

"So do you." He bent and kissed her, not passionately, but nicely. He went to pour drinks. "How've you been?"

She told him. He seemed to be listening, but his mind was on what had happened with Millie. Now that he was less stimulated, he recalled that it hadn't been Millie who started things rolling. It had been him. He'd dived on her like a starving shark. She, with her obvious inexperience, hadn't stood a chance. If she'd kept quiet, there wasn't a chance in hell that he'd have stopped in time. By now, they'd be having a conversation about blood tests and babies. His face flushed at just the thought.

"What's wrong?" Angel asked.

"Nothing," he said quickly, pasting on a smile. "Seen Frank lately?"

She let out a loud breath. "Tony, I've just been telling you about Frank. There's a job opening in Dallas and he wants to take it. The manager of the club's offering him advancement into security work, and he'll train him. It pays well."

"You don't say. He didn't tell me anything about it," he added.

"He's been in Dallas, interviewing. He just got back. I saw him at the club when I went off duty tonight. He's going to tell you tomorrow." She sipped her drink, put it down and brazenly slid into Tony's lap. "Don't let's talk about Frank. I'm lonely." She put her mouth against his with a little moan.

In the old days, that would have set the fires burning. But not tonight. Tony was remembering Millie's wretched expression. She'd be sitting in the bedroom hearing him with Angel and probably crying her eyes out over his insensitivity.

He drew away. "We're going to have to put anything past the drinks and conversation on hold," he said gently. "I'm working a job. There's a woman I'm protecting," he added, jerking his head toward the bedroom. "She's asleep, but she might wake up."

"Is she your girl?" Angel asked.

"She's a librarian," he replied flatly.

"Oh, good Lord, you poor man!" She laughed. "A librarian! How did you ever get talked into a job like this?"

He was offended by her attitude toward Millie. "It's not exactly easy to get those jobs," he said, his eyes narrowing. "My foster mother was a research librarian. She went through college to get the job, and even then she had to beat out the competition for it. So did the woman I'm guarding. It takes a good education," he added.

"Well, excuse me." Angel laughed. "Here I am with my little high school diploma making fun of a college graduate!"

He felt uncomfortable. He pushed her away and got to his feet. "It's just a job."

She got up, too. She gave him an amused smile as

she picked up her purse. She stopped just in front of him. "Just how old is this bookworm you're taking care of?"

"I don't know. Somewhere in her twenties."

"Pretty?"

He frowned. "Inside, she's pretty," he replied.

"Poor man," she sighed. She reached up and kissed his cheek. "I guess we all meet our Waterloo someday. Looks like this is yours." He chuckled. "Good luck."

That same thought was only beginning to form in his own mind. He smiled sheepishly. "Yeah. Thanks." He bent and kissed her cheek. "It was fun while it lasted."

"Same here. See you around," she added, and winked as she let herself out.

Tony stood, staring at the closed door, with his hands in his slacks pockets and his heart even with his shoes. He'd made a terrible mess of things. Millie was going to hate his guts.

He paused outside her door. He wanted to apologize, to tell her that inviting Angel over was mean-spirited and he was sorry about it. He was sorry for pushing her into a corner and making her feel guilty and cheap, when it was his own fault. He was the one who'd caused the problem and he'd blamed her. It was going to hurt, this apology. With a wistful smile, he knocked gently on the door.

"Millie?" he called.

There was no answer. He tried again, with the same result. She might be in the bathroom and couldn't hear him. Gently he opened the door and peered inside. The bed was empty. Millie's coat and purse were gone. He ran to the bathroom. It was empty, too. She'd gone! She'd walked out, probably while he was in the shower gloating about having Angel come over to show Millie he couldn't care less what she thought of him. Now she was walking into danger. If the contract killer was keeping an eye on her, he'd see her leave the hotel, in the dark, all by herself. He'd have a prime opportunity to kill her, and Tony would be responsible.

He grabbed his cell phone and punched the speed dial for Frank's number. God, he hoped Frank had it turned on!

Sure enough, he had his cell phone on. He answered on the second ring.

"Frank!" Tony said at once. "I need you to call your detective friend and tell him that Millie's on her way back to her apartment, alone. I have to get my car out of the parking garage and it will take precious time. He needs to send somebody to her address right now!"

"She's gone home alone?" Frank was all at sea. "But how did she get out past you? And why did she leave in the middle of the night?"

Tony ground his teeth together. "Tell you later," he gritted. "Do what you can about getting somebody to her apartment, will you? She may be perfectly safe, but I've got a feeling... Never mind. Thanks." He hung up before Frank had the chance to ask any more embarrassing questions. Then he ran down the stairs, foregoing the elevator, on his way to the parking garage. He prayed every step of the way that he wouldn't be too late. That sweet, gentle woman wouldn't stand a chance if the contract killer was anywhere nearby!

He broke speed limits and ran red lights across the city getting to Millie's apartment building, and had the good luck not to be seen by a squad car in the process. He parked in the first spot he came to, got out and ran toward the building. He didn't see another car, or another person, on the way in. Maybe, he thought, just maybe he'd get lucky.

He took the staircase up to the fourth floor and walked cautiously down the hall. He stopped in front of Millie's apartment, looking around carefully. He was relieved not to see any activity. He'd just relaxed and was about to knock on the door when he heard voices inside the apartment. One was male.

Tony almost threw his weight against the door to force it in a moment's panic, but that way would get her killed if the voice he heard was the killer's. So he slipped out of his shoes, picked the lock with ridiculous ease—thanking God that she didn't have a dead bolt lock—and slid his sidearm out of its holster as he silently opened the door.

"...never thought it would be this easy." A male voice chuckled. "So much for your boyfriend's skills."

"Could you just shoot me," Millie asked in a world-weary tone, "and not talk me to death?"

"Well, you've got grit," the man said with reluctant admiration. He raised a pistol with a makeshift silencer—an empty two liter soft drink bottle—duct-taped to the muzzle. "Goodbye from John."

"No. Goodbye from me." Tony had the pistol leveled at the man even as he spoke, his hands steady, his voice calm and cool.

As the hit man turned, shocked, and then lifted his gun again, Tony pulled the trigger. The killer fell to the floor and didn't move.

Tony put away his pistol, checked to make sure the hit man wasn't going to get up again and knelt beside Millie, who was sitting frozen on the edge of her bed. Her face was white. Her eyes were blank with shock. She looked at Tony, but she didn't even see him.

There was an urgent knock at the door. "Miss Evans?" a voice called with deep concern.

"Stay put," Tony said gently. "I'll answer it."

He opened the door, and Frank's detective friend was standing there with a patrol officer.

"We heard a gunshot when we got off the elevator. Is Miss Evans…?" the lieutenant began.

"She's fine," Tony said. "But, sadly for him, the hit man didn't hear me come in."

The lieutenant noted the pistol in its holster. Tony reached for his ID, but the lieutenant waved it away. "No need," he said. "I was on the phone with your boss just this afternoon. Where's the deceased?"

"In here." Tony led them into Millie's bedroom. She was sitting, staring into space. "She's pretty shaken," he told the other men.

"Miss Evans, wouldn't you like to sit in the living room while we process the scene?" the lieutenant asked her.

She looked at him blankly. He grimaced.

Tony bent and lifted her into his arms, cradling her a little too close to his massive chest in the aftermath of fear, and carried her tenderly into the living room. He brushed his mouth over her forehead as he put her on the couch. "It will be all right," he said softly. "I promise."

She didn't make a sound. In the space of minutes, her whole life had been turned upside down. The night had gone from a fulfilled dream to a nightmare. Tony, kissing her. Tony, furious and insulting her. Tony, bringing his girlfriend to the apartment to humiliate her. And now, Tony shooting another man in a space of seconds without hesitation, with eyes so cold they didn't even seem alive. She looked down and saw tiny droplets of blood on her overcoat. The killer's blood.

She took it off, with jerky motions, and dropped it quickly on the floor. She shivered. Tony's job had seemed otherworldly to her until tonight. Now she understood how deadly he was, how dangerous he was. Her eyes went involuntarily to the crumpled human figure on the floor of her bedroom, with dark stains growing around it. She shivered again. She'd only ever seen dead people in caskets. This was sickening. Terrifying. She realized that it could be her own body lying on the floor like that, except for Tony's dark skills.

Tony drew in a quiet breath. "I'm so sorry," he said. He

pulled a crocheted afghan off her easy chair and draped it around her. "I never meant tonight to end like this."

She shivered again. She didn't answer Tony, or even look at him.

People came and went. A team of crime scene investigators tramped over the apartment in funny blue pull-on boots, wearing masks and gloves, taking samples of everything, lifting fingerprints, bagging evidence. If Millie hadn't been so shell-shocked, she would have enjoyed watching the process that she'd only ever seen in television dramas.

Through it all, Tony stood with the detective, watching and commenting. At one point, Tony came back in with statement forms and asked if she felt up to writing down what had happened when she got home. She nodded zombielike, took a pen and started writing. Tony filled out his own form from across the room, just to make sure the lieutenant knew he wasn't collaborating on stories with Millie.

Hours later, many hours later, the police and the medical examiner's crew left with the body.

"You can't stay here," Tony told her quietly. "Not after what happened."

There was a tap on the door. Tony opened it and Frank came in. "I just got off work," he said, hesitating when Millie jumped up from the sofa and threw herself into his arms. She cried as if all the tears in the world were suddenly pouring out of her. She clung to Frank, sobbing incoherently. He held her, patting her back, while Tony looked on with anguish. He didn't need to ask why she was suddenly so animated with another man. She'd seen Tony shoot a man. His profession had suddenly become crystal clear to her, and she was afraid of him now. It was a miserable feeling.

"You can't stay here," Frank told her gently. "You can stay with my mother. I already talked to her about it."

"That's so…so kind of her," Millie choked, wiping at her eyes with the back of her hand.

"She likes you. Don't worry about packing anything," he added quickly when she looked, horrified, at her crime-scene-taped bedroom door. "She'll lend you a gown. Come on."

"Okay." She held onto his sleeve. She didn't quite meet Tony's searching eyes. "Thank you for saving my life," she said, like a child reciting a line her parents has prompted her to say.

"You're welcome," he replied in a cool tone. He was more shaken than he let on. He'd just killed a man. It wasn't the first time. But then he'd never seen himself through the eyes of an innocent. Millie couldn't even look at him anymore. He felt less than human.

Frank saw that. "I'll call you later," he told his friend, knowing that Tony would still be awake however long that was.

Tony drew in a long breath. "Sure."

Frank drew Millie out the door with him. He left it open. Tony stood there watching them until they were out of sight.

* * *

He went back to the hotel, but he didn't sleep. He was still awake late in the morning, so he ordered breakfast and sat down to eat it when it came. He called Frank as he made inroads into his second cup of strong black coffee.

"How is she?" he asked his friend.

"Shaken," he replied. "She couldn't stop talking about the way the man got into her apartment so easily, even before she had time to take off her overcoat. She figured he was watching and followed her home."

"That would be my guess, too."

Something in Tony's tone was familiar to the man who'd known him for so many years. "You never really get used to shooting people, do you?" he asked.

Tony sighed. "No. It goes with the job description, I guess, but in recent years I've been more of a planner than a participant. It's been a long time since I had to throw down on an assailant."

"You've got too much heart, and too much conscience, for the line of work you're in," Frank said flatly. "You need to consider a change, before you get so old that they retire you. Imagine having to live on a government pension," he added, and chuckled softly.

Tony laughed, too, but his heart wasn't in it. "Your friend the lieutenant have anything more to say about last night?" he asked.

"About the killer, you mean? He knew the guy, actually. He'd weaseled out of two homicide charges, just in the past year. In one of them, he shot a pregnant woman, killing her and the child. Funny thing, the two witnesses died in strange accidents, about a week before they were going to testify against him. He said the guy would do anything for money, and it's no loss."

"He was still a human being," Tony said in a dull, quiet tone. "He had family that must have loved him, at least when he was little. He had a mother…"

"He pushed her down a flight of stairs and killed her when he was eight," Frank mused. "It was in his juvy record. The psychiatrist figured it was a terrible accident and shouldn't be held against the poor orphan."

"You're kidding me!"

"The psychiatrist was later sued by the victim's family."

"No wonder."

"So stop beating your conscience to death," Frank counseled. "I'd like to tell you about my new job."

"In Dallas, I guess. Angel was over here—" He stopped dead. That had been a slip he shouldn't have made.

There was a long pause. "So that's why Millie went home alone, huh?" Frank asked, and in a different tone of voice. "Don't tell me—you made a heavy pass at Millie, she ran, you called Angel to come over and soothe you so that Millie could hear it all and see what she'd missed."

"Damn!" Tony muttered. Frank knew him right down to his bones, and he didn't like it.

"She's a virgin, you idiot!" Frank grumbled. "That sort of woman isn't going to go running headlong into a one-night stand. She believes it's a sin."

"Yeah, well, I wasn't exactly thinking clearly at the time!" Tony shot back.

"Now you are, and you've blown it," Frank advised him. "She doesn't want to see you again, ever."

Tony's heart felt as if it were weighed down with bricks. "Yeah. I sort of figured that's how she'd feel."

"Someday, you're going to fall for a woman. I hope for your sake that she doesn't treat you the way you've treated Millie," Frank replied. "She's special."

"I guess she'll marry you and live happily ever after, huh?" Tony asked sarcastically.

"Don't I wish," Frank sighed. "Why do you think I'm moving to Dallas? I'm sick of eating my heart out over Millie."

"You might try candy and flowers and soft music," Tony replied, trying to sound lighthearted.

"I've tried everything. She told me once that you can't make people love you," he added bitterly. "She was right. So I'm cutting my losses."

"She'll have nobody left to talk to," Tony said quietly. "She doesn't mix well. She's never had a real girlfriend that she could confide in. She won't let people get close to her."

"You don't know much about her, do you?" Frank asked.

Tony hesitated. "Not really, no."

"Her father was a roughneck, worked on oil rigs. When he came home, he drank. Excessively. Millie's mother tried to leave him, but he kept Millie with him and threatened to cut her up if her mother didn't come back. She was too scared of him not to do what he said. Millie's whole childhood was one of stark terror, of being afraid to trust anyone. It was almost a relief, she told me, when he died of a heart attack. She and her mother finally had some peace, but it was too late for Millie to reform her character. She doesn't trust anybody these days. And especially not after what John did to her. It was her father all over again, only worse."

Tony felt even smaller. "She never told me."

"Why would she? I'm sure she knew that you weren't interested in her."

"Yeah."

There was another long pause. "What's next on your agenda?" Frank asked.

"What? Oh. I've got an assignment over the border. Very hush-hush."

"Most of them are." Frank chuckled. "Well, I'll leave my forwarding address with Angel. You can come see me up in Dallas after the first of the year."

"I'll do that. I won't have any reason left to come back to San Antonio, once you're gone."

They were both talking around the fact that Millie would still live there.

"Can you tell her I'm sorry?" Tony asked after a minute. "I mean, really sorry. I tried to tell her just after I got the hit man, but she was too scared of me to listen."

"Is that surprising? Most people are scared of you."

"I don't mind it with most people," Tony said gruffly.

"She's gone through a lot. More than she should have had to. If I hadn't listened to John, maybe I could have spared her some of it."

"If."

"Yeah. Your lieutenant thinks she's out of the woods, then?"

"He does. One of his men's confidential informants said that the gang boss who was holding the money for the contract killer decided he needed a nice new car, so he wasn't passing the contract along. Good news for Millie."

"Very good." Tony was relieved. At least she'd be safe now, from John and his postmortem attempts on her life.

"So you can get on with your life now."

"I can."

"Keep in touch," Frank said.

"You know I'll do that. See you around, pal."

"You, too."

Tony leaned back and stared blankly at a painting of Japanese flowers and characters in the frame on the wall. It was all over. He'd go back to his assignments, Millie would go back to work, Frank would take up his new job in Dallas, and nothing would draw the men back to San Antonio ever again. Well, Frank's mother still lived there, so he'd go to see her, probably. But he was willing to bet that Frank wouldn't contact Millie again. Anyway, he consoled himself, he wasn't emotionally attached to Millie. It had been a physical need, brought on by abstinence and proximity. He'd be over it in no time.

He got up and started packing.

* * *

Millie was back in her own apartment. Frank had called in a marker and had the people who cleaned the nightclub come over and scrub Millie's apartment. He'd paid them out of his own pocket, but he hadn't told her.

When she left Frank's mother's house, Millie was still getting over the trauma. She wasn't looking forward to having to live where a man had died. But when she got inside, she was surprised. The bedroom had been re-arranged. It was spotlessly clean. There were new curtains, a new bedspread. It looked brand-new.

"Oh, you shouldn't have done this!" she exclaimed, smiling up at Frank.

He shrugged and grinned. "We're friends. It's for old times' sake. I won't be around for much longer."

"I know." She looked sad. "You'll like Dallas. My mother was from there. We used to go visit my grandmother, until she died."

"I'll like it," he agreed.

"This is great." She looked around, touching the curtains, smoothing the bed. Her eyes were sad. "Tony saved my life, and I barely thanked him," she said in a subdued tone. She looked at Frank, worried. "You know, he never blinked an eye. Tony was ice-cold. He never needed a second shot." She wrapped her arms around herself. "I've never seen anybody shot before."

"It's upsetting, the first time," Frank, a combat veteran, replied.

She cocked her head. "You've shot people."

He nodded. "I was in Iraq, in the early nineties," he reminded her.

She managed a smile. "It's not like they show it on TV and in the movies," she said. "Or in those spy films, either. This guy didn't have a metal silencer. He'd made one from a soft drink bottle and duct tape."

"Homemade ones still do the job," Frank told her. "He didn't want to attract attention."

"That gun of Tony's sounded like a cannon," she recalled. "The hall was full of people when we left, all trying to get in to see the crime-scene examiners work. I wish I'd paid attention. I was too shaken."

"So was Tony," Frank replied. "Regardless of the contract killer's background, he's still a human being. Tony used to go through some sort of purification thing. He won't go near the res in North Carolina, but he has cousins from his clan in Oklahoma. He hangs out with a couple of them. They build a sweat lodge and help him get through the emotional pangs."

She was fascinated. "I never knew that. Neither did his foster mother, I guess, because she didn't say anything about it."

"She didn't know," he said simply. "He didn't want her to know what his job actually involved. He told her he worked for the government, and she figured that meant he was a desk jockey."

"He protected her," she said.

"Exactly."

She went back into the living room silently, her eyes

on the sofa where Tony had placed her so gently after the shooting. He'd been supportive, nurturing, and she'd backed away from him. That must have hurt, especially when he'd shot a man to save her life.

"He said to tell you he was sorry," Frank told her.

She glanced at him. "He didn't need to be."

"About Angel," he emphasized.

She flushed. "Oh. The glittery woman."

He scowled. "Excuse me?"

She drew in a long, resigned breath. "You were always introducing him to girls who worked at the club," she recalled with a sad smile. "Those were his sort of women. He told me so. He didn't want ties, ever."

"He may want them someday."

"Not my business," she said quietly. "He brought her to his room to show me how little I meant to him. It wasn't necessary. I already knew that." She turned to Frank and laughed shortly. "I'm a librarian. Doesn't that just say it all?"

He scowled. "If you'll recall, that girl in the mummy movie was a librarian. She was a two-fisted heroine as well."

"Not me," Millie sighed. "Thanks for everything, Frank," she added, tiptoeing to kiss his tanned cheek. "I'll miss you."

He looked at her with anguished longing that he quickly concealed. He grinned. "I'll miss you, too, kid."

CHAPTER SIX

WEEKS passed. Thanksgiving went by in a flash, and suddenly it was almost Christmas. Millie stopped by the window of a department store when she got off the city bus at her stop. It was beautifully decorated in an old-fashioned sort of way, with artificial snow and trees and mountains, and a classic Lionel train set running through the scenery. Millie loved electric trains. One day, if she could ever afford a bigger apartment, she promised herself she was going to buy one and run it every Christmas.

It was cold, even in San Antonio. She tugged her coat closer. It was a new coat, an extravagance, but she couldn't bear to wear the old one ever again, even with the blood spatters removed. She'd given the coat to a charity drive.

She wondered how Frank was doing. He'd already moved up to Dallas. He phoned her and said he liked his new colleagues, and thought he was going to enjoy the job. He did miss San Antonio, though, he added.

Dallas was brassy and cosmopolitan, a sprawling city with odd, futuristic architecture. San Antonio still retained its historic charm. It was also smaller. But what he really meant was that he missed Millie. She was sorry she couldn't care for him as he cared for her. Despite everything, even after his cruel behavior, it was still Tony who lived in her heart.

Tony. She pulled the coat closer as she walked down the sidewalk toward her apartment building. She imagined he was off in some exotic place with some new glittery woman, having a ball. It was a modern sort of life for most women these days, rushing around from one sex partner to the next with no feeling of obligation or permanence. The movies reflected it. So did television and books. But Millie was a romantic. She lived in a past where men and women both abstained before marriage, where family mattered, where two people got to know each other as individual human beings long before they got to know each other physically. In that world, Millie lived. She devoured romance novels with characters who shared her old-fashioned views on life and society. So what if it was only make-believe. The carnal quality of relationships in real life was as empty as an office trash can on Sunday. Empty and sad. Like Tony's life.

For all his adventures, he would never know the joy of holding a baby in his arms and reading to his child at bedtime; watching him grow and learn and laugh. Millie wanted children so badly that it was almost painful to see them with their parents in stores and know that she would never experience that singular delight. She thought back often to the night in Tony's hotel room when she'd chosen virtue over experience, and she wondered what might have been if she hadn't stopped him. Perhaps there would have been a child, and she could have had it in secret and he'd never have known. It made her sad to think about that. She could have loved the child, even if Tony wouldn't let her love him.

She did enjoy her job. She got to read to children there. In fact, on Christmas Eve the library opened up for an orphan's home. Volunteers gathered to give presents to the children. The volunteers also read stories to the children. It was a new program that the library had only just instituted, and they were hoping that it would be a success. Millie was looking forward to it. She'd wear her red Santa Claus hat and a red dress, and for one night she could pretend that she was a mother. It was the only way, she thought wistfully, that she'd ever be one.

A newspaper reporter had shown up with a camera and a notebook computer to cover the event. Several other people were snapping photos with their cell phone cameras and movie cameras, probably to post on the Web. Millie was having the time of her life with two little girls in her lap. She was reading the story of *The Littlest Angel* to them. It had been her favorite as a child. Judging by the expressions on their faces of these small children, it was becoming a favorite of theirs as well.

She wasn't aware of a movement in the entrance of the library. A big man in a tan cashmere coat and a suit was standing there, watching the activity. The sight of Millie with those little girls only reinforced a thought he'd been harboring for some time now—that she would be a wonderful mother.

"Is it okay for me to be here?" he asked a woman wearing a name tag who was standing next to him.

She looked way up into large black eyes in a darkly tanned face, surrounded by wavy black hair in a ponytail. She smiled. "Of course," she said. "Do you know one of the children?"

He shook his head. "I know the lady who's reading to them," he corrected. "We've been friends for a long time."

"Miss Evans, you mean." She nodded. She smiled sadly. "She's had a very bad time in recent years, you know, especially when that man tried to kill her. She's much better now, though."

"Yes."

"You can go in, if you like," she added. "We've invited the public to participate. Actually," she added, "we're hoping that the children may form some attachments here that will benefit them. Donors are always welcomed. And there might be an opportunity for adoptions as well."

He frowned. "I hope you've screened the men."

She grimaced. "I know what you mean," she said softly. "No, that wouldn't have been possible, I'm afraid. But there are two undercover police officers in there," she added with a chuckle. "So if anybody has uncomfortable intentions, they'll be in for a big surprise."

He smiled broadly. "Nice thinking!"

She laughed. He was a very pleasant man. "Why don't you go and speak to Miss Evans? She's been very sad the past few weeks. I found her crying in the ladies' room, just after she came back to work. After the shooting, you know. She said she'd been so wrapped up in herself that she'd failed someone who was very close to her." She looked up at his expression. "That wouldn't be you, would it?"

His broad chest rose and fell. "I failed her," he said quietly.

She patted his big arm. "Life is all about redemption," she said softly. "Go make up."

He grinned at her. "You wouldn't be in the market for a husband, I guess?" he teased.

She laughed merrily. She was seventy if she was a day. Her white hair sparkled in the overhead light. "Get out of here, you varmint."

"Yes, ma'am."

He reached Millie just as she ended the story and kissed little cheeks.

"Go get some cake and punch now," she told them, easing them back on their feet.

They laughed and kissed her back. They were pretty little girls. One had jet-black hair and eyes, the other was a redhead. They held hands on the way to the treat table.

Millie was smiling after them when a shadow fell over her. She looked up into Tony's face and caught her breath.

He knelt in front of her chair. "Yeah," he said deeply, searching her green eyes through the lenses of her glasses. She wasn't wearing contacts tonight. "That's how I feel when I see you, too. It takes my breath away."

She didn't have enough time to guard her response. She was so happy to see him that she began to glow. "I didn't expect to see you," she said.

"Didn't you?" His dark eyes smiled. "I stayed away until I thought I'd given you enough time to get over what I did."

"You saved my life," she protested. "I barely thanked you for it."

"You look good with little kids in your lap," he said quietly. "Natural."

"I like children."

"Me, too."

She searched for something to say. "Why are you here?"

"Because you're here, and it's Christmas Eve," he said.

She didn't understand. "But how did you find me?"

"I work for the government," he pointed out. "I know how to find anybody."

That reminded her of the shooting, which brought back disturbing images.

"I'm mostly administrative these days," he said quickly. "I don't have to use a gun. That night…" He looked tormented. "I didn't have a choice," he began.

She put her hand over his mouth. "I'm sorry!" she said huskily. "I'm so sorry. I didn't mean to make you feel guilty over what you did. If you'd hesitated, we wouldn't even be having this conversation!"

He caught her wrist and kissed the palm hungrily.

Her breath caught again at the hunger his touch ignited in her.

He saw it. His dark eyes began to glow.

For long seconds, they just stared at each other, blind to amused looks and muffled conversation.

"Can you come outside and sit in the car with me for a minute?" he asked, clearing his throat.

"I guess so."

He got up and pulled her up with him. He waited while she got into her coat and spoke to the white-haired lady Tony had been flirting with. The elderly woman gave Tony a thumbs-up sign behind Millie's back and he laughed.

"What was that all about?" Millie asked as they went out the front door.

"I'm thinking of having an affair with that lady you were just talking to," he said with a blatant grin. "She's a hoot."

"Mrs. Mims, you mean?" She laughed. "Isn't she, just! She's president of our 'friends of the library.' Before she retired, she was an investigative reporter."

"Well!" He saw something in Millie's face that made him curious. "What does she do now?"

"She writes mystery novels," she told him. "Very successful ones."

"I should talk to her. I know a lot of mysteries." He

frowned. "Well, most of them are classified. But I could give her a few hints."

"She'd love that."

He unlocked the door of his rental car, a luxury one, and helped Millie into the passenger seat. She was smoothing the wooden dash when he got in on the other side.

"You do travel in style," she mused.

"I can afford to." He turned on the dome light and pulled something out of his pocket. "I've been doing a lot of thinking, about my life," he said as he faced her, with one arm over the back of her bucket seat. "I've been alone and I've enjoyed it. I've had brief liaisons, and I've enjoyed those, too. But I'm getting older. I'm tired of living alone."

She was hardly breathing as she sat, entranced, staring into his black eyes with breathless hope.

He reached out and touched her soft mouth with his fingertips, loving the way her eyes closed and her breath jerked out when he did it.

"Oh, hell, the rest can wait a minute. Come here!"

He dragged her over the console into his big arms and kissed her so hungrily that she actually whimpered with smoldering desire.

His breath caught at the sound. His arms contracted. His mouth opened on her lips, his tongue penetrating, his own moan overwhelming hers in the hot, urgent silence that followed.

After a minute, he shuddered and caught her arms. He put her back into her own seat with visible reluctance. He was almost shaking with the force of his need. She was so unsteady that she fell back against the door, her mouth swollen, her eyes wild and soft, all at once.

"My foster mother was like you," he managed. "Old-fashioned and bristling with principles that seem to be a joke in the modern world. But I happen to like it." He fumbled in his pocket for a gray jeweler's box. He put it into Millie's hands and closed them around it. "Open it."

She fumbled trying to get the spring lid to work. Finally he had to help her—not that his hands were much steadier.

There, in the box, was a set of rings. There was a yellow-gold emerald solitaire with diamond accents, and a gold wedding band with alternating diamonds and emeralds.

"They're beautiful," she whispered. Maybe she was dreaming. Yes. That was probably it. She pinched her own arm and jumped.

"You're not dreaming," he said, amused. "But I've done my share of that, since I messed up things in my hotel room." He made a whistling sound. "That was a closer call than you'll ever know, girl. If you hadn't started protesting, I couldn't have stopped. I'd never lost control like that in my whole life, even when I was in my teens."

Everything went over her head except the last sentence. "Really?"

"Really. You are one hot experience."

"Me?" she asked, surprised. "But I don't know anything."

He grinned slowly. "Yeah. That's the exciting thing."

She blushed. He laughed when he saw the color in her cheeks. He was thinking how rare a thing that was. He couldn't stop thinking about how it had been with her, on that hotel bed. Even in memory, it made his blood run hot.

"I've done bad things in my life," he said then, very solemnly. "I like to think I did them in the service of my country, to protect our way of life. It was exciting work, and profitable. But I've put a lot of money away, and I've gotten the wild streak in me tamed somewhat." He hesitated. It was hard work, putting this into words. "What I'm trying to say…I mean, what I'm trying to ask…"

"I'd marry you if we had to live in a mud hut in a swamp with ten million mosquitos!" she interrupted.

He caught his breath. "Millie!"

He scooped her up again and kissed her so long, and so hard, that the windows all fogged up. Which was probably a good thing. Because when the tap at the window came, they weren't in any condition to be seen.

They scrambled apart, rearranging clothing, trying to look normal.

Tony buzzed the window down, with a carefully calm expression that didn't go well at all with the smear of lipstick across his mouth and face, and his hopelessly stained white shirt and half-undone tie and unbuttoned shirt. "Yes?" he said politely.

The white-haired woman doubled up laughing.

He scowled, trying to neaten himself up. In future years, the story would be told and retold by both partners.

"I just wanted to say…" she choked, trying to stop laughing long enough to be coherent, "that we're opening the presents, and the little girls…would like Millie to help them open theirs."

"We'll be right in. We were just getting rings out of boxes and stuff," he said, ruffled.

She murmured that it looked to her that it was a good idea to get the rings on and the words said in some legal fashion, and pretty quickly. Then she laughed some more and left.

Tony slid the engagement ring onto Millie's finger and kissed her. "So much for surprising your colleagues," he mused. "I imagine Ms. Perry Mason there will have tipped off the whole bunch by the time we get back inside."

"I don't mind," she said shyly.

He was lost in her smile. "Me, neither," he said.

Then he had to kiss her again. But they managed to get back into the library before all the presents were opened, to an unconcealed round of laughter that only the adults in the group truly understood.

They spent Christmas Day together talking about the future in between kisses. Tony offered her a church wedding, but they both decided that it could probably wait until they had more than one friend to ask to attend it. Meanwhile the local probate judge's office did nicely, with an attorney who was looking for a birth certificate and a judge's clerk for witnesses.

It had been Tony who refused to go past some energetic petting before the wedding. He wanted Millie to have things just the way she wanted them, he explained. So they'd wait.

However, the minute they reached Millie's apartment, which was closer than his hotel room, they were undressing even as Tony locked her door. They didn't even make it to the bedroom. Millie had her first intensely intimate experience on the carpeted floor of her apartment, and she never felt the carpet burns until she and Tony were lying in a tangled, sweaty heap under the soft hall-ceiling light.

"Wow," he managed.

"Oh, yes," she whispered while her heartbeat threatened to pound her into the floor.

He stretched his tired muscles, laughing when they cramped. "Hell!" he muttered. "I really tried to make it to the bedroom…"

"I don't care," she said in a tone that almost purred with satisfaction. "On a floor, standing up, in the bathroom…I never dreamed it would feel like that!"

He rolled over, so that he could look down into her soft green eyes. Her glasses and her clothing were strewn around them. "It hurt, at first."

"Did it?" she asked, surprised. "I didn't even notice."

"You flinched," he mused, brushing his warm mouth over her swollen lips. He chuckled softly. "But I knew what to do about that."

She blushed as she recalled exactly what he'd done about that.

His mouth smoothed down over soft, smooth, warm flesh. "I'm still vibrating," he murmured. "It was like swallowing fireworks!"

"Yes." She reached up and pulled him down to her, loving the feel of his muscular, hairy chest over her bare breasts. The contact electrified her. She arched up, catching his legs with hers, curling them around, tugging hopefully.

"It may hurt," he whispered.

"It may not," she whispered back, touching him shyly, but boldly.

He groaned. After that, he wasn't in any condition to protest.

She had to sit down very carefully. He noticed and his pursed lips smiled, reminding her of the restraint he'd tried to exercise.

"You insisted," he charged.

She grimaced. "Yes, but now I know better." She grinned at him anyway. "It was worth it."

He laughed out loud. "Yes, it was. Are you hungry?"

Her eyebrows arched. "I am."

He went into the kitchen and started looking through cabinets and the refrigerator. He laughed. "I can see that you're not impartial to Italian cooking."

"I love it. But you're not Italian."

"Not hardly. I just have that last name, since my mother married the devil." He frowned. "I should have had it changed, I guess. But that SOB who got her pregnant would never have let her use his name, and I don't want it, either." He shrugged. "Nothing wrong with an Italian name. It confuses people who think they know my background." He glanced at her. "I like confusing people," he said.

She got up and went to him, sliding her arms around his middle, pressing her cheek against all that warm strength. "I love you so much," she whispered. "I thought I'd die of it."

His own arms contracted. He kissed her hair. "I didn't say the words," he whispered. "But you must know that I feel them, right to my soul. These past few weeks without you have been pure hell!" He bent and kissed her soft mouth with something like anguish. "God, I love you!"

Tears welled up in her eyes and overflowed. Afterward, he stood just holding her, rocking her in his big arms, while they savored the belonging.

"It's a few days too late, now, but I just remembered that I didn't get you anything for Christmas," he said suddenly, disturbed.

"Yes, you did," she argued. She looked up at him with clear green eyes. "I got you for Christmas." She kissed his chin and grinned. "You're the best belated present I ever had! My very own Silent Night Man." She cuddled close and added impishly, "My very own CIA agent! But I promise not to tell a soul."

He laughed wholeheartedly and wrapped her up close with a sigh. "You're the best present I ever had, too, precious. Merry Christmas."

"Merry Christmas, my darling," she whispered. She closed her eyes. Under her ear she heard the deep, steady beat of his heart. She remembered the instant she'd looked up into his eyes on Christmas Eve, and the glorious happiness she'd felt. It had only gotten better in the days that followed. This had been, she decided, the best Christmas of her whole life. She was holding her happiness in her arms.

* * * * *

Christmas Reunion
CATHERINE GEORGE

Catherine George was born in Wales and early on developed a passion for reading, which eventually fuelled her compulsion to write. Marriage to an engineer led to nine years in Brazil, but on his later travels the education of her son and daughter kept her in the UK. And instead of constant reading to pass her lonely evenings she began to write the first of her romantic novels. When not writing and reading she loves to cook, listen to opera and browse in antiques shops.

Dear Reader,

I felt both privileged and delighted to be asked to write a Christmas story for the Centenary Year of Mills & Boon, particularly when the subject was to be Christmas weddings.

I enjoy writing about weddings as much as writing about Christmas, so this was the icing on the cake for me. To expand the culinary theme, I added a few essential ingredients to my Christmas mix. Along with the joy of a snowy winter wedding with carols, I stirred in the thrill of first love and the rapture of reunion, added an unexpected Christmas Day for two, spiced it with a dash of Shakespeare, and gave it the finishing touch of a New Year's Eve trip to a very romantic location.

I hope the result is a confection you will enjoy reading as much as I enjoyed writing it. Try to steal some time to yourself while your loved ones are napping, or out on the traditional walk!

With warmest good wishes for Christmas and the New Year,

Happy reading,

Catherine George

CHAPTER ONE

WARNING lights flashed overhead as Gideon Ford turned off the motorway and, right on cue, drove straight into thick, freezing fog. Every mile of the route through the Cotswolds had needed such total concentration his eyes were burning by the time he reached Chastlecombe. The steep, deserted main street looked as unreal as a Christmas card through the tendrils of fog wreathing its festive lights, but almost zero visibility met him again when he left the town to turn up the private road to Ridge House. He slowed down to a snail's pace over the uneven surface, then stopped dead and hauled on the handbrake when he saw lights glimmering dimly in The Lodge, which was supposed to be empty over Christmas. With a groan he switched off the engine and got out to investigate. The Maynards were in Australia. So who, exactly, was in the house?

Gideon strode up the path to the front door and rang the bell, rousing a chorus of furious barking in response.

He relaxed slightly. If the dogs were there the Maynards must have come back for some reason.

Felicia Maynard was in the hall on her way to bed when the sudden peal of the doorbell frightened the life out of her. It was too late for carol singers, but burglars would hardly ring the bell. She gritted her teeth. Maybe staying here alone wasn't such a brilliant idea after all. She ran back to the kitchen to clip leashes to the clamouring retrievers and let them tug her along the hall. She hung onto the dogs as she opened the door, and then stood suddenly motionless as she gazed up at a face she hadn't seen in years. Waving dark hair framed chiselled features grown harder and more rugged with maturity, and the hazel eyes even had a line or two at the corners. But her tall, city-suited visitor was still the best-looking man she'd ever met.

Gideon Ford stood turned to stone as he gazed at the barefoot vision in the open doorway. Felicia Maynard's tawny hair spiralled loose on the shoulders of a long green dressing gown, and her dark, almond-shaped eyes were riveted on his in blank astonishment. She stood utterly still, until the panting black retrievers tugged at her impatiently, as if waiting for the word of command to launch on him in attack mode.

'Hello, Flick,' he said at last. 'Sorry to frighten you—'

'I wasn't frightened,' she lied hastily, as her heart resumed normal service. 'Gideon Ford, no less! This is a surprise.'

'Your parents told me the house would be empty over Christmas, so I came to investigate. I've just driven from London,' he added, shivering.

'Scary journey in this weather. All right, boys,' she said to the dogs, unclipping their leads. 'Crisis over.'

Freed from guard duty, the dogs made for Gideon with wagging tails. To Felicia's surprise they made a big fuss of him, submitted to expert ear-scratching, then at her sharp command loped off down the hall to the kitchen.

'You look frozen. Would you like some coffee?' she offered, surprising herself. Gideon even more, by the look on his face.

'I've been dreaming of coffee for the last thirty miles,' he said, after a pause.

'I'll take that as a yes, then,' said Felicia, nettled because he'd hesitated. She opened the door wider to let him in, then shut out the freezing fog and led him to the warm, inviting kitchen. She thrust her feet into the shoes lying under the table and gave her visitor a polite smile.

'Sit down while I boot up mother's new miracle coffee maker. Or are you in a hurry to get home?'

'No.' In no hurry at all now he'd set eyes on Felicia Maynard again.

With his intent eyes following her every move, Felicia was glad when the coffee was ready. She picked up the tray she'd loaded with hands less deft than usual, and took it to the table to join him. 'Mother told me you'd bought Ridge House,' she said, determinedly conversational. 'Apparently the town is agog to know if you're bringing a wife and family to share it.'

Gideon shook his head. 'No wife. No family. How about you?'

Felicia handed him a steaming mug. 'If you've been talking to my parents you probably know I'm not married, either.'

But not unattached. He drank deeply, and set the mug down with a sigh of appreciation. 'Wonderful. Thank you, Flick.'

'Not many people call me that any more.'

'You prefer the authorised version?'

She shook her head and sat down to face him. 'It makes me feel young again.'

His eyes lit with mockery. 'I know exactly how old you are, Miss Maynard, so that won't wash.'

'But you, Mr Ford,' she said very deliberately, 'have a lot more to show for the passing years than I do.'

He shrugged. 'I'm told a group of Harley Street consultants employs you as office manager, which sounds impressive enough to me.'

'Whereas you own a whole chain of pharmacies nationwide: a quantum leap from a single chemist shop in Chastlecombe.' She raised her cup in toast. 'Congratulations.'

'Thank you.' He raised an eyebrow. 'Your parents said you wouldn't be here over Christmas. Change of plan?'

'There was an unexpected shortage of beds where I was staying, so I came home to mine.'

'Do your parents know you're here alone?'

She shook her head vehemently. 'Absolutely not! They've gone to meet their first grandson—my brother's baby. I wouldn't dream of letting anything spoil the trip for them.'

Gideon's curiosity got the better of him. 'Why isn't the man in your life here with you?'

Her eyes shuttered. 'His boss invited a select few to a chalet in Klosters. I was included, but I couldn't go. I'm a bridesmaid at Poppy Robson's wedding tomorrow. So Charles sent the bride his regrets and took off solo to his dream Christmas holiday: skiing by day and furthering his ambitions over dinner every night.'

'What does he have in mind?'

'A partnership in the law firm he works for.'

Scorn gleamed in the striking eyes. 'If he turned down Christmas with you the man's also a total idiot.'

Felicia smiled, feeling absurdly gratified. 'Thanks for the compliment. Have some more coffee.'

'Thank you. I hope the fool hasn't spoiled your Christmas, Flick,' he added.

'Not in the least. I'll enjoy the wedding far more without him.' Damn. She hadn't meant to say that.

'Where does he think you are?'

'At the Robsons' farm. I was supposed to stay with Poppy for the wedding. I did for a couple of days, but some relatives turned up in need of beds so I moved back here. And to calm Poppy and her mother about sleeping alone in the house I fetched the dogs home from kennels.' For heaven's sake stop babbling and shut up, Maynard, she told herself crossly.

'Sensible move,' said Gideon. 'Will there be room for them at kennels when you go back to London? I'm here for a while, so I could take them if not.'

Felicia smiled, surprised. 'How very kind of you.' She hesitated, then shrugged. He might as well know the rest. 'Actually, there's no problem because I'm home until my parents get back. I'm taking time off to give serious thoughts to my future, Gideon.'

His eyes narrowed. 'You're giving up your job?'

'I might. Now my flatmate's married I can't keep the flat up on my own, so it feels like a good time to make a change all round.'

So she hadn't been living with her solicitor boyfriend. Excellent. Gideon leaned back in his chair. 'Do you have something else in mind?'

'Not yet. I'm thinking of leaving London to find work locally.'

'How does your lawyer feel about that?'

'Furious. Conducting a long-distance romance doesn't appeal to him.'

'Not a happy New Year for either of you, then?'

She shrugged. 'No broken hearts involved, I assure you—on either side.' Not much romance, either.

Gideon drained his cup and got up. 'I must let you get to bed. Thanks for the coffee, it was a life-saver.' He took out his wallet and handed her a card. 'If you have a problem, ring me. Any time.'

'I'll be fine,' she assured him.

He smiled. 'I'm sure you will. But I promised your parents I'd keep an eye on the house, so I'll merely be doubly vigilant now I know you're here.'

'On your property, in a way,' she said lightly. 'Though Dad bought The Lodge from the former owners of Ridge House, so I'm not your tenant. I just live in the "willow cabin at your gate".'

'Twelfth Night?' His eyes lit with a gleam so hot it almost sent her backing away. 'I prefer *Romeo and Juliet*. Goodnight, Flick.'

'Goodnight.' She closed the door, locked up, turned out lights and marched upstairs, annoyed to find she felt easier alone now Gideon was in residence up at Ridge House—which was totally illogical and girly. It was a good half-mile away from The Lodge. Nevertheless, she felt a lot safer knowing he was around for a while. Even though his parting shot had turned her knees, and other parts, to jelly.

Gideon Ford drove the short distance to Ridge House in a buoyant mood. His various trips to Chastlecombe over the months had never coincided with the visits Felicia Maynard made to her parents'. But seeing her tonight had given him proof of something he'd always known, deep down. One look at her had been all it took to revive feelings which had merely lain dormant all these years, ready to spring to life the moment they met again. Felicia had been a very pretty teenager, with an air of reserve that had set her apart from her peers. As an adult woman the prettiness had matured into good-looks all the more appealing for the intelligence behind them. And yet the man in her life had left her to spend Christmas alone! Gideon's eyes gleamed. Felicia might be home alone, but he would personally make sure she wouldn't be lonely.

While Gideon opened up Ridge House half a mile away, Felicia got ready for bed, deep in thought. The years had not so much rolled back as swamped her like a tidal wave at first sight of that unforgettable face. The shock of it had struck her dumb at first, then gone to the other extreme and loosened her tongue. Embarrassing. But though she'd prattled away about herself, Gideon had been annoyingly reticent about his own life. She shrugged. A successful entrepreneur with looks like his was bound to have loads of women in it—or even one special one. She slapped moisturiser on her face with an ungentle hand. The lady might be in residence at Ridge House already for all she knew. But Poppy's mother, the fount of all local knowledge, would surely have known about it if she were. Felicia scowled irritably at her reflection. Gideon Ford's private life was nothing to do with her.

She slid into bed, shivering. Tomorrow she just had to buy a hot-water bottle, because if there was such a thing in the house she hadn't found it anywhere. But tomorrow was Christmas Eve. There would be no place to park in the town. Not a problem. She wasn't due at Poppy's until midday, so the walk to town would be the ideal way to pass the time. But it would mean getting up early to exercise the dogs first—taking care to keep them well away from the grounds of Ridge House now the master was in residence.

For a while Felicia tried hard to blank out all thought of Gideon Ford. But her memory refused to co-operate. It rewound inexorably to her teenage years, and with a sigh she surrendered, at last, to nostalgia. Taller than most of his friends, Gideon Ford had excelled at sports, and as well as brawn had not only possessed brains, but looks which had all the girls sighing after him. He'd been skilled with a cricket bat, and a brilliant rugby full-back, but because most matches with other schools had been played on Saturdays he'd refused to put himself up for team selection. Gideon Ford had spent every Saturday in term time, and every day in school holidays, working in the family chemist shop with the father who'd brought his son up single-handedly almost from birth. And most surprising of all, unlike his fellow sixth formers, there had been no girlfriend in Gideon's life.

Consequently it had caused huge excitement when he'd turned up to audition for the Christmas concert. To impress parents, scenes from Shakespeare were to be part of the programme, along with the more usual items from various soloists and the school choir. The day Felicia had been cast as Juliet opposite Gideon as Romeo the envy of her friends had been almost as

intense as her fiercely hidden euphoria. And she knew
that Gideon had been treated to a lot of back-slapping
and horseplay from boys who'd hotly envied him the
chance of making love to Flick Maynard—even if it was
in Shakespearian verse in front of an audience.

Felicia smiled to herself in the dark. Her mole in the
male camp had been Andy Robson, brother of her best
friend Poppy. From the same source Felicia had known
for ages that the boys had called her the Snow Queen.
The title had been no problem to live up to, because
from the day she got to secondary school Felicia had
nourished such a fierce secret passion for Gideon Ford
that none of the other boys had ever stood the slightest
chance with her. But because he was two years ahead
of her, and in her eyes unattainable, she'd become
resigned to her passion remaining not only secret but
hopeless. When the miracle had happened, and she'd
been chosen to play Juliet to Gideon's Romeo, the Snow
Queen had wanted to yell in triumph and turn cart-
wheels round the school playing field instead of just ad-
mitting to Poppy that she was quite pleased with Mr
Johnson's casting.

Rehearsals had been held separately for each scene
after school, and the young drama teacher had been
loud with praise when he'd found that his Romeo and
Juliet were not only word-perfect from the start, but
promised to do him proud. After only a modicum of direction Gideon and Felicia had soon been playing the
balcony scene with all the conviction of young lovers—

but with an aura of innocence about their chemistry that was utter magic, as Paul Johnson had confided to astonished colleagues in the staffroom.

It had been all too easy for Felicia to play a girl madly in love. With Gideon in the role of Romeo no acting had been necessary.

The costumes had been hired from a theatrical agency. Felicia's dress had been pearl-coloured silk, with a low-cut square bodice and long tight sleeves puffed at elbow and shoulder. But Mr Johnson, after pronouncing the dress suitable, had been so keen to assess the reaction when his star performers were revealed to the audience for the first time he'd insisted that Romeo and Juliet wait to get into costume until the last minute before they appeared on stage for the dress rehearsal.

In the audience beforehand Poppy had eyed her friend's tight braids in surprise as they watched her brother Andy winning roars of laughter as Bottom in *A Midsummer Night's Dream*. 'Your make-up is brilliant, Flick, but what about your hair?'

'I'll comb it out and fasten some of Grandma's pearl beads in it, but I just had to catch Andy's star turn first.'

'Leah Porter was so sure Gideon would play Oberon to her Titania she's still steaming because he's your Romeo,' said Poppy, grinning. 'Andy, of course, told her she's jolly lucky to get him as Bottom.'

'She most certainly is. They're brilliant together.'

'Leah's pretty miffed because she hasn't seen you

two in action. Why won't Mr Johnson let anyone near your bit?'

'Because we're not as good as the others, I suppose.'

Poppy rolled her eyes. 'As if!'

Felicia laughed with the rest at pretty blonde Leah wooing Andy in his ass's head, but well before the scene ended she slipped away to change. Miss Nesbitt, Junior English, lowered the gleaming dress over Felicia's head and let it fall into place in folds just clear of her feet, and Felicia unravelled the braids and ran a comb through her hair to send it streaming down her back in gleaming tawny ripples. The young teacher helped thread the pearl beads through it, then looped one string across Felicia's forehead, and smiled in satisfaction.

'There you go, Juliet.'

Felicia smiled nervously, her heart beating a rapid tattoo as Miss Nesbitt opened the door to a tall figure in doublet and hose.

'Very nice indeed, Romeo! Your Juliet's ready and waiting.'

And utterly breathless at the sight of him.

'You look amazing, Flick,' said Gideon, in a tone which set Felicia's pulse racing.

'She certainly does. So do you.' Miss Nesbitt waved them away. 'Break a leg, you two.'

Gideon took Felicia's hand and held it tightly as they stole in taut silence down deserted corridors to wait backstage in the hall.

'You both look fantastic,' whispered the drama

teacher as they arrived. 'Once the wood in Athens has changed to an orchard in Verona pop up to your balcony, Juliet. Can you manage the ladder in that dress?'

Felicia gave him a radiant smile as she nodded. Tonight she could do anything. Gideon gave one last squeeze of her hand, then at the prompter's signal she began the careful climb—Gideon ready to catch her if she slipped. She gained her 'room', and stayed half hidden behind the window as the stage curtains went back and Romeo strolled on stage through the 'orchard'. His hose fitted his muscular athlete's legs like a second skin, and the short brocade doublet flattered a physique which raised a sigh from all the girls in the audience as Gideon looked up at the balcony in longing.

'But soft! What light through yonder window breaks? It is the east, and Juliet is the sun.'

Juliet moved out onto the balcony and leaned down to smile into his upturned face, transported back to fifteenth-century Verona as she risked the wrath of her family to welcome her lover. They played their scene to rapt silence, but wild cheers broke out when Romeo climbed the trellis to the balcony and took Juliet in his arms.

Felicia stirred restlessly at the memory, wondering now if the scene could have possibly been as perfect as she remembered. Both of them had looked the part. She still had the photographs to prove it. And neither of them had fluffed a line or missed one of the careful directions given by their teacher. But the following night, at the actual concert, Gideon had added a move of his own. When Romeo had taken Juliet in his arms on her balcony he had kissed her, the effect electric both on Felicia and the audience.

She had climbed down to the stage afterwards still dazed, and moved in front of the curtain, hand in hand with Romeo, to acknowledge the applause. Gideon had bowed with the grace of a natural athlete as Felicia sank into the deep curtsey practised for weeks in front of her mother's cheval mirror. Then it had been a quick change and back to earth to join in the Christmas carols with the choir and the audience. The following week had felt very flat, with no rehearsals and only the Christmas party to look forward to.

The entire week had been a trial, because their friends watched both of them like hawks, certain that Gideon had thawed the Snow Queen. But to Felicia's disappointment he'd made no move to cash in on the rapport that had made their scene such a triumph. Then the day before the party Gideon had asked her if he could drive her home after it, and all was well with the world. Felicia had known he delivered medicines to housebound patients in his father's van, but the possibility of his taking her home in it had never occurred to her. She had accepted happily, suddenly full of enthusiasm for the party she'd felt none at all for until then.

The Christmas dance had been a great success, which for Felicia had been solely down to Gideon, who'd stayed close to her all evening, whether they were dancing or not. When they collected their coats together at the end of the evening Poppy had been beside herself with excitement because Gideon was driving Felicia home.

'Must dash—Tom's waiting. But tell me all about it tomorrow,' she hissed. 'Every detail!'

But the drive home and the minutes spent in the van at The Lodge were too private to share with anyone. When Gideon kissed her goodnight Felicia's joy in the evening was complete.

'You didn't dance much with anyone else,' she said breathlessly.

'I didn't want to.' He ran his hands through her hair and kissed her again, with a warmth she reacted to hesitantly at first. But gradually she grew bolder, her lips and tongue responding with a shy ardour that aroused Gideon to such a pitch he tore himself away and subsided in his seat, his hand crushing Felicia's. 'I've got to stop,' he panted, 'or I'll want a hell of a lot more than just kisses.'

She glowed with delight. So the paragon was human after all. 'Will I see you again over Christmas?' she asked breathlessly.

He sighed. 'Flick, you know how things are. Christmas is the busiest time of the year in the shop. And now I've persuaded Dad to branch out with the gift side of things it's only fair I pitch in with that, as well as the deliveries—'

'Hey, don't worry. No problem.' She was out of the van at The Lodge gate and running up the path before he could say another word. And gave a better performance than her Juliet as she told her parents she'd had a wonderful time.

Felicia smiled ruefully into the darkness. How young and innocent it all seemed now. But then she *had* been innocent, or at least totally inexperienced. Unlike most of the other girls in her class. How hurt she'd been that night. After kissing her silly Gideon had left her high and dry with her first encounter with lust—though to be fair he hadn't left her long.

The following morning her mother had called her downstairs. 'Visitor for you, darling.'

Felicia dressed quickly and ran downstairs, expecting Poppy. And fought to hide her delight at the sight of Gideon drinking coffee at the kitchen table with her mother.

He jumped up, smiling warily. 'Hi, Flick. You took off last night before I could ask. I'm doing some deliveries for Dad this morning. Do you fancy coming along for the ride? I'd really appreciate your company,' he added, disarming her.

But, determined not to be a push-over, she shook her head. 'I'm going shopping with Mother.'

Which was news to Jess Maynard, but she picked up her cue like a pro. 'That can wait until you get back, darling, or even tomorrow. It's a lovely day for a drive.'

Pride salved, Felicia ran to get her jacket, and virtually danced down the path to the white van.

'You didn't give me time to finish last night,' Gideon

said as they set off. 'I was trying to say that I want to spend what free time I *do* have with you.'

'Oh.'

He put a hand on her knee. 'I wanted to chase after you to tell you that—'

She touched the hand fleetingly. 'I wish you had!'

'Do you mean that?' He turned for a moment to look at her, then returned his attention to the road with a smile when he found she did. 'Friends again, then?'

'Yes.'

'But let's get something straight,' he said, his tone so autocratic it thrilled her to the core. 'I want to be a whole lot more than just your friend.'

Oh, yes, please! She turned dark sparkling eyes on his profile. 'You may have noticed—or maybe you haven't—that I've never had a boyfriend.'

'It's a hot topic in the changing rooms,' he assured her. 'Did you know,' he added, 'that I've never had a girlfriend, either?'

Was he kidding? Of course she knew! 'Why not, Gideon?'

He grinned. 'I play too much sport and work too hard in the shop for problems with excess energy.' He hesitated, then sent her a sidelong look. 'I've never had a girlfriend because I've been waiting for you to grow up.'

Felicia stared at him in wonder, hardly daring to believe him.

He nodded. 'It's true, I swear.'

She swallowed hard. 'I had no idea.'

'Tell me about it! You don't know what effect you have on us poor helpless males.'

'The same helpless males who call me the Snow Queen?'

He chuckled, and put the possessive hand on her knee again. 'Stay that way for them. Keep your warmth for me. So is that settled?'

Felicia eyed his profile warily. 'What, exactly?'

'You and me.'

'You mean we're officially going out together?'

'Yes, Felicia Maynard, and staying in together now and again, too. Agreed?'

She nodded vehemently. 'I could make supper for you and your dad sometimes, when you're busy. If he wouldn't mind. About me, I mean.'

'He'll be all for it. He's always telling me I should spend more time with friends. Everything I do for him, Flick, and with him, is my choice entirely, never because Dad demands it.'

'I'm sure it is. He's always so kind—does he like me, do you think?'

'Of course he does. He thought you were wonderful as Juliet.'

'Only because I had you for my Romeo!'

And that, Felicia thought, punching her pillow again, had been the start of an idyllic phase in her life. All through that Christmas holiday they'd spent every moment possible together, to the satisfaction of Richard Ford, who'd been openly delighted about their friendship. When the shop had grown packed with people hunting for last-minute presents she'd helped out, displaying such a talent for selling expensive cosmetics and perfume he'd insisted on paying her a Christmas bonus.

It had all been like a dream come true, right through the following term, with cinema trips and long walks, and hours spent just talking, utterly happy in each other's company. Then, the night before the Easter holidays, Felicia's parents had suggested she ask Gideon round to The Lodge to keep her company while they were out at a charity dinner dance. Although hours had been spent together, in her room or his, Felicia was burningly aware that this would be their first time totally alone.

By the time Gideon arrived that night Felicia had already been hot with excitement, and both of them had been in too high a state of anticipation to eat much of the supper Jess Maynard had left for them. Afterwards Gideon had rushed her to the sitting room and pulled her down on the sofa, kissing her like a man at the end of his tether. For weeks there'd been lingering goodnight kisses, and stolen caresses that had stoked fires of mutual longing. But this time the knowledge that they were alone, without fear of interruption, had set the fires blazing out of control as soon as they touched. They'd gasped in each other's arms when his hands had slid beneath her sweater, and Felicia's tongue had responded ardently to the demand of his as he undid her bra with unsteady hands. With a groan he'd torn his mouth away, and pushed her sweater up to kiss her breasts.

'Wait,' she panted, and tugged it over her head. 'Take your shirt off,' she ordered, and Gideon obeyed, pulling her up hard against him as he kissed her again, his lips and tongue weaving such magic Felicia was soon desperate to experience the bliss of making love with Gideon for the first time. She caught her breath as she felt him harden against her, and with daring stroked him tentatively.

'Don't,' he gasped harshly. 'I'm not made of stone!'

'Neither am I. Make love to me properly, Gideon, *please*,' she implored.

His eyes glittered darkly as they gazed down into hers. 'Are you sure about this? *Really* sure?'

She nodded wordlessly, her own eyes lambent with such pleading that he kissed her fiercely. He pulled her to her feet and with an unsteady hand fumbled in his jeans pocket, while Felicia took off the rest of her clothes. Face hectically flushed, she stood with her hands behind her back, suddenly shy as he gazed at her in awed silence for a moment. Then with a growl Gideon pounced to pull her against him, and he kept her there with one hand as he tore his clothes off. They sank to the floor together, both of them shaking from head to foot as their naked bodies surged together. Then Gideon began to make love to her in earnest, caressing her breasts with eager hands and hungry, demanding lips that sent chills of delight coursing through her, followed by a streak of pure fire as his hand ventured lower to make sure she really

wanted him. When Felicia made it feverishly plain
that she'd break in little pieces if he didn't quench the
fire he'd started Gideon ordered her to close her eyes
for a minute.

'My hands are shaking,' he panted, taking so long her
impatient fingers dug into his back

'*Please!*' she gasped. 'Just *do* it.'

But in his desperate hurry Gideon made a total hash
of it. Their prolonged foreplay had fired him to such a
state of arousal he lost control the moment their bodies
joined. The first electric jolt of sensation was so intense
for him he was deaf to her cry of pain as lack of experience rocketed him to a frenzied climax which proved
too much for the protection he'd been so careful to use.

Felicia winced as she pulled the covers higher. Poor
kids. No romance as Romeo and Juliet any more. Just
a couple of teenagers whose first experience of sex had
ended in total disaster. Not total, exactly. To lie naked
in Gideon's arms as he caressed her, and to feel his hard
body vibrating with need against hers had been wonderful, just as she'd dreamed it would be. But after the
weeks of anticipation the act of love itself had been
pain and disillusion for her and humiliation and abject
remorse afterwards for Gideon. When the prospect of
consequences had hit them both simultaneously Felicia
had snatched up her clothes, sobbing, as Gideon,
appalled, stammered apologies she'd cut short in her
desperate need for privacy.

'Just go now, please. *Please!*'

And from that moment on Felicia Maynard had never set eyes on Gideon Ford again—until tonight, when he'd appeared out of the fog like a ghost from Christmas past.

CHAPTER TWO

THERE was no question of sleeping late next morning. After what felt like only minutes after Felicia had closed her eyes the dogs woke her, clamouring to go out. In an ideal world, she thought bitterly, she would have been allowed a lie-in after such a bad night. Instead she was forced to stumble downstairs before it was light. She flung open the kitchen door, teeth chattering, as Bran and Jet shot out into the garden, and only managed to lure them back in by rattling their filled bowls on the kitchen floor.

While they devoured their breakfasts, heads down and tails waving, Felicia made tea, then sat at the kitchen table to drink it while she jotted down a list of things she needed in town before she was plunged into the wedding mayhem of the Robson household. Right on cue, the phone rang.

'Are you up?' demanded Poppy.

'Of course I'm up,' said Felicia, yawning. 'The dogs saw to that. What's wrong, bride?'

'Nothing—just too excited to sleep any longer. Are you *sure* you don't want the hairdresser to perform on you as well, Flick? She'll be here at ten.'

'With my hair there's not much point. I'll do it myself when I get back from town.'

'You're not going down there this *morning*? I want you here!'

'I must do a spot of shopping first. But don't panic. I'll be with you at twelve on the dot, hair done and face on.'

'I just so wish you could have stayed here,' said Poppy with regret. 'On the other hand you had a lucky escape. It was bad enough before, but it's a madhouse since Andy arrived to wreak havoc among the girl cousins.'

'I had a lovely peaceful night in my own bed instead. By the way—'

'Must go. I can hear Mother rattling her way up with the bridal breakfast tray. Don't be late!'

Felicia put the phone down, smiling wryly. Poppy had cut her off before she could mention Gideon Ford.

Priority a hot-water bottle, she reminded herself as she went back to her list. More freezing fog was expected today, and the possibility of a white Christmas Day. No matter. As long as the snow kept off today, the weather could do what it liked tomorrow. Once the excitement of Poppy's wedding day was over Felicia was looking forward to lounging about in peace with the dogs, plus a pile of books and the television for company. The prospect was so inviting she patted gleaming heads lovingly as the retrievers came to lean against her legs.

When a look through the freezer turned up some of her mother's herb stuffing, she decided to buy a chicken in town as soon as the shops opened, and go the whole hog with bread sauce for a proper Christmas dinner. Then Bran and Jet could have some titbits for a special treat, and she'd have leftovers for Boxing Day.

Felicia downed the last of her tea, wondering how Gideon was managing for Christmas at Ridge House. He must surely have someone helping him up there. Though why he wanted such a big place with no wife and family to share it was a mystery. Especially when she knew, via an article in the local newspaper, that his main home was a Thames-side apartment in London. Not bad going for a boy who'd spent the early part of his life living over a shop. Good for him!

'I'm off to dress,' she told the dogs. 'Then because it's so early—thanks to you two—I'll take you for a walk. No, not now,' she laughed, as they began cavorting round her. 'Later.'

The walk with the dogs was trying. They wanted to run free in the grounds up at Ridge House, as they'd done the day before, and strained at their leashes when Felicia kept them in check along the lane. Even with the collar of her padded white parka turned up over a thick sweater she felt so chilly it was hard to be patient with the dogs, who investigated every twig and leaf along the hedgerows, it seemed to Felicia, before she put her foot down and turned them for home.

'Hey, I'm pack leader,' she informed them, 'so move it.'

Back at the house, Felicia exchanged Wellingtons and jeans for a short tweed skirt and knee-length suede boots. She pulled a yellow knitted beret over her hair, flung a matching muffler round her neck, and set off at a brisk pace, her spirits lifting as a pale sun broke through the fog.

It was no surprise to find the town already crowded. Her progress was slow, due to greetings from several people on her way to the thronged main square, where boys from the church choir were singing carols at the foot of the brightly lit Christmas tree. She put money in their bucket for the church roof fund, then dived into the warmth of the packed bookshop to buy extra paper-backs for her lazy Christmas Day. In a sudden spurt of extravagance, she added a history of Chastlecombe with exquisite watercolour illustrations for her father's January birthday. A look at her watch sent her off at a run to the arcade, where she forced herself to pass tempting windows displaying hand-made sweaters and classic clothes. Hot-water bottle, she reminded herself sternly, and made for Ford's Pharmacy, once a modest-sized chemist shop on one side of the arcade, but long since enlarged to take in premises on either side. As well as dispensing prescriptions and selling medical supplies of all kinds, it stocked a wide range of cameras and el-ectronic and household goods. It also held franchises for several brands of expensive cosmetics, and one window was given over to photographs of gorgeous, sultry models advertising perfume, alongside more mature beauties sponsoring anti-ageing miracle cream.

Felicia peered past them, trying to see if Gideon was in the shop. When—*if*—they met again, she was determined to be poised and casual instead of turning into a frozen lump at the mere sight of him. Satisfied there was no sign of him inside, she threaded her way along the thronged aisles to pick up a couple of hot-water bottles in fleecy covers, and then joined a line of people waiting to pay at the cash desks. The line was already so long that one of the assistants rang for help, and Felicia's heart leapt when Gideon Ford, suited up in Savile Row pinstripes, came to take over one of the tills. As she inched forward she grew resigned to her fate. Unless she turned tail and legged it right that minute, Gideon would be the one taking her money.

He looked up with the smile he gave everyone, but his eyes lit with extra warmth as she slid her hot-water bottles across the counter. 'Why, hello there, Flick. You're an early bird this morning.'

'Hi.' She smiled brightly. 'I didn't expect to find the boss manning a till.'

'At Christmas we take any help we can get,' he countered. 'Fancy pitching in yourself? I pay good rates.'

'Sorry. I've got a wedding to go to. And before I get to that I need to shop for my Christmas dinner.'

'You've left it a bit late,' he commented, handing her change over.

'True. There's a queue a mile long outside the butcher, so I just hope the supermarket still has a chicken or two left before I walk home.' She smiled at him. 'Merry Christmas, Gideon.'

'And to you, Flick.'

Felicia left for the supermarket at a run, annoyed now that she hadn't driven down. Instead of pushing a trolley round the store she took a wire basket to make sure she didn't buy more than she could carry home. Already laden with a bag of books and the hot-water bottles, once she acquired a large corn-fed chicken and a bag of groceries she felt like a pack mule.

'Taxi?' said a familiar voice, as she hurried from the store.

Felicia spun round to see Gideon getting out of a car, and gave him a radiant smile. 'Oh, yes, *please*,' she said thankfully. 'I didn't drive down because I thought parking would be a nightmare.'

'It is,' he assured her, and took her bags. 'Isn't all this a bit ambitious just before the wedding?'

She nodded ruefully. 'But I was up early with the dogs. I walked them first, too, so I suppose hiking into town afterwards was a bit silly. And of course I bought more than I intended.' She eyed him curiously as he got in the car. 'I didn't see you in the supermarket.'

'I wasn't there. At the thought of you hiking home laden with shopping I deserted my post to drive you.'

Felicia stared at him in surprise. 'Why, thank you, Gideon. Have you finished for the day, then?'

'No.' He turned the car into the stream of traffic. 'I'll drop you off and then help out in the shop again for an hour or so.'

'You're very kind.'

'A regular paragon,' he agreed with mockery.

She chuckled. 'That's what the girls in school used to call you—amongst other things.'

'What other things?'

'I won't sully my lips by repeating them,' she said primly.

He let out a crack of laughter. 'Good God! I wish I'd known.'

'What would you have done if you had?'

'Nothing different.' He shot her a sidelong glance. 'You were the only one I ever wanted.'

Felicia blinked, struck dumb by this matter-of-fact announcement, and she grew so conscious of his proximity, and the scent of warm, immaculately groomed male in the close confines of the car, she was anything but a frozen lump by the time they reached her gate. Gideon helped her out, then collected her bags and carried them to the front door.

'Thank you,' she said breathlessly, as she unlocked it.

His eyes lit with a hot gleam she was sure they'd never possessed when he was young. 'By the way, we didn't discuss a fare in advance.'

'True. Is your fee high?' she demanded, expecting— hoping?—that he'd ask for a kiss.

He gave her a slow, unnerving smile. 'It depends on

how you look at it. There is a charge, but are you prepared to pay it?'

Felicia eyed him suspiciously. 'What do you have in mind?'

'Information. I want you to fill some gaps for me. I know you're tied up with the Robson wedding today, but what are you doing tomorrow?'

'It's Christmas Day!'

His lips twitched. 'So they tell me. Where are you spending it?'

'Here.'

'Alone?'

'Yes,' she said defensively. 'Mrs Robson wanted me to go back to the farm for lunch, but I declined with grateful thanks. She's got a houseful already, and it would have been a bit strange without Poppy, so I opted for peaceful solitude with Bran and Jet.'

'Why did Poppy choose Christmas Eve for her wedding day? Honeymoon travel must be a challenge.'

'They're not travelling anywhere other than back to the house they moved into a month ago. They've only just got it straight, and Poppy wanted to spend their first married Christmas Day alone there together.' Felicia smiled. 'Tom was all for it.'

'I'm sure he was.' Gideon gave her a straight look. 'You and I are alone tomorrow, too, Flick. So postpone the chicken to Boxing Day and have lunch at Ridge House with me. And afterwards you can fill those gaps I mentioned. I'll fetch you about eleven.'

She stared at him in astonishment. 'You're serious?'

He grinned, looking so much like the teenager she'd adored that Felicia's heart contracted. 'Dead serious. What do you say?'

'Well, yes, I suppose,' she said warily, and made a rapid mental inventory of her shopping. 'But you'd better come here to eat—because of the dogs.'

'I'm only too delighted,' he assured her. 'Christmas dinner at The Lodge it is, then. Though I still want to show you round my house.'

'I'd love to see it some other time.' She smiled. 'Come about midday tomorrow. I should have the meal well in hand by then.'

CHAPTER THREE

FELICIA went inside to let the clamouring dogs out, then put her shopping away in a daze, not sure how she felt about spending Christmas Day with Gideon Ford. What gaps did he mean, exactly? she wondered, as she raced upstairs to transform herself into a presentable bridesmaid. Compared with his impressive empire-building her life had been uneventful. School, college, work, some boyfriends along the way, but no relationships of any significance—mainly because Juliet had found it so desperately hard to get over her Romeo. All the men she'd met in the years since, up to and including Charles Beattie, had failed to measure up to her memory of Gideon Ford—whether they were taller than him or not. And now that he'd grown into his bones Gideon was a very impressive man, she conceded with a sigh, not sure that she'd been wise to say yes to Christmas dinner with him. Oh, why not? she thought impatiently. She wasn't accountable to anyone—certainly not to Charles now. Besides, it was no big deal for two old friends to eat together, Christmas Day or not.

The Robson farm, as expected, was in total chaos when Felicia arrived. Andy came bounding out to give Felicia a rib-threatening hug, his small daughter toddling behind, and Christmas music blared from the house as Mrs Robson, looking flustered, urgently beckoned to Felicia.

'Thank heavens you're here! I can't get Poppy out of the barn; I'm sure she's ruining her hair. You know I wanted to have the reception at a hotel, but would she listen? The caterers have put out some snacks for us, so please coax her into the house to have something to eat before she gets dressed. You too, dear. I don't want any fainting on the way down the aisle!'

Felicia gave her a kiss. 'Don't worry, I'll winkle her out.' She held out a hand to the little girl. 'Come on, sweetheart, let's capture Auntie Poppy and drag her into the house.'

'We'll capture my wife at the same time,' said Andy, picking up his daughter. 'She's in there, too, fussing over last-minute details. Lord knows why. It all looked perfect to me hours ago.'

'It looked perfect yesterday,' Felicia assured him. 'Once we put the decorations up we spent ages juggling with place cards.'

The bride, her old jeans and sweater incongruous with her elegantly piled hair, was standing just inside the barn doors beside a giant, lavishly decorated Christmas tree, deep in consultation with her similarly coiffed sister-in-law.

'Come on, you two,' called Felicia. 'It looks perfect, so come and eat something.'

Poppy turned in relief, smiling. 'About time you got here, bridesmaid!'

'Hi, Leah,' said Felicia, and gave Andy's wife a hug. 'You both look very glamorous about the head. Will my home-made effort pass?'

Poppy cast an eye over the tawny curling hair Felicia had caught up into a looser knot than usual, with a few spiralling tendrils allowed to soften it for this special day. 'Gorgeous.'

Andy gave Leah a kiss. 'Come on, darling. Mother's convinced you girls will pass out in church if you don't choke down a lobster puff, or whatever.' He waved a hand at the transformed barn. 'You've done a really good job, sis.'

Green garlands studded with red and gold baubles looped the old stone walls. More baubles gleamed among the holly and mistletoe suspended from the rafters over tables laid with crimson cloths and spectacular central decorations of holly and ivy wreathed round fat red candles. Sheaves of corn trailing fairy lights stood in pairs in corners and along the walls, and as a finishing touch the fire basket under the great iron cowl and chimney used for pheasant shoots was stacked with logs ready to blaze in welcome later.

'Flick has been a huge help,' said Poppy, and gave her bridesmaid a grateful hug as they all went back to the house. 'You should have seen her shinning up and down ladders to hang holly and mistletoe yester-day!'

'He obviously wishes he had,' said Leah, laughing, and gave her leering husband a shove. 'Put your tongue back in, Robson.'

The bride's mother, elegant in violet suit and hat, was driven to church later, with her elderly fur-coated aunts, followed by Rob and Leah and their daughter, plus a trio of young cousins. In the sudden peace that followed Felicia was still trying to zip up the bride's dress when Poppy casually mentioned an extra wedding guest.

'You'll never guess who Tom met this morning when he drove down into town to collect his grandmother's medication.' Her expectant eyes met Felicia's in the mirror. 'Gideon Ford was actually in the shop—manning a till, would you believe!'

Felicia's hand paused. 'I would, actually. He was there when I went in for a hot-water bottle. Keep *still*, Poppy, this catch is tricky. I don't want to tear the lace.'

'You've met him, then,' said her friend, crestfallen.

'Yes, last night. He called at the house to check up because I had lights on and Mum and Dad had told him the place would be empty. It was a big surprise to find Gideon Ford on the doorstep.' Total shock, rather.

Poppy spun round, her skirt swirling dramatically. 'You never said a word this morning!' she accused.

'You didn't give me a chance.'

'So what happened?'

'Nothing much. He'd just driven from London, and looked frozen, so I asked him in for coffee.'

'*Really?* He's been here a few times, sorting Ridge House, but never when I'm around. How does he look these days?' Poppy asked eagerly.

'Good,' said Felicia tersely.

'Tom said he seemed delighted with the invitation.'

'Should you have been talking to your bridegroom at that point?'

'As long as we didn't actually *see* each other today before the ceremony a phone call doesn't matter.' Poppy sat down again, to let Felicia secure a small coronet of rosebuds and ivy in her hair, then got to her feet, eyeing herself in the mirror. 'That's it, then. How do I look?'

'Sensational!' Which was the literal truth. Poppy's dress was dramatic. The top half had long tight sleeves and a low neckline in heavy white lace, in striking contrast to the crimson velvet skirt.

'Thank you, Felicia. You look pretty good yourself!'

Felicia's ivy-green dress was long and narrow-skirted, and all velvet. Poppy fastened a trio of rosebuds in her bridesmaid's loose knot of hair, then stood back and smiled happily at their reflections.

'We look pretty damn good,' she said with satisfaction.

Felicia helped her into the red velvet jacket that completed her bridal finery, and with a last look at her reflection Poppy picked up her bouquet of trailing ivy and crimson roses, then made for the door when her father shouted up to say the car was ready and waiting.

'I shouldn't be coming in the same car. You're supposed to ride in stately splendour with your dad,' said Felicia as they went downstairs.

'Poppy and I wanted you with us, dear,' said George Robson, smiling at her, then blinked hard as he saw his daughter. 'Oh, my lovely girl—you're an absolute picture,' he said gruffly.

'Thank you, Dad.' Poppy kissed his cheek lovingly.

He cleared his throat. 'You make sure Tom Henshawe takes good care of you.'

'It's all Tom's ever wanted to do,' Felicia assured him.

They arrived at the church to a joyous peal of bells, and smiles and waves from the crowds who'd taken time off from last-minute shopping to see the bride.

Felicia slid from the car to help arrange Poppy's skirt, and fell in behind as George Robson proudly led his daughter up the path to the garlanded porch where Andy waited with his own daughter. The toddler looked like a walking doll in her green velvet dress and slippers, a garland of rosebuds in her gold curls and her hands in the little velvet muff she was so proud of. Andy handed her over to Felicia, kissed his sister, then went inside with his fellow ushers and joined his wife.

When the familiar strains of Mendelssohn accompanied the bridal party down the aisle Felicia's throat tightened, and the bridegroom greeted his radiant bride with a smile of such tenderness his mother sniffed audibly in the pew behind him. Felicia had spotted Gideon the moment she was inside the church, and gave him a fleeting smile as she passed by, then the organist stopped playing as they reached the smiling vicar at the altar steps. Poppy handed her bouquet to the senior bridesmaid, the junior brides-maid decided she wanted to sit on her mother's knee, and the service began.

The church choir led the congregation in Poppy's choice of seasonal carols, and later, while the register was signed, the smallest boy in the choir sang 'In The Bleak Midwinter' in a treble so pure there was hardly a dry eye in the church. As a grand finale everyone joined in a lively rendition of 'O Come All Ye Faithful' before the wedding party emerged from the vestry to walk down the aisle to the triumphal strains of Wagner.

When the fading light shortened the photographic session in the porch the photographer left to continue at the reception. And once the bride and groom had driven off in a cloud of confetti to follow them Mrs Robson began organising a place in one of the cars for Felicia.

Gideon stepped forward. 'I've got room in mine, Mrs Robson.'

'How kind,' she said, beaming. 'All right with you, Felicia? A pity to crush that dress by squashing in with us. Thank you very much, Mr Ford.'

'Gideon, please,' he said, smiling at her.

'It's a pleasure to see you again,' she said warmly. 'I'm so glad Tom met up with you this morning.'

'Are *you*?' said Gideon, as he held his car door for Felicia.

'Am I what?' she asked, shivering.

'Glad that Tom met and invited me this morning?'

'Of course I am.' She smiled gratefully as he turned up the heating. 'Thank you. I was getting a bit cold.'

'I could see that. I jumped in with my offer before you succumbed to frostbite.'

Felicia wondered if he'd noticed the gleeful look Mrs Robson exchanged with Leah when he'd done so. 'So is all this taking you back? It's like a school reunion.'

'It's interesting to meet up with old friends,' he agreed.

'You must see a difference in some people.'

'Some thinner, some fatter, everyone older, but basically pretty much the same.' He smiled. 'I knew Tom Henshawe was crazy about Poppy, but Andy Robson married to Leah Porter surprised me. I thought she had aspirations to be an actress.'

'She had. She even went to drama school after her degree. But after a while she decided it wasn't for her, went back to teaching, and met up with Andy again.'

Gideon glanced at Felicia as they left the town behind. 'Are you warmer now?'

'I certainly am. And there'll be hot mulled wine when we get to the barn.' Felicia smiled at him. 'When you see inside you'll understand why Poppy wanted to get married on Christmas Eve.'

'The message came over loud and clear in church, with the carols.'

'Poppy's favourites every one. Though she joked that "O Come All Ye Faithful" was a hint to Tom—as if he needed it. There's never been anyone else for him since they were in nursery school.'

'So why has it taken so long to get to this stage?'

'They've been living together since they got officially engaged last year. Poppy had this bee in her bonnet about not wanting anything to rock the boat, on the principle that if it ain't broke don't mend it, but Tom put his foot down when she started talking about children. And Poppy caved in the minute he said marry me or else. Do you remember the way to the farm?' she added.

'Of course I do,' said Gideon, in a tone which won him a startled glance. 'I remember every last thing about my life here.'

'Could I ask you a really big favour?' said Felicia, quelling the shiver his remark had sent skittering down her spine. 'I need to let the dogs out before I join the party, so could we make a detour past The Lodge? It's starting to snow.'

'Do you have your keys with you?'

She nodded, and jingled them in her rose-trimmed velvet purse.

'Then I'll drop you off at the farm and drive back to let them out.'

'But I can't impose on you to do that!'

'Of course you can. You're not dressed for dog-walking.'

Gideon drove down the lane to the farm, and parked right outside the barn doors. He came round to let Felicia out and, ignoring her protests, picked her up to carry her through the falling snow to set her down alongside Poppy and Tom in the warmth and light inside the barn.

'Hey,' said the bridegroom, grinning. 'That's supposed to be the bride's prerogative!'

'I thought you might object if I gave Poppy the same treatment,' said Gideon, laughing. He gave the pair good wishes for their happiness as he shook Tom's hand and kissed Poppy, had a word with both sets of parents, then excused himself to run an errand before joining them for their wedding supper.

'Wow,' muttered Poppy. 'How romantic was that?'

'It was only to save my posh velvet shoes,' said Felicia. 'Say cheese!' she added as the photographer resumed his work.

Once the photo shoot was over the guests were served with copious quantities of hot mulled wine, which soon combined with the warmth emanating from the roaring log fire to heighten the festive atmosphere.

Poppy had been worried over seating the day before because Charles Beattie's absence meant that her bridesmaid had no partner. The usual choice, the best man, had a wife, whose place was obviously beside him, but Felicia had promptly solved the problem by asking to sit with Andy and Leah at their table.

When the best man announced in stentorian tones that everyone should take their places so the vicar could say grace, it came as no surprise to find that Poppy had added an extra setting alongside Felicia's—with Gideon Ford's name printed on the place card. She looked up with a smile as Gideon waited for the vicar to finish. He held her chair for her and sat down, confirming that the dogs were fine. He greeted everyone at the table, then smiled across at the little girl eyeing him with the open curiosity of the very young.

'Hello, Miss Bridesmaid. You're a very beautiful young lady. Will you tell me your name?'

'She doesn't talk much yet,' warned Leah.

'Unlike her mother,' teased her husband, and turned to his little daughter. 'Go on, pet. Tell the gentleman your name.'

A mischievous smile lit the elfin face as she pointed to the table decoration and then to herself.

Gideon pretended to ponder. 'Is your name Candle?' he asked, surprised.

She shook her head, and pointed again.

'I've got it,' he said in triumph. 'You're Ivy!'

Another shake of the garlanded curls.

'I give up,' he said, throwing up his hands.

'*Holly,*' she said, giggling in delight when he got up to bow.

'Of course you are! How do you do, Holly?'

While the first course of steaming soup was served, Gideon told Felicia he'd fed the dogs. 'They were so insistent I had no choice.'

'I forgot to mention that,' she said, laughing. 'How did you know where to find their food?'

'They practically opened the cupboard door for me!'

Aware of Leah's searching gaze fixed on them,

Felicia began introducing Gideon to the other guests at the table. The convivial bunch included Tom's two younger brothers, who knew the builders working on Ridge House and asked Gideon about their progress. He was currently converting the attic floor to an office area, he told them, so that he could conduct his business affairs from Chastlecombe when necessary, as easily as from his headquarters in London.

'So you've decided to come home at last?' said Leah. 'What took you so long?'

'I had one or two things to do first,' he said dryly.

'If you've both been in London all this time,' said Andy, 'it's surprising you and Flick have never run into each other.'

'Oh, come on,' said Felicia, laughing. 'What are the odds on that? London's a big city, Andy.'

'Did you know she worked there, Gideon?' asked Leah.

'Yes, her parents told me,' he said casually. 'Though until yesterday we hadn't actually met up again since we were in school.'

'Turned out quite well, hasn't she?' said Andy, grinning. 'Ah, good. Here comes more food.'

The lavish main course was eventually followed by individual Christmas puddings, which arrived at the table in dramatic flames. Holly, visibly flagging, clapped her hands at the sight, but by the time the speeches began she was fast asleep on her father's shoulder.

The bride's father was sentimental, the best man humorous and very complimentary to the ravishing bridesmaids, but when the bridegroom got up he simply drew a long breath and said, 'At last!' gazing down at his bride with eyes blazing with such happiness that David Henshawe jumped up to lead the cheers and applause when it became obvious that his brother was too emotional to say more.

'What happens now?' asked Gideon in an undertone as the noise died down.

'The bride and groom cut the cake, then the dancing begins. Nothing sophisticated,' added Felicia. 'Just Tom's young brother Jake as DJ.' She smiled at him. 'Poppy wanted simple.'

'She was right. The best man was right, too. You do look ravishing,' he added softly. 'Your lawyer is an idiot.'

She shrugged indifferently. 'He's probably having the time of his life right now.'

The intent eyes looked into hers. 'How about you?'

It suddenly struck Felicia that she was, too. 'I'm enjoying all this enormously,' she assured him. 'Do you dance much these days?'

'No.' He gave her the unnerving smile again. 'But I'll make up for it tonight.'

On the bride's instructions Jake Henshawe had made a compilation of Fred Astaire songs to start the proceedings. When he asked the bride and groom to take the floor, Poppy took off her jacket, made a sweeping curtsey in response to the applause, then melted into Tom's outstretched arms to dance to the sophisticated strains of 'The Way You Look Tonight.' When the song changed to 'Let's Face the Music and Dance' the best man came to claim Felicia, but when 'Change Partners' followed it he handed her over to Gideon and went off to dance with his wife.

By this time everyone was on the floor, displaying various levels of expertise, and several of the older guests were happily singing along with Fred Astaire.

'We get contemporary stuff later on,' Felicia told Gideon.

'I prefer this kind,' he said, pulling her closer. 'What man wants to hop about on his own when he can hold a beautiful woman in his arms?'

There was general laughter when David Henshawe ordered everyone to obey as 'Change Partners' began again. Jake had cut the CD to make the change every other song, and Felicia danced with several different partners, including the euphoric bridegroom and the bride's surprisingly nimble father, before she got back to the table to down the glass of water Gideon had poured for her.

'Thank you,' she said breathlessly. 'Wow, that was fun.'

'It certainly was,' he agreed, and grinned at Leah. 'Your mother's a regular Ginger Rogers.'

'Which is more than can be said for you, David Henshawe,' she said, wincing. 'My toes may never recover from our foxtrot.'

The young man grinned cheerfully. 'Is that what we were doing? I'm better at the other stuff. Look out when Jake plays the real dance music!'

Leah gave a theatrical moan.

'Where's the little bridesmaid, Mummy?' asked Felicia.

Leah smiled fondly. 'Fast asleep over at the house, with Tom's young cousin watching over her, phone at the ready if I'm needed. His grandma nobly offered, but bookworm Kitty assured me she prefers reading to dancing. The snow's stopped, by the way.'

'Good news for guests with a drive at the end of the evening—not least the bride and groom,' said Andy, complacent at the thought of his old bed close at hand over at the house. 'Poppy insists on driving back to Chipping Camden tonight.'

'To hang up her stocking at the foot of her own bed,' said Felicia, smiling as Poppy and Tom came towards them.

'And Tom will have masses to stuff in it, as usual,' said David, shaking his head. 'How he dotes on that woman.'

'What woman?' demanded Poppy behind him.

He spun round in dismay. 'Only you,' he assured her.

Tom laughed. 'Dead right,' he told his bride regretfully. 'Women are expensive. I can only afford one!'

'But I'm worth it,' she said, beaming up at him. Then she began moving round the table to chat with everyone, her eyes sparkling as Gideon stood up when she reached him. 'Long time no see. How are you, then, Gideon Ford?'

He kissed the hand she gave him. 'All the better for Tom's invitation to your wedding. It's a great privilege to share in your day.'

'I'm really delighted that you're here. Take good care of my bridesmaid,' she ordered.

'With infinite pleasure, Mrs Henshawe.'

Tom clapped him on the back and grabbed Poppy's hand as the music started. 'Back on the floor, wife.'

From then on the music was loud and noisy, and older guests were showing signs of fatigue by the time a recorded drum roll announced the reappearance of the bride and groom in their travelling clothes. Poppy and Tom took to the middle of the floor, to thank their guests for coming and to wish them Happy Christmas and a safe journey home, then made a run for it as everyone stampeded to follow the pair outside to a car adorned with old boots and horseshoes and a light covering of snow. There were cheers as Poppy flung her bouquet high in the air behind her. Andy caught it and with a grin presented it to Felicia, then there were kisses all round and the newlyweds drove clanking away up the snow-covered track.

Gideon took Felicia aside. 'I need to get moving. My car's in the way. Can I drive you to The Lodge?'

'No need, thanks. My car's here. I'll just collect my things from the house and get home under my own steam.' She smiled up at him, conscious of interested eyes turned in their direction. 'I'll see you in the morning,' she whispered.

Gideon squeezed her hand. 'I'm looking forward to it.' He turned away to take his leave of everyone, then drove off to make way for other departing guests.

'How about a nightcap?' said Andy as the three of them walked over to the house. 'Or if asked really nicely I could be persuaded to make my famed hot chocolate.'

'Tempting, but no, thanks,' said Felicia, yawning. 'I've got to get back to let the dogs out. I'll just change my glad rags, then I'm for home.'

Leah eyed her, frowning, as they went upstairs together. 'Are you sure you won't join us here tomorrow, Flick? I don't like to think of you up there on your own.'

'That's very sweet of you, but I'll be fine. Life's been so hectic lately I really relish the idea of peace and quiet for once.'

'If you change your mind any time just get in the car and come—promise?'

'Cross my heart!'

On the drive home Felicia's early start to the day began making itself felt. But her fatigue vanished at the sight of Gideon's car parked outside The Lodge. She drove into the garage, smiling warmly as he came to help her out.

'How disappointing. You're wearing boots,' he commented, eyeing her feet. 'I was hoping to carry you to your door before I went home.'

She laughed. 'Be thankful I've let you off, Gideon.'

He watched her unlock the door, then bent to kiss her cheek. 'Merry Christmas, Felicia Maynard.'

'Merry Christmas, Gideon Ford.' It was on the tip of her tongue to ask him if he wanted coffee, but the bouquet she was holding decided her against it. No point in frightening him off. 'Thank you for waiting for me.'

'A habit I learned early on in life where you're concerned. So, goodnight—though "parting is such sweet sorrow", Juliet,' he added.

'"Then I shall say goodnight till it be morrow"!' She went inside, smiling at him as she closed the door.

CHAPTER FOUR

NEXT morning Jess Maynard rang from the other side of the world. Eventually, due to lengthy descriptions of the gorgeous baby, followed by more of Poppy's wedding, the phone call grew far too expensive for Hugh Maynard's liking, and he came on the line to wish his daughter a happy Christmas, then told his wife to say goodbye—very briefly—so he could get some sleep. Laughing, Felicia assured her mother she was fine, sent her love to James and Olivia, a big kiss for baby Robert, and promised to ring later in the week.

Felicia collected her presents, but feeling suddenly forlorn at the thought of opening them alone, took them downstairs and stacked them round the base of the tree. She eyed the little pile for a moment, then hunted out some suitably masculine Christmas paper to wrap the book of Chastlecombe watercolours. Just in case. It wouldn't do to be embarrassed if Gideon by any chance brought her a present. And if he didn't she'd keep the book for her father.

With carols on the radio for accompaniment in the kitchen, she added more butter to the defrosted herb and leek stuffing, then worked it with care under the loosened breast skin and put the chicken in the oven to roast.

'That's for me,' she told the keenly attentive dogs as she made bread sauce. 'You can have some goodies later.'

While the sauce simmered Felicia prepared vegetables and thought about what to wear. On her own she would have gone for heavy cords and a thick sweater, but the present unforeseen and still unbelievable circumstances definitely called for something more special.

When potatoes and parsnips were roasting, and green beans were sliced ready to cook, she ran upstairs to get ready. She tied her hair back with a velvet ribbon, added a few touches to her face, then wriggled into the clinging chocolate cashmere dress she'd bought to wear for the staff Christmas lunch hosted by the consultants she worked for. She fastened her bridesmaid's present—a chunky gold and amber pendant—at the deep scoop neckline, pulled on her suede boots, and went down to put a match to the sitting-room fire.

If she'd had any doubts about her appearance, Gideon's reaction reassured her when she opened the door to him later.

'Merry Christmas, Miss Maynard. You look even more ravishing than yesterday,' he said, smiling over the large box he was carrying.

'Merry Christmas, Mr Ford. You look good yourself.' Instead of the formal suits she'd seen so far he wore cords and a checked shirt, topped by a fawn cable sweater and an ancient waxed jacket.

'Where shall I put the box, Flick? It's just some wine and a few Christmas bits and pieces. I've brought some tiramisu from Orsini's, so I'll put that in your refrigerator. Shall I take the rest into the sitting room?'

'Of course.'

Once Gideon had made enough fuss of the dogs to satisfy them, he opened the wine while Felicia lit red candles in white pottery holders on the kitchen table she'd laid with a green cloth, shiny red Christmas crackers, and her mother's best china and silver.

'Off you go,' she told the dogs, and they subsided obediently in their usual places near the stove, their noses raised to the delicious smells wafting from the oven. 'Instead of deserting the dogs I thought we'd eat in here—but not a word to Mother!' Felicia checked on the potatoes roasting under the chicken, put the beans to cook, then turned the volume down on the radio and raised the glass Gideon had filled for her.

He touched it with his, smiling. 'To state the obvious, this is an unexpected pleasure, Felicia.'

'Isn't it just?' she agreed. 'By the way, no Christmas pudding—so we'll eat your tiramisu instead, if you don't mind.'

'It's why I brought it.'

'I love the stuff, though I rarely eat at Orsini's.' She smiled. 'My father is probably the only man in the known world who doesn't care for Italian cuisine, so we tend to patronise the King's Head for special family occasions.'

'Is that where you eat when you bring your lawyer here?'

'No.' Her smile faded. 'He's never been to Chastlecombe.'

Gideon's eyebrows rose. 'So how long have you known him?'

'A few months or so. My parents have met him, of course,' she said casually. 'They come to see me in London quite often.'

'Speaking as an old friend, Miss Maynard, the man doesn't come across as the love of your life,' commented Gideon, and topped up her glass.

'He's not. He's just a friend.' She smiled at him cheerfully. 'Some day my prince will come—I hope.' At sixteen she'd believed he already had. He was sitting opposite her right now, looking just as perfect for the role ten years on as he had as a teenager. 'So why *did* you buy Ridge House, Gideon? It's a bit big for one man. Or do you have plans to marry and fill it with children?'

'Eventually, yes. But that wasn't the primary reason. Once I had enough money I always intended to buy it if it came up for sale.' He smiled a little. 'When they were first married my mother used to tease Dad about buying Ridge House for her when he'd made his fortune. But she died when I was little, and as you know Dad died suddenly just before I left school so it was up to me to buy the house.'

'You bought it as a memorial to them?' Felicia put out a hand to touch his.

Gideon nodded sombrely, then smiled. 'Let's talk about more cheerful things.'

'Like food,' she said briskly. 'How are you with a carving knife?'

'Expert!'

'Of course you are. Right, then, you get carving. I'll make the gravy and decant the vegetables and we'll be there.'

When they were at the table with full plates in front of them Gideon brandished his Christmas cracker. 'Pull!' He laughed as a pirate hat fell out. 'I haven't worn a paper hat since I was a kid,' he said, grinning, and managed to look dashing rather than ridiculous in it as he pulled Felicia's cracker with her.

To her relief her hat was a gold foil crown, which looked so good with her dress that Gideon accused her of rigging the crackers beforehand.

'I'm innocent!' she exclaimed, holding up her hands. 'Now, let's eat before my efforts get cold. No Brussels sprouts, I'm afraid.'

'Thank God for that!'

Gideon ate with appreciation as they laughed over the corny jokes in the crackers.

'That was superb,' he said later, after a second helping of everything. 'But you ate about half as much as me, so how about some tiramisu?'

'I don't think I can manage any yet,' she said regretfully.

'I most certainly can't, so let's clear away. Then we can lounge in front of the fire afterwards with a clear conscience.'

'I can clear up later. It's mostly just stacking the dishwasher,' she said quickly, but Gideon shook his head, dislodging his hat in the process.

'Let's both do it now.'

While they worked the dogs were given titbits from the chicken, then sent out into the garden. When Gideon whistled them in Felicia took off her crown and apron and sighed with relief. 'Right. Let's take the rest of the wine with us. Or would you like coffee?'

He shook his head. 'Not yet. What about these lads?'

She laughed, and patted their heads. 'We'll leave them here. If we let them in there with us they'll hog the fire.'

'I'd like some dogs myself, but I'm not here enough to make that feasible yet. Great tree,' he added, as they reached the other room.

'Mum and Dad had it ready the weekend I came home to wish them *bon voyage.*'

Felicia sank onto the sofa while Gideon added more logs to the fire. When the flames flared up to outline his profile, she tried to look at him objectively. At eighteen he'd been handsome enough, but in the years since then hard work and maturity had added a whole new dimension to his looks. But her reaction to them remained unchanged.

He got up. 'Where will I find more logs? We'll need more than just this basketful.'

'Um—in the garden shed, I suppose,' she said, hoping she was right. 'You'll find torches in the scullery.'

'I'll stack these on the hearth and take the basket to fetch more.'

When he came back he wore a look of purpose Felicia viewed with misgiving as he shared the last of the wine between their glasses. He put hers on the table at her elbow and sat down beside her. 'Right, then. Talk to me.'

She tensed, wishing she hadn't eaten so much as her heart began to thump. 'What do you want to know?'

'Exactly what happened after our last encounter, right here in this room. I know you were ill. But you didn't make it back to school for the entire summer term, and as soon as I'd finished my exams I had to leave Chastlecombe,' he reminded her.

She put out a hand. 'I was so deeply sorry about your father, Gideon.'

'Thank you.' He took the hand and held it. 'Unknown to me, Dad had suffered with heart trouble for years. When he made his will he stipulated that should he die while I was still studying I was to complete my education before I took the business over myself, if I wished to do that. I did, of course, so with the solicitor's help a manager was engaged to run the shop, and because the flat over it went with the job I left Chastlecombe to live with my aunt in York and went on to university from there.' He turned, his eyes suddenly relentless as they fastened on hers. 'But what *really* happened with you, Flick? What was your mysterious illness?'

She heaved in a deep breath. 'Nothing mysterious about it. I was terribly hot that evening before you came, but I thought it was just with—well, with excitement at the prospect of being alone with you,' she said, flushing. 'Anyway, I was so wretchedly ill the next day my parents were afraid of pneumonia, but it turned out to be glandular fever. Highly infectious, which meant Mother couldn't even let Poppy through the door. Fortunately my brother James was backpacking in Australia in his gap year, so he was out of the loop. And you carried on at school, so I knew I hadn't infected you—though it's a miracle I didn't. They call it the kissing disease.'

His hand tightened on hers. 'But in the end we did a hell of a lot more than just kiss, Felicia.'

She nodded dumbly, heat rushing through her at the memory of what had happened between them, right here in this room.

'Your mother told me what was wrong when I rang,' he went on, 'but when she said you were too ill to speak to me I took that to mean you wanted nothing more to do with me.'

She shook her head. 'Gideon, it wasn't like that at all. My glands were so swollen I really did have difficulty in talking for a while. I was dizzy, and felt sick most of the time, so wrapped up in my misery I didn't even try to ring you once I knew Mother had let you know what was wrong.'

'I convinced myself it was a cover-up.' His eyes

blazed suddenly. 'Surely you knew I was afraid I'd made you pregnant? When you didn't go back to school after Easter I was convinced you'd been whisked away somewhere to have a termination.'

'No.' Her eyes fell as heat rose in her face. 'Though it was six weeks before I knew for certain that I wasn't pregnant. The illness affected my system, and I had a long time to worry before it started working normally again.'

His mouth tightened. 'It never occurred to you to let me know when it did?'

'I did ring the flat, but got no answer,' she said defensively, and raised her eyes to his. 'I could hardly leave the news in a message your dad might pick up. In any case,' she added tartly, 'I hadn't heard from you in ages, so I thought you'd given *me* up in disgust. When your father died I was convalescing at my grandparents' house on the Gower coast, which is why I missed the funeral. When I got back you'd already left and I didn't know your address. But you knew mine!'

Gideon shrugged. 'I had my pride, Flick.' He gave her a sardonic smile. 'To shore up my battered ego I bedded as many willing girls as possible in my first term at university, to make up for the fiasco with you.'

'Good for you,' she said, deliberately flippant to cover a sharp pang of jealousy at the mere thought of it.

'But after a while,' he went on soberly, 'I pulled myself together and got down to some serious work. My goal was to enlarge Dad's business once I qualified, as my personal memorial to him. My aunt was all for it.

She lent me some money when I told her I planned to expand and buy another business, and it all mushroomed from there. I was soon able to pay her back and buy another, and on it went. But winning concessions in some of the supermarket chains was the big boost to Ford's Pharmacies.'

Felicia nodded gravely. 'Your dad would have been so proud, Gideon.'

'I know.' His eyes softened. 'He was a great role model. But he was also a warning I'm taking to heart. Dad was the ultimate workaholic, and for years I've been pretty much the same. But now I mean to relax more and take time to enjoy life. Which is where Ridge House comes in, as a weekend retreat.'

'Mother said you'd had a lot of work done there.'

He nodded. 'But it's on stop until after New Year. My first priority is fitting the top floor up as an office, so I can spend more time here once I'm married.'

A statement which hit Felicia like a body blow.

'Unfortunately,' he added silkily, watching her like a hawk, 'I don't have someone lined up for the role of wife quite yet.'

'Really?' she said, wanting to hit him. 'Surely there must be women queuing up to audition, Gideon? In fact, why are you on your own here for Christmas? You must have had invitations.'

'I did—several. But like you I opted for peace and quiet. The thought of behaving as the perfect house guest over the holiday sent me running for the hills!' He looked her in the eye. 'But it's good to share Christmas Day with *you*, Flick.'

'My pleasure,' she said lightly.

'Tomorrow you can come over to Ridge House and I'll play host. The dogs can come, too,' he added. 'They know the place well. Your father often brings them over when I'm here.'

Does he really? thought Felicia. He could have mentioned it. 'Thank you, Gideon. I'd like to come.' Which was putting it mildly. Quite apart from having his company on Boxing Day, she was wild with curiosity about his house. 'I'll walk over with the dogs, then. When do you want me?'

Felicia could have bitten her tongue the moment the words were out, as thoughts of their youthful disaster brought colour rushing to her face again.

'Good question,' said Gideon, and smiled that smile again. 'Don't worry,' he said softly. 'You're quite safe. I make mistakes, as you well know, but rarely the same one twice.'

Get a grip, she told herself fiercely, and smiled. 'I meant what time shall I come.'

'I know you did. I'll come and drive you over mid-morning.' He glanced at the presents stacked under the tree. 'Isn't it time you opened those?'

She wished now that she'd opened them before he'd arrived, and kept things on a more impersonal level. 'It didn't seem like much fun on my own.'

He smiled indulgently. 'So the girl I once knew still lives inside the sophisticated lady!'

'Christmas tends to put me in touch with my inner child,' she agreed. 'You don't have to fetch me tomorrow, Gideon. The dogs are messy passengers.'

'I keep a pick-up down here. They can ride in the back.' He leaned back with a sigh of pleasure, long legs outstretched. 'Christmas this year is a lot different from my expectations.'

'Mine too,' she said honestly. 'I expected it to be different, of course, due to Poppy's wedding and my parents away baby-worshipping in Australia. But not this different.'

'Spending Christmas Day with your first love?'

Felicia's heart did a somersault as he raised an eyebrow.

'I was your first love, wasn't I?'

She nodded reluctantly. 'You know you were.'

'You were certainly mine.' His mouth twisted. 'That was the problem. If I'd had some experience beforehand, like every other normal male animal my age, what happened between us wouldn't have been such a disaster. Did I turn you off men for a while?'

'Yes.' Other men, anyway. She eyed him challengingly. 'Would any of it have happened if we hadn't played Romeo and Juliet together?'

'Damn right it would,' he assured her. 'I was just waiting—impatiently—for you to turn sixteen before I made my move. Then the drama teacher—what was his name?'

'Mr Johnson.'

'Right. He told me in confidence that he wanted me

to play Romeo opposite Leah Porter in the Christmas concert. I agreed—but only on condition that you played Juliet.'

'So that's how I landed the role!' Felicia shook her head in wonder. 'And Leah played Titania opposite Andy instead, and now she's married to him. Odd how fate arranges things.'

'I couldn't wait for fate,' Gideon said, gazing into the fire. 'My plan was to get you used to me as a lover onstage, then coax you into the role in real life.'

She stared at him, amazed. 'And I never knew! Not that coaxing was necessary. I'd been hiding an outsize crush on you for years. I could hardly believe my luck when my name was read out for Juliet.'

Gideon swivelled to look at her. 'So my elaborate plan to thaw the Snow Queen was never even necessary?'

'All you had to do was ask,' Felicia said candidly. 'But I just adored doing the balcony scene with you. I was a romantic teenager, remember?'

'So was I—until our last night here,' he said morosely. 'Not much romance about our final scene together.'

She smiled ruefully. 'Two amateurs together just had to be a recipe for disaster—more *Babes in the Wood* than *Romeo and Juliet*.'

Gideon laughed. 'How right you are.' He was quiet for a moment. 'I told you I made up for it later—'

'So you did,' she said, her eyes kindling at the thought. 'How about you?'

'It had quite the opposite effect on me.'

He winced. 'I put you off sex for life?'

'Not for life,' she said demurely. 'But certainly for a while.' And not for the reasons he meant. Her problem had been finding any man who appealed to her after Gideon Ford. He'd been a hard act to follow.

They both gazed into the flames, the silence between them almost tangible. Then a log fell with a sudden crash. Gideon got up to mend the fire, and afterwards turned to her, smiling persuasively.

'So, then, little Miss Maynard, are you ready now to see what Santa Claus has brought you?'

Felicia shrugged. 'I suppose I should, after my parents went to so much trouble. Will it bore you to watch?'

'I could never be bored in *your* company, Flick—' He paused. 'Your parents never call you that.'

'No. It was purely a school thing.'

'Felicia suits you far better,' he said, and sat down beside her. 'Right. Off you go.'

Feeling ridiculously self-conscious, she went over to the tree. And discovered extra parcels behind it. She shot a questioning glance at Gideon, but he just smiled and waved her on. She started on the parcels from her parents, and took out a sweater in a subtle creamy pink shade from the shop in Chastlecombe arcade. She held it up against her, eyebrows raised, and Gideon nodded in warm approval.

The other parcels contained books, both printed and audio, and some CDs she'd hinted about—and a set of lacy underwear Felicia passed over in a hurry, to

Gideon's amusement. Her parents' final parcel contained a suede jacket she'd been coveting from the same source as the sweater.

'Wow—how gorgeous! Mum and Dad have really gone overboard this year to make it up to me.' She smiled ruefully. 'They were longing to see their first grandchild, but had terrible qualms about abandoning me over Christmas.'

'Instead you're spending it with me,' said Gideon matter-of-factly. 'Keep going, Felicia.'

She eyed the remaining pile warily. 'I hope you haven't been too extravagant, Gideon.'

'Just a few tokens of gratitude,' he said with sudden formality, and got up to join her. 'If they embarrass you, I'll open them for you.'

'Of course they don't. It's very sweet of you,' she said hastily, and opened a package in the distinctive gift wrapping of Fox's Lair, the source of her sweater and jacket. She took out a vast, dramatic pashmina in cashmere in a distinctive shade of muted pink. 'How lovely!'

'I asked Elise Fox if she knew you, and she suggested this,' he said blandly. 'I wouldn't have chosen that colour with your hair, but she said you'd like it.'

'She's right. I do!'

Two of the gifts were less personal: a trio of soaps with a famous name, and a large box of chocolates. But the last parcel contained a plate hand-painted with a portrait of William Shakespeare. Scenes from some of his plays decorated the circumference; with the balcony scene from *Romeo and Juliet* in pride of place above the Bard's head. Felicia gazed at it in silence for a moment, then reached up and kissed Gideon's cheek. 'Where on earth did you find it?'

'In the antiques place in the arcade. I bought it on my first trip back here quite a while ago. It's early Victorian, and not quite perfect—'

'Oh, yes, it is,' she said fiercely. 'Thank you so much, Gideon. I shall hang it on my bedroom wall.'

'I'm glad you like it. You have another present left,' he added.

'That's for you.' Felicia handed it to him. 'I thought you might like this now you're going to live here part of the time.'

Gideon unwrapped the large book, then looked at the beautiful watercolour prints inside in such silence Felicia began to wonder if she'd made a huge mistake.

'These are just wonderful,' he said at last, clearing his throat. He examined every one, then very carefully put the book down on a table. 'Thank you, Felicia. I shall keep it in a prominent place for all to admire.' He gave her a wry look. 'What did you give the lawyer?'

'A case of the wine he likes. And he gave me perfume I don't like,' she said flatly.

'We did a lot better for each other,' said Gideon, quietly and bent to kiss her cheek.

For both of them the second kiss, fleeting though it was, acted like a match to kindling. Gideon took her in his arms and kissed her mouth, and Felicia kissed him back with a warmth she could no more have helped than draw breath. But far too soon for her he raised his head and let her go.

'I'd better take the dogs out,' he said unevenly.

'Right.' She gave him a bright, unsteady smile. 'While you're doing that I'll make some coffee. Unless you're in a hurry to get home?'

Gideon gave her a scathing look. 'What possible reason could I have for wanting to go back to an empty house instead of staying here with you? When you tell me to go I will, but not before.'

'Then why are you rushing off to walk the dogs?' she demanded. 'They let me know when they want to go out.'

'Because,' he said tightly, 'you're even more irresistible now than you were at sixteen, Felicia. I need a few minutes in the cold night air to recover the head I nearly lost again just then.'

Surely, thought Felicia crossly as she followed him out to the kitchen, Gideon Ford had moved on a bit from the extraordinary paragon he'd been as a boy? It was humiliating to want a man who called a halt before she did. Earlier he'd made it plain without words that he wanted her. But he had no intention of acting on it, obviously. Whereas right now she would have been rather happy with a kiss or two. A romantic little interlude would be nice, if only for old times' sake.

'Should I clip their leads on?' said Gideon, as the dogs frolicked around him.

'No. They haven't had their proper dinner yet, so they

won't even stay out long, let alone wander off,' she assured him.

While he was outside Felicia filled the dogs' bowls, then switched on the coffee maker. After that embarrassing little episode, what should they do now? Her original plan had been to watch television at this point— probably a sentimental Christmas movie, or the inevitable James Bond. But did her guest enjoy such things? Knowing him when they were teenagers, with only a few weeks together in anything like a relationship, gave her no clue to Gideon Ford's tastes now they were both adults.

When he came back in he was shivering as the dogs rushed past him to their bowls. 'It looks like snow again,' he announced.

'This is nearly ready. Would you like some brandy with it?'

'No, thanks. Just your wonderful coffee.'

'Right. I'll bring it in a minute. You go ahead and make up the fire. Please,' she added with a smile.

'Certainly, madam.' Gideon chuckled as Bran and Jet stretched out along the base of the Aga. 'And they call it a dog's life!'

Felicia patted their heads, then put the coffee pot on the tray and followed him into the sitting room. 'That looks good,' she said, nodding at the cheerful blaze. 'If we get enough snow to knock out the power I can at least be warm.'

'If it gets to that point you'd better bring the dogs and

stay with me. I invested in an emergency generator at Ridge House.' He got up from his crouch in front of the fire, looking slightly dishevelled, and even more mouth-watering to Felicia because of it. 'Are you still coming over tomorrow?'

'Yes, of course.' She looked him in the eye. 'Any reason why I shouldn't?'

He smiled crookedly. 'None at all. How about some tiramisu?'

'Right now I'd rather have some of those gorgeous chocolates. But you have some—or I can make you a chicken sandwich,' she offered.

He shook his head and resumed his place on the sofa. 'I'll just settle for coffee.'

'So, what would you like to do now?' she asked as she poured.

'What was your original plan for the day?'

'Reading was my pastime of choice. But if I'd got tired of that probably a film on television.'

'We could still do that, if you like,' offered Gideon.

'You're just being polite. Tell me what *you'd* like to do,' she said firmly.

He held out his cup for a refill. 'I just want to talk and catch up on all those years since we were last together—how many boyfriends you've had, what your flatmate was like, whether you enjoy your job in Harley Street.'

She looked at him thoughtfully. 'And if I tell you all that will you respond in kind, Mr Ford?'

'You know most of it already.'

Too much, when it came to his bedding college girls. 'Ah, but I want to know about the current girlfriend, and this apartment of yours in London, and so on.'

'Done.' He got up to put their cups on the tray, then put another log on the fire and sat down again beside her. 'Fire away.'

Felicia told him she'd had a couple of boyfriends during her years at university. But the only lasting relationship had been with Katherine Fry, a college friend who'd become her eventual flatmate in London. For years personal assistant to the owner of an art gallery, Katherine was now his wife. 'She got married a month ago, and I miss her badly,' said Felicia with a sigh. 'Your turn. Tell me about these other invitations you had.'

Two of them, Gideon told her, had been to join family parties, but he'd turned them down with grateful thanks and as much tact as possible. 'I had to be pretty blunt about one of them,' he said, his mouth turning down. 'It was from someone you might class as "the current girl-friend" because I'd been seeing her occasionally on what I mistakenly imagined was a casual, no-strings basis. But I found she'd planned an intimate Christmas for two, and was making it frighteningly plain that she expected a ring as a present.'

'Oops! Which kind? Engagement or wedding?' said Felicia, eyes dancing.

'Judging by those from two former husbands, a huge rock to start with, followed by a third wedding ring,' Gideon smiled wryly. 'I told her that this had never been an option, and never would be, at which point she made such an ugly scene I beat a hasty retreat.'

Her lips twitched. 'So you're not always a paragon, then, Gideon?'

'Not even close. Paragons don't achieve my kind of success in the business world, Felicia. I can be as ruthless as the next man,' he assured her, 'but I keep to the law, play by the rules, and I've never misled a woman about my intentions—including Helena. But enough about that; tell me about the men in your life. If the lawyer is that recent there must have been others in London before him?'

'I'm a big girl, Gideon. Of course there were others. But not many,' she added honestly, and he laughed.

'A big girl who tells the truth?'

'That's me.' She hesitated. 'But, to continue with the truth thing, after you it was a long time before I let anyone else get close to me.'

'Because I hurt you so much?'

'No. Because it was so hard to get over you.'

Gideon sat very still. 'But you managed it eventually?'

'Of course I did. I was a bit late getting round to it, but I grew up in the end.' She looked at him squarely. 'Enough to know that a few kisses are not life-altering experiences, Gideon.'

'If you're referring to my restraint just now—'

'Of course I am.'

'Then think about it from my point of view.' He pointed to the hearthrug. 'Is that the same one?'

'Yes,' she admitted, horrified to find herself blushing vividly again.

He turned to seize both her hands. 'I was a clumsy adolescent then—'

'Whereas now you're a past master?'

'Enough to want to take you to bed when we make love again, rather than revisit the scene of my crime right here.'

Felicia licked suddenly dry lips, every nerve-end in her body quivering as she gazed at him like a deer caught in the headlights. The air was suddenly so thick with sexual tension she found it hard to breathe. *'When?'* she said huskily, when she could trust her voice to function. 'Don't you mean *if*?'

'No.' He pulled her into his arms. 'I'm no paragon, Felicia. Just an ordinary man with a full set of phero-mones, testosterone and every other damn thing in a normal man's equipment. But throwing you on that rug again is out of the question after you've not only fed me royally, but given me the most thoughtful present I've had in a long time.' He kissed her hard, then let her go. 'Next time we make love it's going to be memorable in a different way from last time, Felicia.'

'You seem very sure there *will* be a next time,' she said, her heart hammering at the mere thought of it, and at the same time resentful because he seemed so sure of her.

'I'm utterly certain. Fate has brought us back together.' He smiled that slow smile of his that rendered her boneless. 'And I'm going to take full advantage of it.'

'But not today,' she said forcibly, determined to exert some kind of control.

Gideon laughed and squeezed her hand. 'But not today. So, if you want to watch *It's a Wonderful Life*, or whatever, I'm only too happy to watch it with you.'

'Deal,' said Felicia, seizing gratefully on the offer. 'But, because there's nothing I really fancy on television right now, I'll let you choose from that stack of DVDs in the corner.' She laughed when he chose *Butch Cassidy and the Sundance Kid*. 'I haven't seen this for years,' she told him, as they settled down to watch. 'Robert Redford was really something, wasn't he? Or do you prefer Paul Newman?'

'Personally, I go for Katherine Ross.' Gideon smiled nostalgically. 'All we need now is some popcorn.'

And your arm around me, thought Felicia, and tensed as he moved closer and slid his arm along the back of sofa behind her. 'I always loved this film,' she said with difficulty.

'I was tempted to go for *High Noon*.'

'We can watch that next time.'

'Tomorrow, at my place,' he agreed.

The rest of the day passed in surprising harmony for a situation with such simmering undercurrents behind the tacit truce. The underlying tension was no curb on their appetites, and Felicia made chicken sandwiches for a late supper she ate with as much enthusiasm as Gideon, with one of her new CDs playing in the background. Eventually Gideon took the dogs out one last time, but refused a nightcap when he came in again.

'Of course—you must have driven here with that box,' she said, not sure whether she felt relieved or forlorn because he was leaving.

'I didn't. I carried it. But I won't have a drink because it's time I went home, Felicia,' he said, and took her hand. 'Thank you for my best Christmas Day in a long time.'

'Mine, too.' She smiled up at him, her dark eyes candid as she told him the simple truth. 'It's so good to see you again, Gideon.'

He responded by taking her in his arms to kiss her with a thoroughness that sent a thrill right down to her toes. 'When you opened the door to me the other night,' he said huskily, raising his head at last, 'I discovered the reason for my urge to spend Christmas at Ridge House. Sleep well. I'll be here in the morning.'

CHAPTER FIVE

INSTEAD of lying awake and restless, as she'd expected, Felicia slept like a log and woke next morning to find the dogs had given her an extra Christmas present of an hour longer in bed. When she let them out she found the garden covered in snow, and, feeling utterly at peace with the cold, silent world, watched the dogs frisking, their coats shining like black silk against the blanket of white until they started rolling in it. They came bounding back to her, smiling from ear to ear, and submitted happily as she rubbed them down, then followed her into the kitchen to wait, tails wagging, while she filled their bowls.

Felicia tried to read one of her new books over breakfast, but in the end gave up and thought about Gideon instead: a habit she'd worked so hard to break all those years ago. Madly in love with him though she'd been as a teenager, she'd also liked him enormously. It was the quality in Gideon that made him different from any other man she'd met since. They might have been Romeo and Juliet, but they'd also been the best of friends. And she was going to see him again soon, so it was time to stop daydreaming, clean out the fire in the sitting room and relay it, and take a shower and do her hair and make herself appealing enough for him to forget his scruples and give her a kiss which lasted a bit longer.

Felicia was ready and waiting in heavy cord jeans and the new pink sweater when Gideon was due, pleased she was in good time when the dogs started barking as the doorbell rang. She threw open the door, but instead of Gideon found Andy on her doorstep, with his daughter in his arms and his smiling wife alongside him.

'Hi,' said Leah. 'We've come to check up on you.'

Felicia regrouped hurriedly as she ushered them inside. 'How very sweet of you. And don't you look pretty, Holly Robson?'

The little girl beamed, and struggled to get down. 'Doggies!'

'It's OK,' said Andy, and set her on the floor. 'She's used to dogs at the farm.'

Felicia's heart leapt as the bell rang again. She opened the door and smiled brightly at Gideon, her eyes locking significantly with his. 'Hello. How nice to see you. Andy and Leah have just arrived.'

'Nice to see you, too,' said Gideon, without missing a beat. 'Greetings, all you Robsons. I thought I recognised the car.'

'We came to see if Flick was all right up here on her own,' said Leah, smiling up at him. 'Is that why you're here?'

'Actually, I came to ask if she fancied a look round Ridge House, followed by pot luck for lunch.'

'We're on our way to lunch with Leah's parents,' said Andy. 'You're invited, too, Flick. And I'm sure they'd be pleased to see you, too, Gideon.'

'Doggies,' repeated Holly imperiously.

'Bring her in the kitchen,' said Felicia. 'It's warmer in there.'

Bran and Jet were delighted to see everyone, especially Gideon. Something Leah homed in on right away.

'They seem to know you rather well, Gideon.'

'They certainly do,' he said, roughing them up. 'Felicia's father sometimes brings them over to Ridge House to run in the gardens.'

'It's so kind of your parents to invite me, Leah,' said Felicia, avoiding Gideon's eye. 'But I just can't leave the dogs that length of time—'

'Why doesn't everyone come over to my place for a drink?' he suggested. 'You can all have a look round the house, then you two can take Holly on to her grandparents afterwards.'

'Great idea,' said Leah, eyes sparkling. 'I've been dying to see round your house. I'll ring Mother and say we'll be a bit late. Holly, leave those poor dogs alone.'

'I've brought the pick-up,' said Gideon, 'so the dogs can come too if you like, Felicia. Bring their food.'

'How long are you hoping to keep her at your place, then?' demanded Leah.

'As long as she agrees to stay,' he said promptly. 'I

should put your hiking boots on, Felicia, and bring slippers or whatever with you.'

'Yes, sir,' she said, saluting smartly.

He grinned. 'If you Robsons would like to go first, we'll follow on. Park at the front of the house, Andy; I'll take the pick-up round the back.'

Felicia rolled her eyes as she joined Gideon in the kitchen. 'I didn't know whether you'd want me to mention yesterday or not, so I kept quiet.'

'Ditto,' said Gideon. 'Not that I care a damn if the whole world knows I spent Christmas Day with you—'

'Good, because if Leah finds out that's exactly what will happen,' she warned. 'I'll just run upstairs and get my parka. Will you collect the dogs' things?'

A few rushed minutes later Felicia was in the cab of Gideon's pick-up, along with the dogs' equipment and a bag containing the tiramisu, she saw with amusement. She turned to see Bran and Jet thoroughly enjoying the novelty of the short ride. When Gideon drove up the snowy drive to park at the back of the house they leapt down and raced round the front with joyous barks to greet the visitors.

'It's a big old place, Gideon,' said Andy, eyeing the façade with respect. 'When was it built?'

'Seventeen-ninety. The irregular bits are Edwardian extensions.'

'I love it,' said Leah, impressed.

So did Felicia. She'd loved it from childhood, when

the former owners had used to let her play in the gardens with her brother James.

'You must all be cold,' said Gideon. 'Bring Holly inside.' He ushered them into a wide hall full of light streaming from the Victorian lantern ceiling on the landing above. 'Luckily the snowfall was light, and soon cleared from the glass up there. Come this way.' He took them into a vast empty drawing room, with a marble Gothic revival fireplace and a multi-paned bay window which took up the entire front wall.

'Gosh, this is grand. If you'll tell me where the kitchen is I'll put the dogs in there out of harm's way,' said Felicia, eyeing the gleaming wood floor.

Gideon led them down the hall to the kitchen, clicking his fingers for the dogs to follow, with Holly toddling after them as fast as her legs could carry her.

'Never known my wife lost for words before,' Andy murmured to Felicia.

She grinned at him. 'Great house, isn't it?'

'In every way!'

In the kitchen it was obvious that the dogs felt completely at home, and Felicia could see why. The room was bigger in dimension, but otherwise it was an exact replica of the kitchen at The Lodge, complete with red Aga in a recessed alcove, oak cupboards and dresser, and an oblong kitchen table surrounded by rush-seated chairs. It even had the same warm atmosphere of welcome. The dogs obviously agreed, because they made a beeline for the Aga and sank down beside it.

Holly plopped down beside them, crooning as she stroked them.

'This is just lovely,' said Leah, sighing.

'Thank you. It was only finished a couple of weeks ago, but I'm pleased with the result,' said Gideon. 'Right. Let's take a quick tour of the other rooms, then I'll give everyone a drink.'

'You'd better ring your mother, Leah,' Andy reminded her.

'And please explain about the dogs and thank her for me,' said Felicia quickly.

The tour was short—not only because Holly protested volubly at being parted from the dogs, but because other than the fully furnished master bedroom and bathroom, which took up the area above the drawing room, the rest of the house was newly decorated but empty.

'The attic floor is still a work in progress—euphemism for a shambles—so we'll leave that for another day,' Gideon informed them. 'Now, let's get back to the kitchen for that drink. I can provide you with most things. Or I can make coffee.'

'Better for the driver,' agreed Andy.

Once Holly was settled back down with the dogs, Leah looked round the kitchen with curiosity. 'Do you spend your evenings in here, Gideon? There's no place to sit in the house otherwise.'

He turned round from the coffee maker with a smile. 'I tend to watch television in bed for the time being. I haven't spent much time here yet. Once I get the place in shape I'll come back more often.'

'It must have been a bit odd to spend Christmas Day here in this great place all by yourself,' remarked Andy.

'Actually, I didn't,' said Gideon casually. 'Felicia gave me lunch at The Lodge.'

Both Robsons stared at her in surprise.

'So that's why you turned down your invitation to the farm, Flick!' said Leah, eyes gleaming.

'No,' said Felicia, unruffled. 'I always intended to spend the day at home.'

'I asked her to have lunch with me here,' said Gideon, 'but she wouldn't leave her dogs, so she took pity on me and let me join her at The Lodge. I rather forced her hand.'

'No forcing necessary,' said Felicia promptly. 'It seemed only sensible when we were both on our own. We're old friends, after all.'

'You were a bit more than just friends once upon a time,' said Leah pointedly.

'We were indeed,' said Gideon, smiling at Felicia. 'She was the love of my life back then.'

'How lovely,' sighed Leah, and cast an eye at her husband. 'Was I yours, Andy?'

'Of course—still are,' he assured her, and got up. 'And now I think it's time to drag the other love of my life away from those long-suffering dogs. Come on, poppet. Time to go to Granny's.'

'Granny not got doggies,' said Holly sadly, and waved at the retrievers. 'Bye-bye.'

She brightened as they wagged their tails in response, and Andy picked her up, hugging her close. 'Say bye-bye to Gideon and Felicia, pet.'

'I notice you use her proper name these days, Gideon,' said Leah.

'Because her parents refer to her that way, I suppose,' he said casually, smiling as they saw his guests to the door. 'Have a good day, and come again when I've got the place more in shape.'

Gideon turned to Felicia with a wry grin as they went back to the kitchen, their footsteps echoing in the empty house. 'That's it, then. Our secret is out.'

'What secret?'

'Our Christmas Day together, and also that you were the love of my life. You didn't say I was yours!'

'I didn't have to.' Her answering smile was equally wry. 'Leah knew that only too well.'

'Was I, Felicia?' he said, suddenly serious.

'Of course you were.' She looked at him very directly. 'I thought I made that pretty plain at the time.'

'But that was a teenager talking. Looking back now, as a woman, would you say the same?'

'Yes, Gideon. When I was sixteen you were most definitely the love of my life.' She eyed him challeng-ingly. 'Satisfied?'

Instead of answering he opened the kitchen door and ushered her inside. 'Tell me what you think of my kitchen.'

She smiled. 'My jaw dropped when you brought us in here. It's bigger, of course, but otherwise an almost exact replica of the one at home.'

Gideon nodded, and pulled out a chair at the table for her. 'Would you like a drink before lunch?'

'Not really.' She eyed him hopefully. 'Some tea would be good. Do you have any?'

'Of course I do. A kitchen like this must be able to provide tea!' He switched on the kettle and took tall porcelain mugs from a cupboard.

'Any biscuits?'

'Yes, but you're not having any. It's nearly time for lunch.'

'Spoilsport.'

Gideon put two mugs of tea on the table. 'There's milk on the tray.'

'So, what are we eating?'

'Wait and see. Renzo Orsini gave me some tips on how to impress you.'

Felicia smiled. 'You were lucky to get tips from a top chef along with the tiramisu. I didn't know he did takeaway food.'

'He doesn't. It was a special favour for me.' Gideon sat down, smiling reminiscently. 'His father used to let my dad have the odd pasta meal to take out. Renzo always brought it round, so we got to know each other well. He's married now, with two children. I'll introduce you some time.'

'I'd like to meet him. Now explain this kitchen to me.'

'Its similarity to your mother's?'

'It's identical, not similar, Gideon!'

He nodded. 'If you think back to our flat over the shop, the kitchen was a cramped little galley, with barely enough room for the appliances. When your mother asked me into your kitchen at The Lodge, that first day after the party, I fell in love with it. Your lovely mother had been baking, and she gave me coffee and cakes still warm from the oven—' Gideon broke off, smiling wryly. 'I decided then and there that one day I would own a kitchen just like it. So here it is. Your parents thought it was a great idea.'

She eyed him narrowly. 'It seems to me you've been having a whole lot more to do with them than they've ever let on. They never said a word about the kitchen, or anything else about you.'

'Maybe they thought you wouldn't be interested.'

'Hardly likely,' she said with scorn. 'After all, you're the local boy made good...' She halted as the penny dropped. When Gideon had left town without contacting her she'd made it tearfully plain that she never wanted to hear his name again, and Jess Maynard had taken her daughter's words as gospel. Any articles Felicia had read about him in the local paper had been left lying about in prominent places at home, rather than posted to her in London.

'I assume,' said Gideon dryly, 'that you told your mother my name was never to cross her lips after that fateful night.'

'More or less,' she said honestly. 'I was wild with curiosity when I heard you'd bought this place, but Mother's very reticent on the subject. She's obviously convinced I still feel hostile towards you.'

'Do you?' asked Gideon casually.

Felicia shook her head. 'No. As I told you before, I managed to grow up eventually, and admit that I was equally to blame for what happened.' Her eyes narrowed. 'You obviously got the hang of it pretty quickly once you got to college.'

He nodded smugly. 'I'm a fast learner.'

'And I bet you soon got top marks.' She smiled brightly, ignoring the persistent little jealous pang. 'So, come on, Gideon Ford. What *are* we having for lunch, and what can I do to help?'

He got up, holding out his hand. 'Before that you must see my attic.'

'You don't mind showing *me* your shambles, then?'

'Actually, it's not quite the shambles I made out. But there are some parts of my house I prefer to keep strictly private other than to you.'

'Why me?'

'Because you were once the love of my life,' he said promptly. 'So, come with me, Miss Maynard. I assume we let sleeping dogs lie?'

She glanced at the pair snoring together in the warmth of the Aga. 'They obviously think they're at home.' She frowned. 'Have they been in here before?'

'More than once,' admitted Gideon.

'No wonder they settled down so quickly. All right, then, show me your inner sanctum.'

Gideon led the way upstairs, past the master bedroom to a narrower flight of stairs at the end of the upper hall. At the top he ushered Felicia into a thickly carpeted room furnished with a handsome modern desk, complete with computer, telephones and captain's chair, and a huge, inviting sofa in exactly the right place for watching the plasma television screen hung on the far wall.

'Definitely not a shambles,' said Felicia, surprised. 'So where's the mess?'

'Through here.' Gideon opened a connecting door into a larger room full of unpacked boxes, metal work-stations and swivel chairs, with electrical cables snaking in confusion over bare boards. 'This is where I'll run my little empire from home when necessary, with room for staff. I bought strictly functional stuff for this room, but the desk in the study is a David Conway original, from the furniture shop in town.'

'Great choice,' she said, impressed, as they went back downstairs. 'By the way, I thought you only watched television in bed.'

'Only sometimes. We'll watch the one in the study after lunch. Talking of which,' Gideon added, 'let's go down and do something about that.'

'Let me help.'

'By all means—though it's just a single man's special,' Gideon warned as they went into the kitchen. He fetched two luscious steaks from the butler's pantry. 'They've been marinating in rosemary-flavoured oil and a hint of garlic, as instructed by Renzo. Would you rummage in the fridge and put a salad together while I take the dogs for a run out there?' he asked. 'I'll switch the griddle on now, so when I come back I'll just slap the steaks on it for a minute or two and we're there.'

Felicia nodded with enthusiasm. 'Sounds good. Shall I make some dressing?'

'Use this,' he said, handing her a plain glass jar. 'Renzo gave me some of his.'

Felicia got busy, wondering if things were more relaxed between them today simply because they were in his house, well away from the scene of their youthful disaster in her own home. Whatever the reason, she felt light-hearted as she worked, and by the time Gideon returned she had filled a bowl with baby spinach, rocket, lamb's lettuce and slices of ripe avocado, and put out silverware she'd found in the kitchen table drawer, in exactly the same place everyday things were kept at home.

She rubbed the dogs down and gave them a chew each, while Gideon washed his hands and patted the steaks dry with kitchen paper. He slung the meat on the hot griddle, then put glasses and an opened bottle of red wine on the table. He added a loaf of crusty, artisan-style bread on a board with a pot of butter, and transferred a dish of baked potatoes from oven to table.

'Are the steaks done?' she asked, salivating at the aromatic smell as she tossed dressing into the salad.

Gideon flipped the steaks over and let them cook for a minute, then put them between two hot plates to relax for a moment while he filled their glasses. 'Happy Boxing Day, Felicia,' he said, raising his glass in toast.

'Same to you, Gideon.' She smiled at him radiantly as she raised her own. 'How long must we wait for those steaks? I'm starving.'

When Gideon had pronounced them rested enough, the steaks, blackened on the outside and juicily pink on the inside, were the best Felicia had ever eaten she informed him as she doctored her potato with butter.

'Maybe it's something to do with the company.' He topped up her glass, then began outlining his plans for decorating the reception rooms in the house.

'You're choosing everything yourself?' she said, surprised. 'No interior decorator?'

'I did that in my London place, but the result is a bit impersonal. My kitchen there, for instance, is functional rather than welcoming. Here I want my own personal taste everywhere, successful or not. But I'm open to suggestions. So let's take a walk through the other rooms later, and you can tell me what you think.'

They were on their way out of the kitchen when the dogs barked sharply—as they always did when Felicia's phone rang. She took it out of her bag, and sighed as she saw the caller ID. 'Hello, Charles. Shouldn't you be out on the *piste*?' she asked, making a face at Gideon.

'Hi, Felicia. Blizzard conditions here, so we called it a day. I thought I'd ring to see how the wedding went.'

'It was just wonderful. A really happy, joyous occasion.'

'Good, good. Sorry I missed it. Are you still at your friend's farm?'

'No. Too many relatives turned up needing beds, so I'm at home.' *Sort of*, she mouthed at Gideon, fluttering her eyelashes.

'Alone?'

'No. I'm with a friend.'

'Girlfriend?'

'No.'

Slight pause. 'Someone you met at the wedding?'

'No. An old friend.'

Gideon moved behind her, slid his arms round her waist and laid his cheek on her hair. 'Close friend,' he whispered in her ear.

'Oh, right,' said Charles, after another pause. 'Did you spend Christmas Day with this friend?'

'Yes, actually. Why?'

'So I take it you haven't missed me, then.'

'Charles…what's this about?' she said, inhaling sharply as Gideon kissed her neck.

'I've missed you,' Charles said, surprising her.

'That's a little hard to believe.'

'Well, I'm the odd one out here because you wouldn't come—'

'*Couldn't* come, Charles.'

'Whatever,' he went on hastily. 'Now the wedding's over fly over and join the party here for New Year's Eve. My room's a double, so no problem.'

Only from his point of view. 'New Year's Eve?' Felicia said coolly, and felt Gideon stiffen. 'For one thing I doubt that I'd get a flight—'

Gideon took the phone from her and disconnected, then turned her in his arms. 'And for another you're spending New Year's Eve with me.'

'When I could be sharing Charles's bed at the chalet?' she said, her voice stifled against Gideon's chest.

'To hell with that,' he said harshly, and turned her face up to kiss her at such length that when the phone rang again Felicia ignored it, so lost in her response to Gideon's dominating mouth that she sagged against him like a rag doll when he let her go.

'Well?' he demanded.

Felicia switched off her phone, gazing up in silence at the face that had gained so much in character over the years. The aquiline nose now had a slight dent at the bridge, and a slight scar dissected one dark eyebrow, but the defects merely added a sexy hint of toughness that appealed to her even more strongly. 'How did you get the scars?'

'Playing rugby for the first fifteen in college,' he informed her, his hold relaxing slightly.

'As well as bedding every girl in sight?'

'I acquired some scars that way, too,' he said, eyes glinting. 'Want to see?'

'Certainly not,' she retorted, pursing her lips primly.

'If you do that I'll kiss you,' he warned.

'Promises, promises,' she taunted, and gave a smothered shriek as he crushed her close and kissed her with a savagery that brought the dogs to their feet, growling softly.

Gideon's arms fell away. 'Sorry, lads. Calm down. I'm not going to hurt her.'

'Good boys!' Felicia laughed as she bent to stroke the dogs.

'Will you misinterpret my motives if I suggest we go up to the study *without* the good boys?' he asked.

'No, because I know exactly what you have in mind,' she teased, taking a DVD from her bag. 'You want to watch *High Noon*!'

But when they reached the study Gideon switched on lamps and pulled curtains, and then drew her down on the sofa beside him. 'Before we get into the film I have a suggestion to make, Felicia. I must be in London on January the fifth, but I have something on before that. Months ago I planned a kind of pilgrimage to celebrate New Year.'

'You mean back here?'

He shook his head. 'No. This was just a brief escape over Christmas. My assistant at the London office is the only one who actually knows where I am right now. And he won't contact me unless absolutely necessary.'

'Your assistant's a man? I pictured you with a glossy power-suited lady,' said Felicia, surprised.

'I had an assistant just like that at one time. Denise was good-looking, and efficient as hell, but she got married, and then pregnant soon afterwards. When she resigned I advertised for a replacement and got Peter. He's not as pretty as Denise, but he's damned good at his job.' Gideon put out a long arm and drew her close. 'Felicia,' he said huskily, 'if I had made you pregnant, our child would be about nine by now.'

Struck dumb by the sudden change of subject, she nodded silently.

'You must have felt enormous relief when nature showed you mercy.'

'I did—of course,' she said, after a pause.

Gideon turned her face up to his. 'Do I hear a but?'

'For a split second of teenage hormonal madness I felt a twinge of regret, too,' she confessed, eyes falling.

His arm tightened for a moment. 'Do you want children one day?'

'Yes.'

'Does your lawyer want them, too?'

'No idea. It's not a subject we ever discussed.'

Gideon shook his head. 'What kind of relationship do you have with this man?'

'None at all now,' she said tartly, and reached in her bag to switch her phone on. 'But I'd better hear him out before I tell him it's finally over.'

'What will you say to him?'

'What do you suggest?'

'Tell him you're booked for New Year's Eve.'

Right on cue, the phone rang again.

'Hello, Charles,' she said, resigned.

'What happened?' he demanded.

'Sorry, the phone must have disconnected—and then I got talking to Gideon.'

'Who the hell's Gideon?'

'He's the friend who joined me for Christmas Day.'

There was silence for a moment, while Charles held on to the temper that all too often got the better of him. 'Look, I know you were upset because I came here for Christmas without you—'

'Not in the least, Charles. You're perfectly entitled to spend it wherever you want. Just as I'm entitled to spend New Year's Eve wherever I want, and that's definitely not with you at the chalet.'

'*What?* But, hell, Felicia, I've told Mr Henderson I've asked you to come!'

'What on earth possessed you to do that?'

'He's paying for the chalet, so it seemed only polite—'

'Politic, you mean?'

He breathed in audibly. 'Look, Felicia, when you get back to London—'

'When I do, I won't be seeing you any more, Charles.'

'Oh, I *see*,' he sneered, after a pause. 'This is my slapped wrist for not turning up at your friend's wedding!'

'Don't be so childish,' she said wearily.

'Sorry—sorry! Look, Felicia, I apologise for not turning up at the wedding. Sincerely. But don't hold that against me. Just do this favour for me, *please*! The thing is,' he added urgently, 'Mr Henderson's keen to meet you.'

'What on earth for?'

'Before he offers someone a partnership he likes to meet the wife. Or in this case fiancée. Now, don't fly off the handle, but I jumped the gun a bit and told him we were getting engaged—'

'*What?* You had absolutely no right to do that,' she said, enraged. 'And now I suppose he wants to vet me, to make sure I come up to the firm's standards.'

'It's not like that, Felicia!' he pleaded.

Gideon's arm tightened around her shoulder.

'Tell him to go to hell,' he said in her ear.

'What was that?' demanded Charles.

'Gideon was making a suggestion.'

'He's there with you right *now*?'

'Yes. And he's given me some very good advice, so stop spluttering and listen. I'm not coming, Charles.'

'Oh, come *on*, Felicia, at least think it over!' he pleaded.

'Not a chance. The answer's no. Tell Mr Henderson I can't get a flight, or I've got flu. Better still, tell him I've jilted you—or you've jilted me, if that suits you better. It all boils down to the same thing. It's over between us—for good. I won't be seeing you again. Happy New Year, Charles.' Felicia cut his incensed protests off and tossed the phone into her bag, then turned to Gideon with a militant light in her eyes. 'There. I've burned my boats.'

'Magnificently!' approved Gideon.

'But don't worry. It doesn't mean you're obliged to spend New Year's Eve with me.'

Instead of assuring her it was what he wanted most in the world, Gideon gave her a searching look. 'If you'd been here on your own, and we hadn't met up again, would you have flown to join him?'

'No way. It was over for me long before that,' she said flatly. 'We had a major row—and not just about Poppy's wedding. Charles was not only furious about the long-distance romance issue, the real bone of contention was my refusal to move in with him.' She caught her breath as Gideon lifted her onto his lap.

'So why didn't you?' he asked, settling her against him.

It was such heaven to relax against the heat and strength of Gideon's body that Felicia's thought processes stopped functioning for a moment. 'Promise not to laugh?' she said at last.

He laid a hand on his heart. 'Promise.'

'You know better than anyone that I was a late developer in certain areas,' she said, grimacing. 'I was probably the only girl in my class, apart from Poppy, who hadn't—well—'

'Had sex?' he said helpfully.

She glared up at him so ferociously he kissed her swiftly in apology.

'Sorry. Go on.'

'I've met a few interesting men through my job. I liked one of them a lot.'

'But you wouldn't live with him, either?'

Felicia shook her head, feeling a strong desire to purr when Gideon smoothed a hand through her hair.

'Why not?' he asked.

'Because—and this is the point where you mustn't laugh—to me, living with a man is a commitment. One I've never wanted to make yet.'

'So, did the interesting gentleman propose marriage?'

'Yes. But, much as I liked Dominic, I hadn't the slightest desire to marry him.'

'Did you have a physical relationship with him?'

'Eventually, yes. But after a while it ended things between us, because it didn't work for me.'

'After a while?'

Her colour rose. 'Remember how good I was at Juliet?'

'Vividly.'

'My acting skills came in useful in bed, too. But only until…well—'

'Dominic caught on?'

Felicia nodded, sighing. 'And took it very much to heart. He said I was a Sleeping Beauty who needed the right man to wake me up.'

'But Charles wasn't the man, either?'

'Good Lord, no. To me he was always just a friend. But lately he's been trying to rush me to bed, and I've kept saying no—hence the row.'

'So what happened to Dominic?'

'He's married now, with a baby son.'

Gideon's arms tightened. 'Lucky man. Though not *so* lucky,' he amended, 'if you turned him down.'

'I almost didn't,' she confessed. 'My parents liked him so much I was really tempted to say yes to him in the hope that things would work out.'

'How about the lawyer? Do they like him?'

'Not nearly as much as they liked Dominic.'

'Your parents like *me*,' said Gideon smugly.

Her eyes gleamed. 'Do they really?'

'How about you?' he asked, tightening his hold a fraction. 'Do *you* like me, Felicia? You did once.'

'I liked you very much indeed,' she said softly. 'That was the trouble.'

'Trouble?'

'We were such good friends, as well as—as—'

'Lovers?'

She smiled ruefully. 'I thought of us as sweethearts, not lovers, Gideon. Lord, I was naive.'

'But so delectable I had a hell of a fight to wait all that time for you to grow up,' he said, in a tone which raised the hairs on her neck.

Felicia took in a deep breath, her eyes steady on his. 'I'm all grown up now, Gideon Ford.'

CHAPTER SIX

WHEN Gideon made no move to pick up the gauntlet she'd flung down, Felicia tried to slide from his lap, but he held her fast.

'Much as I want to pounce on you and gobble you up,' he said roughly, 'let's talk first.'

'"Is that all you blighters can do?"' she demanded.

'Fighting talk, Felicia!'

'I was quoting from *My Fair Lady*. Juliet wasn't the only string to my bow. I played Eliza Dolittle in the school production a couple of years later.'

'A lady of many talents,' he said with respect. 'Now, then, Felicia Maynard, we need to settle something. I started on the subject earlier, but got sidetracked. So stop looking at me like that and let me say my piece.'

'All right. You said you're returning to London on January the fifth—'

'When do your parents come back?'

'Two days later. Then I go back to London, too.'

'Right. Until January the fifth you're going to spend all your time with me.'

She smiled up at him demurely. 'Does that mean we're going out together?'

Gideon grinned. 'And staying in together.'

'This is all a bit sudden,' she said, suddenly doubtful.

'Not sudden at all—just ten years or so overdue,' he corrected. 'When I saw you standing in your doorway the other night something clicked into place so loudly I wonder you didn't hear it. For weeks I'd felt this compulsion to spend Christmas here alone. The moment I saw you I knew why.'

'But it's only by chance that I was alone for Christmas, too,' she said, frowning.

He nodded sombrely, and drew her closer. 'So let's grab this second chance we've been given and get to know each other all over again for a while before we actually become lovers. And this time,' he added, 'I do mean lovers. I'm better at it now.'

'So am I.'

His eyes took on a molten gleam. 'Ah, but when you make love with me there'll be no faking it, Juliet.'

Felicia laughed, and rubbed her cheek against his. 'So what you're suggesting is a "fine romance but no kisses".'

'Hell, no!' He turned her mouth round to his. 'I'm not taking you to bed yet, but I can't do without this.' He kissed her swiftly. 'As you can tell, I want you right now. But there was always more to our relationship than the physical, even when we were a couple of hormone-crazed teenagers. Now, listen. When I suggested spending time together—'

'Demanded, you mean!'

He shrugged. 'Whatever works. Have you anything planned for New Year's Eve?'

She laughed. 'You just heard me turn down *one* pressing invitation.'

'Surely you've had others?'

'Poppy and Tom asked me to a party at their place, but I'd already had an invitation from Katherine.' Felicia smiled up at him. 'Are you offering me a fourth option?'

Gideon nodded. 'This year I decided on a trip to Italy for the New Year. And before you ask,' he said quickly, 'I was going alone. But Peter reserved a double room for me because I like a big bed.'

'To sleep in alone? An odd thing to do on New Year's Eve!'

'I won't be alone if you come with me, Felicia.'

'To Italy?' she said, startled.

'Yes. This morning I rang the friend I'm flying with, and he says there's room for you on his plane. I also contacted the hotel to confirm the booking, and stressed that it was for two.' Gideon drew her closer and kissed her. Then, as she responded helplessly, went on kissing her with a persuasion far more powerful than any words. When he raised his head a fraction they were both breathing raggedly. 'Say yes,' he said against her lips.

She pretended to think it over, then nodded. 'It's certainly a more tempting offer than joining Mr

Henderson. I might have been forced to kiss him as the clock struck twelve.'

'The only man you'll be kissing on New Year's Eve is me,' he informed her.

Felicia could hardly believe she was actually in Italy when Gideon drove her from the airport at Breschia a few days later. In the interim Gideon Ford had demonstrated very clearly how he'd achieved his success in life. He'd organised everything about the trip down to the smallest detail—including the dogs. Their original place at the kennels had been snapped up as soon as Felicia had taken them home for Christmas, but because Bran and Jet were regular visitors the owner of the kennels had offered to put them up in her own house. The fact that Gideon had gone with her to make the request had probably had a lot to do with Mrs Hartley's offer, as Felicia had told him afterwards.

'One smile from you and she was putty in your hands!'

Felicia sat back, yawning, as they left the airport behind. 'How far is the hotel?'

'Far enough for you to have a snooze.' He smoothed a hand over her knee. 'Lie back and sleep. I'll wake you in good time.'

'I can't waste time sleeping! I still can't believe I'm here. Poppy couldn't believe it, either, when I rang her.'

Gideon chuckled. 'Doesn't she think you'll be safe with me?'

'She has doubts. And, to be fair to her, even if I do

get impulses, normally I don't act on them. Especially,' she added, casting a narrowed eye at him, 'when I don't even know yet where I'm going. Am I smart enough in my Christmas finery?'

Gideon cast a glance at the new suede jacket and sweater, and returned his eyes to the road. 'You look perfect.'

'Even for Italy?'

'For anywhere at all. Now, close your eyes and sleep for a bit. Perfect you may be, but I see shadows under your eyes, Juliet.'

'I was too excited to sleep last night.' She looked at him anxiously. 'Are you tired, Gideon?'

'No. I'll be glad to get there, but don't worry, I won't doze off at the wheel.'

As they drove through the darkness Felicia couldn't keep her eyes open. When she woke Gideon was threading his way through a complex maze of medieval streets, and she sat up hurriedly. 'Wherever it is, we've obviously arrived.'

'We have now,' said Gideon, and came to a halt in front of modest glass portals flanked by tubs of evergreens trained to twist up supporting poles like fluted columns. A young man emerged to help her out, and take the keys to park the car, but Felicia was standing at the reception desk before she saw the actual name of the hotel.

'Welcome to the Giulietta e Romeo,' said the receptionist in English.

Felicia smiled, startled, and exchanged a significant

glance with Gideon as he came to stand beside her. He signed the register, then dispensed with the services of a porter and carried their luggage up to their room. Felicia beamed at him as they went inside. The room was charming, with a gleaming wood floor and a large white-covered bed. Flowers and a tray of fruit waited alongside the television on the dressing table, and to her delight glass doors opened onto a balcony. Gideon opened them and beckoned Felicia outside to look down into the narrow street.

'It's lovely,' she said huskily, and turned to him with a smile, her eyes wet. 'I'm in the Romeo and Juliet Hotel, on a balcony, so we must be in Verona.'

He took her in his arms, rubbing his cheek over her hair. 'Are you happy about that?'

'Happy? It's the most gloriously romantic thing that's happened to me since you kissed me on that other balcony at school!' She reached up and kissed him fervently to make her point, then drew back, frowning. 'But originally you were coming here alone?'

Gideon drew her inside, closed the windows, and drew her down to sit on the bed beside him. 'I always go away alone for New Year. I prefer anonymity in a strange city to forced jollity at a party. So I went to Sydney one year, Times Square in New York another, even once to Edinburgh, among the crowds for Hogmanay. But this year, after my visits to Chastlecombe and meeting up with your parents again, you've been so much on my mind I chose Verona for this year's getaway.'

Felicia leaned wearily against his shoulder. 'I'm so glad you wanted me to come with you.'

'You like your surprise?'

'I can't tell you how much!'

'I thought of changing the booking to a bigger hotel—'

'But that wouldn't have been the same,' she protested, and got up. 'I like this one. I'd like it even more if they could provide me with some tea while I unpack.'

'How about something to eat?'

She shook her head. 'We had such a huge meal on our way to the airport I just need tea.' She gave a sudden engulfing yawn, and apologised, embarrassed, but Gideon took her in his arms, holding her lightly.

'You need sleep. And, just in case you have qualms about sharing that bed with me, I promise that sleep is all I have on my mind. Tonight, anyway,' he added, smoothing a hand over her hair.

Felicia smiled at him gratefully. 'I hope I don't snore!'

'I hope I don't, either.' Gideon released her, smiling. 'Now, I'll ring Room Service, then we'll get on with the unpacking, drink the tea and take turns in the bathroom. And after that,' he added, stroking her cheek, 'We'll get some sleep. You do look tired, Felicia.'

'I am,' she admitted. 'I didn't sleep well without the dogs last night.'

'I'll guard you from all harm tonight, Juliet,' he promised.

* * *

Felicia woke alone next morning to the sound of water running, astonished to find she'd fallen asleep as soon as Gideon had kissed her goodnight. She still had no idea whether he snored or not. She stretched out happily as she listened to the bustle of a busy hotel going on all around her, and looked at her watch. Nearly eight! And she was hungry.

Gideon opened the bathroom door, fully dressed, and stood smiling at her as he rubbed at his damp hair.

'Come on, dormouse, breakfast time. How did you sleep?'

She smiled sheepishly. 'Like a log. Which is pretty amazing. You'd think that the first time I actually sleep with you I'd at least keep awake. But I went out like a light the moment my head touched the pillow.'

'Good. It shows how comfortable you feel with me,' said Gideon with satisfaction. 'So be quick in the shower—I want my breakfast!'

Having slept through the pleasure of sharing a bed with him, Felicia revelled in every minute of the intimacy of eating breakfast with Gideon. She smiled at him so radiantly over their coffee and rolls that he reached out a hand to take hers, his eyes caressing.

'You look happy this morning, Felicia.'

'I am. Though I'm not usually a morning person. It takes a lot of coffee to launch me into my working day. But this,' she added, holding his eyes, 'is an unusual occasion. And I mean to make the most of it.' She picked up the guidebook he'd brought with him. 'So where do we start?'

Afterwards Felicia could never decide whether Verona was really the most beautiful city in the world, or whether exploring it in Gideon's company made it seem that way. They started with the ancient Arena, in crisp morning sunshine, and marvelled at the antiquity of the outer walls, then the sheer stupefying size of the interior—which, at the time it was built, Gideon informed her, courtesy of the guide book, could hold almost the entire population of Verona.

Felicia revolved slowly, looking up at the tiers of seats in wonder. 'What a place. To think it's been here for two thousand years! It must be an incredible experience to see and hear an opera here.'

'We'll come back in the season and do that,' said Gideon matter-of-factly. 'Now for the Via Mazzini— which is pedestrian only, to allow for concentrated designer window shopping.'

'Men don't like window shopping,' protested Felicia.

Gideon caught her in his arms, careless of passers by, and kissed her briefly. 'For you this man will make an exception.' He put his arm round her as they strolled along the narrow street of ancient buildings, which housed some of the most famous names in Italian fashion. And, though she protested, he insisted on buying her a memento of the day.

'You can't leave the Via Mazzini without something to show for it,' he insisted, and minutes later Felicia was in possession of a suede handbag the colour of bitter chocolate, with a designer label she'd often coveted but never aspired to. 'Perfect with those boots of yours,' said Gideon with satisfaction.

'Thank you,' she said huskily, then reached on tiptoe and kissed him square on the mouth, much to the delight of other shoppers. 'But the same rule applies to you.' She paused in front of the next window. 'How about that briefcase?'

'Too expensive.'

'That wallet?'

'I own three already.'

Felicia scowled at him. 'There must be something you'd like.'

'There.' He pointed to a leather photograph frame. 'I'd like two of those, complete with photographs of you. One for my desk in London; the other for Ridge House.'

She beamed at him. 'What a lovely idea. Wait here.' She hurried inside, managed to make her requirements known to the handsome young man who came to help her, and then signed the credit card slip with only the merest wince, and hurried out to Gideon with the parcel. 'Just a small token of appreciation for bringing me here. Normally I'm not a huge fan of New Year's Eve, but this one is the absolute best.'

Gideon put his arm round her and held her tight against him. 'It certainly beats all those others I spent alone.'

'Mine, too,' she said with a happy sigh. 'What now?'

'If we carry along here we come into the Piazza Erbe,

and all its cafés, so before any more sightseeing I suggest a stop for coffee.'

The Piazza Erbe, Gideon informed Felicia as they sat at a table watching the crowds go by, was named for the city's old herb market. 'If you crane past all the umbrellas shading the market stalls, the fountain in the middle of the *piazza* has a statue dating from Roman times.'

'I'm impressed! I just love the idea of antiquities all mixed up with modern bustle and noise. And there's a heavenly smell of roasting meat coming from somewhere,' said Felicia.

'Suckling pig, probably. They sell slices of it in bread rolls.' Gideon grinned. 'Shall I buy you one to munch on while we wander round?'

'Much as I'd like that, no, thanks,' she said regretfully. 'I'd probably ruin my new suede jacket.'

'Which would be sacrilege. So we'll do some more sightseeing for a while, then sit down somewhere for lunch.'

'Perfect.'

Felicia tried to take in all the sights and scents around her, not least the feel of his hand in hers, as they approached San Zeno Maggiore, which Gideon informed her was the most ornate Romanesque church in Northern Italy. She duly admired the bronze plates on the doors, and the relief above them of San Zeno conquering the devil, but once inside the vast, soaring interior she felt cold, so Gideon suggested they take the mandatory look at the famous Mantegna altarpiece inside, and the arches

of the equally famous cloister outside, and then go in
search of more secular pleasure in the shape of lunch—
which Gideon decreed must be pasta.

'*Bigoli,*' he informed Felicia, 'is a sort of wide spa-
ghetti, served here with tomato and aubergine. I've had
it before. It's good.'

Ready to fall in with anything he suggested by now,
Felicia agreed to the *bigoli*, and enjoyed it enormously—though after it she wanted nothing more than
to put her head down on the table and go to sleep. 'It
must be the air here or something,' she said guiltily. 'I
seem to need more sleep than at home.'

Gideon moved closer and put his arm round her as
they drank coffee. 'Just one more sight to see, then we'll
go back to the hotel and you can have a nap.'

'Lovely,' she sighed, and leaned her head against his
shoulder. 'Do you want a nap, too?'

'No. While you do your Sleeping Beauty bit I've got
more shopping to do. I want to get Peter something. He
got the usual bonus, of course, but I think he deserves
something personal to show my appreciation.' Gideon
rose to his feet and held out his hand. 'Up you come.
The final call is on our way back to the hotel.'

'And I know what it is,' said Felicia, grinning. 'I was
pretty sure we wouldn't leave Verona without a look at
Juliet's balcony!'

Gideon laughed. 'Damn! You've guessed.'

It was a short walk through the thronged streets to the
Via Cappello, where the crowd was even denser in front

of a building with the statue of a young girl in the court-yard. Felicia did a little polite jostling to get a better view of the simple picturesque façade, and the famous balcony, then looked up at Gideon with a grin.

'A good thing you didn't have to climb up to *that* balcony, Romeo!'

'It was scary enough as it was. The trellis they knocked up in the school workshop was a bit flimsy.' He smiled down at her. 'Darling, I hate to disillusion you, but the building is apparently a restored thirteenth century inn, and the balcony might be marble, but it was tacked on to the house in the twenties.'

'Oh, dear. How about the long balcony higher up?'

'It certainly fits the period better, but I pity poor Romeo if he had to shin up to that one,' said Gideon, grinning. 'He wouldn't have been much use to Juliet when he got there.'

'You have no romance in your soul,' she accused.

'Oh, yes, I have,' he said softly, and put his arm round her to walk back to the hotel. 'I take one look at you, Felicia Maynard, and I get so romantic I have to be very stern with myself. Now, move it,' he added with a change of tone. 'You take your nap, I'll do my shopping, and there'll be just time for a shower and so on before we go out to dinner. Peter booked a table at seven for me when he made the hotel reservation. Early by local standards, but the only table available tonight.'

'Where?'

'A *trattoria* just down the street from the hotel. Not

grand, but good food, so the hotel management assured him.' He smiled at her, looking so much like the boy he'd been she wanted to jump up and hug him. 'This is one New Year's Eve I intend to enjoy to the full.'

'So do I,' she said with feeling.

Once Gideon had taken her up to their room, he told her to get her head down for the sleep she needed. 'I'll leave you in peace for a couple of hours, so make the most of it. I'll knock when I come back.'

Felicia did as he said, but after an hour she'd had all the sleep she wanted, and made good use of Gideon's absence by taking her time to get ready for the evening.

She twisted a towel over her hair to keep it dry, and sang in the shower, so happy that her face wore a glow as she made it up that had nothing to do with cosmetics. By the time Gideon knocked on the door she was ready to go out on the town in the cashmere dress, knowing she looked her best.

Gideon looked at her in awe as she let him in. 'I've heard about beauty sleep, but I've never witnessed the effect first hand before. You look so lovely I could eat you with a spoon, Felicia.'

She smiled at him in delight. 'Thank you, kind sir!'

'Give me a few minutes to shower and shave, and I'll try to transform myself into an escort worthy of you, Juliet.'

'No transforming necessary,' she said, abruptly serious. 'Gideon, you're the most beautiful man I've ever met in my life.'

He stared at her in shock for a moment. 'You mean that?'

'Every word.'

He smiled crookedly. 'You've taken my breath away.' He took her in his arms very carefully. 'I promise not to spoil such a work of art, but I just have to hold you for a moment.'

'As long as you like,' she assured him, and melted against him with such warmth his eyes darkened and his arms tightened for an instant before he put her away from him.

'Unhand me, temptress,' he said, not quite lightly, and made for the bathroom.

Felicia opened the window and stood on the balcony to gaze up at the stars, still finding it hard to believe that this was all happening. She'd been head over heels in love with Gideon Ford when she was sixteen, and it had taken only one look when she opened her door to him the week before to fall back in love with him again. Or had the feelings been there all along, just waiting for one sight of him to spring back to life?

She was so lost in her reverie that she didn't hear Gideon join her until he slid his arms round her waist and kissed the back of her neck.

'It must be cold on that balcony, Juliet. Come back inside.'

She obeyed, smiling, and eyed his formal suit with warm approval. 'I'll be the envy of all the local *signoras*.'

'As I think I've said before, I'm only interested in you,' he said, with a note in his voice that set her hormones humming.

'Likewise, Mr Ford.' She fastened the chunky pendant round her neck. 'If I wear my suede jacket, casually sling your wonderful suede bag over one shoulder and drape your pashmina over the other, will I look elegant enough for New Year's Eve in Verona?'

'You look ravishing,' he told her, and took her in his arms. 'Sorry, I just have to do this again.'

'Good.' She smiled at him luminously, but then her stomach rumbled, and he laughed and released her.

'Dinnertime!'

The *trattoria* was so near at hand Felicia could have made it comfortably in high heels, but the night was chilly enough to make her glad of the suede boots she'd given herself for Christmas. The restaurant was small, but smart and sophisticated—and very busy. And, just as she'd forecast, more than one pair of appreciative feminine eyes turned in Gideon's direction as they were shown to their table. To her amusement he was embarrassed when she teased him about it.

'And I suppose you didn't notice the *male* heads turning as you arrived?'

She smiled demurely. 'Certainly not. Now, what do we eat? Not *bigoli* again, I think.'

'No. I'd rather you stayed awake for a while!' Gideon moved closer to show her the wine list, which to Felicia's delight was written on parchment. 'This is the heartland of good wine, so tell me what you'd like to eat and we'll choose something to go with it.'

With the waiter's help they both chose beefsteak with truffles and rocket salad, and a bottle of Bardolino Superiore. For sentimental reasons they ordered the inevitable tiramisu for pudding.

'I hope it's as good as Renzo's, but I'm sure the steak won't taste any better than yours,' Felicia told him as they waited for the meal. She nibbled on olives as she looked around, delighted with the bustle and noise of Veronese night life, the animated voices and the tantalising smells of cooking. She smiled radiantly at Gideon as he topped up their wine glasses. 'Is this where you would have eaten tonight if you'd come alone?'

He leaned closer, his eyes holding hers. 'Yes. But now you're here with me I can't imagine it without you.'

'Don't make me cry,' she begged. 'My mascara will run.'

'No crying allowed—our steak is on the way!'

The food was all Felicia had expected it to be, but, excellent though it was, it was secondary to the sheer joy of sharing the long, leisurely meal with Gideon, against the background noise of high-spirited Italian diners enjoying each other's company over the food they took so seriously. The entire evening had a magical quality to it, even the waiter's surprise when they got up to leave long before midnight.

'He thinks we're mad English,' whispered Felicia.

'I just want you to myself when the bells chime in

the New Year,' he said, as they walked back hand in hand along the ancient moonlit street. 'I'm not sure exactly what happens around here at midnight, but when I came back this afternoon I ordered champagne for a toast.' He halted, turning her to smile down into her eyes. 'It seemed appropriate to drink it on a balcony.'

Felicia reached up to slide her arms round his neck. 'Full circle, Gideon,' she whispered as his mouth met hers.

They broke apart as a group of laughing party-goers passed by, and Gideon took her hand to hurry her to the hotel. The receptionist greeted them warmly, and told them in careful English that their champagne came with the compliments of the hotel and awaited them in their room. They thanked him and wished him a happy New Year. Gideon discreetly slid a sizeable tip across the desk and took Felicia's hand to make for the stairs.

She applauded warmly when Gideon removed the cork from the champagne bottle with just the merest whisper of sound.

'*Bravo*. You've obviously had practice with champagne corks.'

'I've had practice in various fields since we were teenagers,' he said, eyes glinting as he filled their glasses. 'Let's take these out on the balcony and drink our toast in the moonlight.'

They moved outside just as the first chimes of midnight sounded from the nearest belltower. The final chime was followed by a staccato, ear-splitting fusillade as fireworks lit the sky with wave upon wave of light that turned the night into day.

'Happy New Year, Felicia,' said Gideon against her ear. He raised his glass to her and she touched it with hers.

'Happy New Year, Gideon.'

He kissed her briefly, then held her close as they watched the display. But after a while Felicia shivered slightly, and Gideon led her inside and shut the windows on the gaudy magical night.

When he put their empty glasses on the tray and switched off one of the bedside lamps the bed suddenly seemed to fill the entire room, and Felicia took in a deep breath to slow the heartbeat that was threatening to choke her.

'Are you nervous?' he asked, his voice amused, to her relief.

'Yes,' she said bluntly, and looked him in the eye. 'I don't want anything to spoil this lovely night.'

Gideon sat down on the edge of the bed and drew her down beside him. 'How could anything do that?'

She leaned her head against his shoulder. 'If you want the truth, I love being touched by you and kissed by you, but when it comes to the crunch I'm afraid I'll disappoint you, because I'm hopeless at what comes next.'

'You won't be with me,' he said matter-of-factly.

She looked up at him, smiling wryly. 'You're *that* good?'

'That's not what I meant.' Gideon stood up and took off his jacket and hung it away, then took off his shoes and knelt in front of her to remove her boots. 'Give me your jacket and let's get comfortable to talk this over.'

'I don't think talking about it will do any good,' Felicia said rather desperately as she handed it over. 'It's only making me more tense.'

'Were you like this with the others?' he asked casually, as he sat beside her.

'It wasn't a cast of thousands!' she said, eyes flashing, and he smiled.

'That's better. I prefer you angry to tense and frightened.'

'Not frightened, just nervous.'

Gideon switched off the other light, then propped up the pillows and put an arm round her to lean back against them. 'After the dramatic end to our relationship all those years ago I couldn't stop thinking of you, driving myself mad by wondering what you were doing.'

'I was the same about you,' she confessed, relaxing slightly. 'I knew—from Poppy, of course—that you didn't have another girlfriend while you were still in school, although there were plenty panting to fill my shoes.'

Gideon pulled her closer, his lips brushing her hair. 'I was working too damned hard to get good exam results to notice. Besides, if I couldn't have you I didn't want anyone else.'

Felicia turned to look up at him, her eyes rueful. 'And I thought you didn't want me at all any more. What a star-crossed pair we were!'

Gideon kissed her nose. 'With no technology to help

us out, either. A simple text message would explain everything in seconds these days, but I didn't even own a mobile phone until my aunt gave me one to take to college.'

Felicia lay relaxed against him, her eyes on the moonlight silvering the polished floor. 'Maybe fate thought it was a good idea to separate us at that point.'

'So I could concentrate on my goal?'

'And work on those other skills you mentioned!'

'However hard I worked, and no matter how many women I met along the way, I could never forget you, Felicia. In fact when Ridge House came up for sale in Chastlecombe my first thought was the prospect of running into you again. But your visits home never coincided with mine. I was grateful for any scraps of information that came my way from your parents—not least the fact that you weren't married.'

'But they must have told you about Charles?'

'If he wasn't your husband I didn't consider him an impediment to getting to know you again. If, of course, I still wanted that once we met up again. You might have changed out of all recognition from the girl I knew.' He let out a deep, contented sigh, and shifted her more comfortably in his arms. 'But the moment you opened your door to me you were still so much all I'd ever wanted it was a good thing you had the dogs with you.'

'What would have happened if they hadn't been there?'

'Something like this,' he whispered, and kissed her.

Felicia surrendered to the skilled, unhurried possession of his mouth, some deep, hidden chord inside her moved by his delight when her lips parted in response. Suddenly all her qualms about not pleasing him vanished as his leisurely tongue caressed hers. When he ran a hand over her breasts fire shot through her and she moved closer, suddenly impatient with the barrier of clothes between them. She sat up, and Gideon jerked upright, his eyes questioning until they met the molten look in hers.

'Undress me,' she ordered.

'Yes, ma'am!' he said huskily. 'Where's your zip?'

'Haven't got one. You sort of peel the dress off.'

Gideon's eyes blazed as he pulled her to her feet beside the bed. He reached for the hem of her dress and raised it with such care that Felicia lost patience and tugged the dress over her head to toss it on a chair. He laid her back on the bed, both of them breathing raggedly as he drew her stockings off with unsteady hands. Then he began kissing her fiercely as he removed the rest, and she kissed him back with equal fire, no longer caring whether she had to fake the next bit or not—though from the storm of sensations rushing through her it seemed this might, just might, be the one time when she didn't have to fake anything at all.

She quivered with anticipation when she was naked at last, revelling in the demand of his devouring mouth as it traced a hot path down her throat, and pinched herself surreptitiously to assure herself that this was no dream, but Gideon actually in her arms at last. She gasped as his hands stroked her breasts into quivering life, teasing their tips until they were erect and almost unbearably sensitive. His lips and grazing teeth made love to each one in turn, and at last, just when she thought she could bear the delicious torment no longer, he moved his skilled, inciting hands lower, invading her secret heat to caress the erect little bud no one had ever found before. At last she reared up in frenzy, and Gideon's eyes lit with triumph as he stripped his clothes off.

'I need to say something,' Felicia managed, before his mouth closed over hers again.

'I thought talking about it made you nervous,' he whispered. 'Are you afraid I'll make the same mistake as last time?'

'No, I'm not.' She breathed in sharply, a streak of fire shooting through her. 'Because I take care of that part myself these days. But—' Gideon's mouth silenced her, and Felicia abandoned herself to the fiery joy of skilled caresses which drove her closer and closer to a peak she'd never reached before, until at last she was trembling on the very brink of something wonderful that remained, tantalisingly, just out of reach.

She felt the brush of Gideon's hair on her thighs as he kissed each one in turn, then gasped as he parted them and with one sure, smooth stroke thrust between them right to her core, sending shock waves rushing through every vein and sinew as he took such total possession of her. She clung to him, her eyes locked on his and her fingers digging into his back as each unhurried, masterful thrust took her closer and closer to the brink again. The rhythm of his loving accelerated, growing in-exorably faster, until she let out a cry of hoarse, in-credulous joy and went free-falling into a whirlpool of sensation they drowned in together.

A long time later, when she'd regained the power of speech, Felicia turned her face on the pillow to meet Gideon's possessive eyes. 'You were right,' she said, in a voice she hardly recognised as her own.

'I usually am,' he agreed, as he pushed curling strands of tawny hair back from her forehead. 'About what, in this instance?'

'I didn't have to fake anything at all,' she said, taking in a deep breath of pure pleasure.

'I know.'

'How do you know?'

Gideon's lips twitched. 'Discounting the finger-nails digging holes in my back, I felt your climax rippling all around me in the split second before I came apart.'

'Oh!' She flushed, then looked him in the eye. 'I never told Dominic.'

He frowned, and turned her face up to his. 'Told him what?'

'That I take the pill.'

'Why not?'

'I made it clear the responsibility was his.' Felicia held his eyes. 'I withheld the ultimate intimacy. I realise now,' she added, 'that I was waiting to share that with someone special.'

'Like me?'

She smiled victoriously. 'There isn't anyone like you, Gideon.'

He pulled her closer, burying his face in her hair. 'There's never been anyone like you for me, either. God! I can't believe that I left it to chance.'

'Left what to chance?'

'Meeting you again. I should have asked your parents for your address and turned up on your doorstep demanding to see you.'

'I wish you had.' Felicia stroked his hair. 'Then we could have got to this stage so much sooner.'

He raised his head to look into her eyes. 'But can you see, now, why I waited to make love to you until we came here to Verona? Call me a romantic fool, if you like, but it seemed the right setting to achieve perfection this time round.'

Felicia held his eyes steadily. 'It is. And it was perfect. And it's shown me why it wouldn't work for me with anyone else.' She sighed, her eyes troubled. 'I wish now that there'd never been anyone else.'

He smiled, and kissed her, taking his time over it. 'You weren't designed for celibacy, Felicia.'

'I'd really begun to think so,' she said, rubbing her cheek against his. 'Making love was the kiss of death for me in past relationships.'

'Not with ours,' said Gideon with utter certainty. He traced a fingertip over her lips. 'We have a lot more going for us than just this. Miraculous though "this" happens to be. You're the friend I need as well as the lover I want more than anything I've ever wanted before. Except for one thing. As soon as I can bring you round to the idea, I want you to be the wife I cherish for the rest of my life.'

Felicia's eyes widened as she gazed into his. 'Wife?'

'You did say you'd never live with a man unless you were committed to him,' he reminded her. 'We've been given a second chance, and I'm damned sure we're not going to waste it. I meant what I said. You were the love of my life when I was eighteen, Felicia, and the moment I saw you again I realised that you still were. And always will be,' he added, and pulled her close. 'Don't cry, darling!'

'A few tears are to be expected when I'm so happy,' she said, then melted against him as he began to lick them away.

'You taste delicious,' he whispered. 'I think it's time I started on the gobbling up I once mentioned.'

'Before you do I have something to say,' she said with difficulty.

'By all means. As long as it's yes.'

'Of course I'm saying yes. You're not getting away a second time, Romeo,' she assured him, and he laughed and hugged her tight.

'Do I look as though I'm trying?'

'But I have something to add.'

Gideon looked down into her eyes. 'I know you approved of Poppy's wedding, but for God's sake don't say I have to wait until next Christmas before you'll marry me!'

'No. But you know I've had been thinking of changing my job and finding one nearer home. Which would mean that long-distance romance Charles objected to so strongly.'

'Unlike your lawyer, I'm willing to settle for that until we can be permanently together.' He kissed her hungrily. 'Every weekend will be a reunion. A very passionate reunion.' He went on kissing her until they were so desperate for each other they were soon caught up in the same inexorable rapture that Felicia had never expected to experience once, let alone twice in quick succession.

When their breathing had slowed, and they were relatively quiet in each other's arms, Felicia stirred at last.

'I've changed my mind, Gideon. I don't fancy the idea of weekends only now we've found each other again.'

'Neither do I,' he said with feeling.

'In that case I think I might stay on in Harley Street for a while after all.' She smiled crookedly. 'But if I do, I'll need a place to live.'

'Not a problem,' he said promptly. 'I can recommend a certain top-floor apartment with river view—on one condition. You share a bed with your landlord.'

'I was rather counting on that—' She gave a smothered shriek as he kissed her hard. 'I hadn't finished,' she said huskily, and smiled into his eyes. 'You interrupted me.'

He smiled, and smoothed her hair back from her

damp forehead. 'I just wanted to kiss you. We've got a lot of kissing to make up, remember? And making love, too, now we're both so good at it. But talk away, my beautiful girl.'

'Do you remember when I said—fairly flippantly, as I remember—that I hoped one day my prince would come?'

His eyes narrowed. 'Go on.'

'When I was just sixteen he came. But then he went away. And now he's come back.' Felicia smiled and hugged him close. 'And this time I'm going to keep him!'

Gideon held her tightly for a moment, then slid from the bed and went over to the jacket he'd thrown on a chair. He came back and dived in beside her, shivering a little.

'Give me your hand, darling,' he whispered.

Felicia held it out promptly.

'No, the left one.'

Her eyes wide, she obeyed, then caught her breath as he kissed it and slid a ring on the third finger. Through a mist of sudden tears she gazed down in awe at a pear-shaped solitaire diamond.

'Do you like it?' he demanded fiercely.

'How could I not? It's utterly glorious.' She kissed him hard, hugging him so tightly neither of them could breathe.

'It seemed appropriate to buy you a ring in Verona, Juliet,' he said unevenly. 'Though I know life won't always be like this. I want the ordinary things in life as well—a wife to share things with, a couple of children in due course, and tramping in the mud at Ridge House as well as dining out in London.'

'I much prefer our story to Shakespeare's,' said Felicia with satisfaction, eyeing her ring. 'By the way, did you remember to buy Peter something, too?'

'I did. He gets the briefcase you fancied so much.'

She laughed, and sank back against a broad shoulder with a sigh of pure content. 'I don't mean to be rude, darling, but I think I need to sleep again.'

He kissed her and held her close. 'Goodnight, my lovely girl. Sleep well.'

'Something to say first,' she said, yawning.

'You'd better make it short and sweet; you're half asleep already,' he said, laughing.

'I just wanted to say I love you, Gideon Ford.'

'Words don't get much sweeter than that,' he said huskily. 'I love you, too, Felicia Maynard. Always have, always will.'

She gave a heartfelt sigh of pure happiness. 'This is the most wonderful night of my life. Happy New Year, Romeo.'

His arms tightened as he rubbed his cheek against hers. 'Now we're together again, Juliet, all our New Years will be happy.'

* * * * *

A Mistletoe Masquerade

LOUISE ALLEN

Louise Allen has been immersing herself in history, real and fictional, for as long as she can remember, and finds landscapes and places evoke powerful images of the past. Louise lives in Bedfordshire and works as a property manager, but spends as much time as possible with her husband at the cottage they are renovating on the north Norfolk coast, or travelling abroad. Venice, Burgundy and the Greek islands are favourite atmospheric destinations. Please visit Louise's website – www.louiseallenregency.co.uk – for the latest news!

Dear Reader,

Upstairs and downstairs in the Regency household mirrored each other in numerous ways – although, of the two, downstairs was possibly the more rigid and stratified. And while the domestic staff had to think about their employers and their guests every minute of their working day, the privileged inhabitants of the upstairs world could go about their lives blissfully unconcerned about what the staff thought of them.

Lucas and Rowan think they know what is best for their friends and intend to set their love lives straight by plunging into the looking-glass world below stairs. I hope you enjoy their Christmas masquerade as they battle with the mysteries of the brushing room and the boot cupboard, the etiquette of Pug's Parlour, the formalities of the Servants Ball and the mortifying insight into the servants'-eye view of their masters' lives.

Their love affair seems doomed by circumstance, but this is Christmas after all, and under the mistletoe wishes can come true.

Louise

CHAPTER ONE

December 12th 1816

'YOUR stepmother expects you to marry a *murderer*?'
Lady Rowan Chilcourt stared at her white-faced friend.
'I go away for two years and when I come back I find
you meekly allowing yourself to be led to the slaughter
like some lamb?'

'Slaughter? Oh, do not say such things, Rowan! And
how can I prevent it?' Miss Maylin turned even paler,
although how that was physically possible it was hard to
see. 'We do not know he is a murderer—surely he is
not—but the stories are alarming, and Lord Danescroft—
Oh, Rowan, if you could only see him for yourself—he
is bleak, unsmiling, utterly sinister.'

'You must say *no*,' Rowan retorted as she paced, the
skirts of her Parisian carriage dress swaying. This was
so typical of Penny: she was the sweetest, most loyal
friend anyone could hope for, but she was painfully shy
and utterly incapable of saying boo to a goose, let alone

to a formidable creature like Lady Maylin. And what Penny's stepmother lacked in breeding she more than made up for in sheer bullying determination.

'I cannot decline, for he has not yet proposed. I have not even met him—not face to face. I have only seen him from a distance at receptions during the Season. Not that he stayed very long when he did come. And he never talks to people. Or dances,' she added plaintively. 'Or smiles.'

'I read about his wife's death at the time.' Rowan frowned, trying to recall the stories she had perused. Acting as hostess to her father Lord Chilcourt, in the midst of the glamour of the Congress of Vienna, had been an engrossing whirl of activity far removed from the sedate and regulated pleasures a single lady of twenty-four might enjoy in London. The English news had seemed far away and alien.

Even so, Lady Danescroft's death had been a sensational and scandalous mystery, and as well as lingering on the horrid details of how she had been found by the butler at the foot of the servants' stair, with her neck broken, the reports had been full of veiled hints and coded phrases. Lady Danescroft had been 'lively', 'well-known amidst the younger set', and famed for her 'wide circle of friends of both sexes'.

The Earl of Danescroft had apparently shown no emotion at either the inquest or the funeral, had declined to speculate upon why his wife should have been on the servants' stair at all in the middle of the night, and had simply become chillier and more abrupt on the subject as time went on.

'Are they really saying he killed her?' Rowan demanded. 'The papers were full of innuendo, but nothing about an outright accusation, let alone a trial.'

'Not exactly.' Penny frowned. 'They say that it is very strange he does nothing to rebut the rumours. He did not go into mourning for her. And—' she blushed '—they say he dismissed his valet the very next day, and the valet was very good-looking.'

'He did not murder the valet as well, then?' Rowan asked, half joking.

'No! Oh, Rowan, do be serious for a moment.' Penelope dragged a curtain closed to hide the swirling snow outside. 'I am sure—well, almost sure—he is not a murderer. He's an earl, for goodness' sake. But he looks haunted by dark thoughts, seems plunged in gloom, and they say his small daughter is kept locked up all the time. Poor little mite.' She sat down, dragging a shawl around the shoulders of her gown. Rowan noticed it was at least one Season out of fashion, and not the work of a leading *modiste,* either. 'How could I marry a man like that?'

'He sounds like the villain of a gothic sensation novel. But one has to admit it would be an astonishingly good match,' Rowan pointed out, sitting down in a flurry of fine merino skirts with considerably more grace than her friend. 'You will forgive me being frank, but—'

'I am one of the unimportant Maylins,' Penny interrupted, nodding in agreement. 'I know. We have all sorts of grand distant connections, but we haven't any money—and no pretensions either. At least,' she added scrupulously, 'we had none until Papa married again.'

They were silent for a minute, contemplating the ambitions of the second Lady Maylin. If she had thought that by marrying a second cousin of the Duke of Farthinghoe she would be catapulted into High Society she had soon been comprehensively disillusioned. But that did not stop her from trying.

'So why should the Earl's eye alight upon you?'

'My godmother is the grandmother of Lord Danescroft. Apparently she has persuaded him that he must remarry for the sake of his motherless daughter and to get himself an heir.'

'Yes, but *you*—'

'I know. I haven't any looks or money, I'm so shy I go scarlet if a man speaks to me, and I have just had a disastrous Season,' Penelope catalogued with ruthless honesty. 'If I looked like you, Rowan—if I had your spirit—I could understand it.'

'They want a doormat because no one else of breeding will have him,' Rowan said grimly. There was no point in trying to persuade Penny that she was a beauty. She was not. She had mouse-brown hair, a figure that at the kindest could be called *slight*, and was so self-effacing it was a wonder anyone noticed her at all. She was also sweet-tempered, caring, wonderful with children and the most loyal of friends. None of these endearing characteristics was of the slightest value in the Marriage Mart, of course.

'Yes. And because I *am* such a doormat I know I will say yes if he asks me. No one will support me. Godmama has arranged for me to be invited to the Christmas house party at Tollesbury Court. He will be there, too, and he is going to propose.'

'What if he does not think you will suit?' Rowan asked. 'They might be able to bully you, but surely not him? Earls can do what they like.'

'Godmama says she has already discussed me with him and he says I sound eminently suitable. She says he is tired of all this horrid gossip and wants a sensible young woman who will not treat him to vapours and who will get on with running the house and looking after the child.' Penny sighed. 'It sounds very dreary: I wonder he does not simply hire a superior governess and a housekeeper.'

'Because they won't give him a male heir,' Rowan pointed out with brutal honesty. 'There must be something wrong with him if his wife was driven to taking the valet as a lover. Perhaps he beat her? Perhaps he squandered her marriage portion? Surely your papa would not force you if such things were the case?'

'No, he would not. But he says I am being hysterical about the mysterious death, and I cannot get him to see that I have taken Lord Danescroft in complete abhorrence.'

'Then we must find out something to the Earl's discredit. Then you will have a logical reason that your father cannot but see is an obstacle to your happiness.'

They fell silent, gazing into the fire. Rowan stretched out a hand and picked up a buttered teacake, biting into it as though into his lordship. 'Is your stepmother to accompany you?'

'No. Godmama said that would be certain to put Lord Danescroft's back up and that she will chaperon me. Even Papa was forced to agree, given what a good match it would be. Stepmama was furious.'

Rowan licked butter off her fingers and pondered the idea that had crept, fully formed, into her head. 'Remind me who your godmother is.'

'Lady Rolesby.'

'Hmm. She has not seen me since before I went to Vienna with Papa. I doubt she would recognise me now—nor would anyone else, come to that.'

'No,' Penny agreed. 'For you have grown so much. You were pretty before, Rowan, and you are truly beautiful now. But what has that to do with anything?'

Rowan ignored the compliment: Penny had always admired her vivid looks. 'Why, I shall go as your dresser. The servants always know everything—I will hear all the gossip, investigate Lord Danescroft and prove how unsuitable he is for you!'

'Oh, Rowan!' Penelope's unremarkable face lit up. 'Would you? *Could* you? I don't expect there is anything to find out about him really, but it would be so wonderful to have someone with me to confide in. But what are your plans for Christmas? Surely your father cannot have intended for you to simply go home alone?'

'No, Aunt Moore in Yorkshire is expecting me.' Rowan grimaced. 'I will write and tell her I have been invited to a house party full of eligible young men and she will be delighted. My handwriting can be atrocious if I try—she will not be able to read where we are going.'

'I am supposed to leave in ten days. Is that enough time, do you think?'

'To learn to be a dresser? Surely it must be? How hard can it be?'

'Miss Maylin? You cannot be serious—have you met her mother?' Lucas Dacre, Viscount Stoneley, crossed one booted foot over the other and stared at his friend. 'She's the most vulgar, scheming creature in creation.'

'Stepmother, I understand. But how do you know her? You've hardly been back in the country ten days.' The Earl of Danescroft raised an eyebrow. It was the greatest show of emotion he had exhibited since he had wrung Lucas's hand three days before. Lucas kept his own face bland, hiding his anxiety at the change in his friend. The last time he had seen him, five years before, he had been his groomsman and had danced at his wedding.

Now Will was gaunt, unsmiling, his expressive brown eyes shuttered, and all the joy had gone out of him. It was hardly surprising: Lucas had spent several hours at his club, buried in the newspaper archives, familiarising himself with the scandal Will obviously had no wish to speak about.

He had not been surprised to discover that Belle had

proved to be as careless with her husband's heart and honour as she had with his money. He had tried to hint at her character when he had seen Will becoming attached—it had led to the only row they had ever had and he had held his peace from then on. *I told you so* was not going to be helpful now.

'I went to a reception at Fotheringham's last night. Frightful bore, but I promised Mama I'd look them up when I was in Town. Lady Maylin was such a sight— all purple satin and plumes and vulgarity—that I asked who she was. Then I overheard her in loud conversation with her cronies. Such a catch she had engineered for her dear Penelope. Such wealth, such a lineage. I removed myself—if I had known she was talking about you I would have stayed longer behind my potted fern.'

The Earl grimaced. 'My grandmother has assured me she will not be invited to Tollesbury.'

'Your grandmother, if you will pardon my saying so, must be all about in the head if she thinks a daughter of that house will be suitable for you.' *Or deserving of you*, Lucas thought bitterly. Will needed someone to love him, not a gold-digging nonentity who just happened to be sufficiently on the shelf to swallow the scandal in return for the title and the wealth.

'I am assured Miss Maylin is not at all like her step-mother. And she is apparently good with children. Louisa needs a mother.' Will might have been describing the appointment of a governess. There was no animation in his voice, no emotion.

Lucas felt the anger stirring inside him. This was the friend who had always seemed to be laughing, the man who had helped him out of scrapes more numerous than he could count. His best friend—the brother he had never had—who deserved someone to cherish him, someone to bring the laughter back. Someone to thaw his heart.

'And if she proves not to be what she is reported to be?' he asked harshly.

'Then I would not offer for her.' Will looked surprised he needed to ask. 'I cannot settle for anyone who would not be a suitable mother for Louisa.' He shook his head. 'But there is no fear of that: I trust my grandmother's opinion.'

'I'm going with you.' *Damn it, all he can think about is whether his new wife will make a good mother to the child. What about himself? Wasn't he hurt enough last time?*

'But you haven't been invited.' Then Will shrugged. 'No doubt it will be easy for you to secure an invitation. Even though you've been in the West Indies all this time no one will have forgotten you. And they will be unsurprised to see you again, now you have come into the title.'

'They'll have forgotten me sufficiently not to recognise me, I hope. At least so long as they see me where they would not expect to.' Lucas smiled, flexing his fingers. He imagined them curling around Miss Maylin's greedy little throat, but he kept his tone amused. 'I shall go as your valet, Will—below stairs they know all about their masters' and mistresses' dirty linen, and I'll wager are more than willing to gossip about it. After a few days there I'll know every secret your Miss Maylin has to hide, believe me. And if Perrott will entrust me with his blacking recipe, you'll have a decent shine on your boots into the bargain.'

Ten days later

It was important to remember one's place. Miss Maylin's dresser, a young lady calling herself Daisy Lawrence, clutched the morocco jewel case to her midriff and stood amidst the shabby valises and the old trunk that made up her mistress's luggage. In front of her the dressers serving Lady Meredith Hughes and the Honourable Miss Geraldine Mather were already supervising the footmen. The impressive sets of matching luggage in their care were carried up the stairs to the guest bedchambers with respectful attention.

They had arrived after she had, but here at Tollesbury Court, as everywhere in polite society, servants took the precedence accorded to their employers. Miss Penelope Maylin was very far down the social ladder indeed, which meant that her dresser waited with patience until her betters had been attended to.

Fires blazed in the hearths facing each other across the flagged floor at the other end of the vast baronial hall. You could have roasted an ox in either, Daisy thought, but at this end of the chamber Cook might safely store the evening's ices and jellies with no fear of them melting. Her toes in their jean half boots were frozen, and she could only be thankful that she did not suffer from chilblains. Yet.

Between the fires the guests were being greeted by their hosts and passed on to the care of the Groom of the Chambers, who was organising footmen to lead them to their rooms. It all took time, and a knot of people formed between the hearths while they shed cloaks and muffs and chatted amongst themselves. There, too, rank was plain. Miss Maylin stood uncomfortably close to the heat, too meek to dodge around the formidable bulk of an older lady who was determined to get as close to her hosts as possible.

Penny—*Miss Penelope*, Daisy corrected herself— was roasting, whilst she was freezing. At this rate she was not going to be upstairs in time to have anything unpacked by the time Miss Penelope got to her room, desperate for a change of clothing and a cup of tea. On top of that, hairpins were sticking into her scalp, her head ached from the severity of her braided hairstyle, and she was as badly in need of that tea as her mistress. But it would surely be her turn next: the other women were vanishing upstairs, dressing cases in hand, without a backward glance at their humble colleague.

There was a stir near the front door, another draught of icy air around Daisy's ankles, and footmen bearing down on her with yet more luggage. Shiny, expensive luggage. Lots of it. *Drat.* Fuming, she stood aside to let all six of them past. And sauntering along in their wake, a handsome dressing case in hand, was an individual

Daisy had no hesitation in recognising as a very superior valet indeed.

He was tall, he was dark, he was lean, and he moved not like a man who spent his life polishing boots and arranging neck cloths, but like one who was at home in the saddle. He was unsmiling, his regular features handsome enough if you liked that sort of thing, she thought critically, watching from the side of the stairs. Then he saw her. Daisy frowned as a pair of deep blue eyes swept over her from head to foot in a comprehensive and very male assessment. *Impertinent wretch!* Her lips were parted as she almost spoke the set-down aloud, and then in the nick of time she remembered who and where she was.

Her teeth snapped shut, catching the tip of her tongue painfully. Eyes watering, Daisy stood in fulminating silence as the valet passed. And then he winked at her. Nothing else on his face moved except for that one lid, and then he was vanishing up the stairs, long legs taking them two at a time.

She had just been winked at by a valet. A *valet*! It was the outside of enough. And this would be just the start. She had half a mind to—

'This all there is, then?' Six foot of liveried footman was standing at her elbow. 'Where's yours?' She pointed to a pair of even more battered valises. His lip curled. 'Right, then. Jim, you take those up to miss's room in the North Turret and we'll take the others. For some reason,' he added over his shoulder as they climbed, 'your mistress has got the Pink Suite. Very nice, too. Seems a bit odd, though—one of the best suites in the place and she's no one much, is she? Still, I expect they've got their reasons.'

Yes, they have indeed, Daisy thought grimly as she followed. *And it will take more than some pink suite to ensnare poor Penny in their plans if I've got anything to do with it.* Impertinent upper servants and chilblains must be endured. This was all her own idea, but she knew who to blame for it. Oh, yes indeed. The Earl of Danescroft was going to regret the day he decided that Miss Maylin would make a conformable and grateful wife.

CHAPTER TWO

'ROWAN, this is going to be ghastly!' Penelope cast herself down on the chaise and fumbled blindly in her reticule for a handkerchief. Her cheeks were unbecomingly flushed from the heat of the great fire and her eyes were suspiciously moist. 'Lord Danescroft is here, and he is even more forbidding close to than I ever dreamt.'

'You must call me, Daisy,' Rowan reminded her, casting an eye at the door. It was securely closed. 'Or Lawrence if you are going to pretend to be starchy. When did the Earl arrive?'

'Just before you went upstairs. I saw you waiting at the other end of the hall, and then they took your things up after his.' Penny blew her nose and looked around at the rose-pink draperies and the gilded furniture. 'What a beautiful room. Do you think they made a mistake, putting me here?'

'No, I think this is a room suitable for a young lady an earl is about to propose to,' Rowan said, provoking a little gasp from Penny. She put away the last of her friend's meagre store of silk stockings and turned to lift the lawn petticoats out of the valise. 'I did not see his lordship, but I have seen his valet, the impertinent wretch. He winked at me.'

That at least made Penny smile. 'Well, you do look very pretty. That severe hairstyle suits you. Let me help you with those; you shouldn't wait on me.' She reached for an unopened valise, but Rowan gave her a little push towards the chair.

'No, you must act the lady and forget who I really am. If anyone observes any undue familiarity—' There was a tap and the door opened. 'Ah, the tea—put it there, please.' Rowan gestured to the table beside Penny's chair and waited until the maid left with a bobbed curtsey. 'You see—you never know when they are going to pop up. Mind you, they gave me a very odd look when I asked for two cups.' She poured, handed Penny her tea, and sank down on the padded fender. 'Bliss.'

Penny was still looking miserable, even after two cups of tea. 'Lie down and rest,' Rowan ordered, 'and I'll shake out your evening things and put away your day clothes.'

By the time Penny was undressed and tucked up in bed, the simpler of the two evening dresses unpacked and hung up and the rest of the accessories laid out, Rowan was beginning to feel considerable sympathy for her own dresser, the unflappable Alice Loveday. She was used to finding everything to her hand, just when she needed it, but trying to recall exactly what Penny would need required more effort.

Done at last, she glanced at the clock—more than enough time to put away the day clothes and go to her own room and organise her modest wardrobe, before changing and coming down again to organise Penny's evening toilette.

'Oh, rats!'

'What?' Penny sat bolt upright in bed, eyes wide.

'Look at the hem of your pelisse! All muddy splashes. And your boots.'

'That was when I got out of the carriage,' her friend apologised. 'A stone slab tipped under my foot and sprayed up dirty water.'

'Oh, well. Time to explore below stairs,' Rowan said, feigning more confidence than she felt. Intensive study of the Maylins' servants' quarters in the company of Miss Loveday was not, she strongly suspected, going to be much help when confronted with the complexities of Tollesbury Court. Nor was her own experience very relevant. Her father's position with the diplomatic mission meant that they had a steward who dealt with every domestic detail, leaving Rowan to make final decisions on menus, flowers and draperies and very little else.

'I need the brushing room and the boot boy. I will not be long.' Fortunately she remembered to use the back stairs, emerging slightly dizzy from its tight twists into organised chaos below. After being comprehensively ignored for several minutes, Rowan stepped firmly in front of a footman, his arms clasped around two filled flower vases. 'Where will I find the boot boy?' she asked crisply.

'Back there—first on the left past the pantry,' he replied, blowing ferns away from his mouth.

After some false turns she located the pantry, then the boot boy in his cubbyhole, panting slightly as he leathered a pair of tall boots on a jack. 'These are for Miss Maylin, the Pink Suite. And where is the brushing room?'

This time she found her way more easily, having spotted some of the landmarks already. It was thankfully empty, so Rowan was able to turn up the lamps against the winter gloom and explore the racks of mystifying brushes and leathers until she found something that looked stiff enough to remove mud without damaging the nap of the cloth.

The tables were padded and covered with baize, so she selected one, laid out the pelisse and began to attack the hem. With all this equipment it was surely going to be the work of minutes.

Lucas strolled through the passageways, Will's buckskin breeches draped over his arm, receiving a gratifying amount of attention from the resident domestics. Below stairs, as above, status was everything, and he was an earl by association. It amused him that as a servant he'd acquired a higher rank than his own, and he allowed an amiable condescension to creep into his manner. If he were to engage his fellow staff in gossip about their employers, and specifically Miss Maylin, he needed to make a good impression: top lofty enough to demand answers to questions, pleasant enough so as not to cause resentment.

A housemaid with a pert manner and a dimple showed him to the brushing room, then bustled off with a swing of her hips and a backward glance over her shoulder. He was smiling faintly from the encounter as he stepped inside and saw the room was already occupied.

The young woman had her back to him, bent over the garment on a long table and presenting a vision which drove the memory of the housemaid right out of his mind. Slender, curvaceous, and clad in a dull black that served only to focus all attention on her figure, she had not heard him come in.

She was muttering under her breath as she brushed. Lucas suspected her words were curses, for she seemed to be more than a little hot and bothered. Her honey-brown hair had been braided and strained back into an elaborate knot but had begun to come down. Little wisps clung to the damp skin of her neck. He moved closer, his feet silent on the oilskin floorcloth.

'Damn and blast and botheration…'

It was a very pretty neck. He found himself trans-fixed by the nape, the tender white skin, the faint sheen of perspiration. What would it be like to bite? Just very, very, gently.

'Oh, drat!' She banged down the brush and straightened up so fast that she had to take a balancing step backwards—straight into Lucas. 'Oh! What on earth do you think you are doing?'

'Ow!' The cry of anguish was wrung out of him. She might be slender, but the top of her head banging back into his nose packed a powerful force. Lucas was fond of his nose. In his opinion it was one of his more distinguished features, and having it broken by an irritable dresser would be distressing.

'Don't blame me,' she continued, with no sympathy for his pain. She turned round and glared at him. 'It is entirely your fault, creeping up on me.' Her eyes were an intriguing hazel colour, her brows arched, her nose small and straight. Right now she was glowering down it. He lowered his hand, reassured that his own nose was still intact. As she saw his face properly her expression became even more severe. 'It is you again! I should have known. You libertine.'

Libertine? 'Are you a dresser?' But of course she was. He remembered her now—the striking girl with the scowl, surrounded by shabby bags. He had winked at her. Obviously a mistake.

'Of course I am!'

'Well, you do not sound like it,' he retorted frankly, dumping the breeches on another table and reaching for a brush. Her accent was crisp, assured and educated, even if her language when he had entered had been decidedly unladylike.

'I was raised in a gentleman's house,' she informed him, picking up the garment she had been dealing with and giving it a vigorous shake. 'And educated with the young ladies. Not that it is any business of yours. A dresser is expected to be genteel.'

'You aren't *genteel*.' Lucas scrubbed at one muddy knee. 'You sound like a dowager duchess at Almack's.'

'It was a very superior household.' She pushed back the damp hair from her forehead and held a hem up to the lamp. The garment appeared to be a drab pelisse of unfashionable cut. 'I do not believe this is mud at all. I think it must be glue.'

'Let me see.' Lucas reached for the pelisse. He had no clue how to remove stubborn stains from ladies' garments—instinctively he was attacking Will's breeches with the same method he'd have used on a muddy horse—but he wanted to keep her there talking. 'Try this fine one, with the thin stiff bristles.'

'Thank you.' She accepted it warily and retreated behind her table, apparently the better to keep an eye on him. 'Why were you creeping up on me?'

'I wasn't,' he denied, attempting to look innocent. He did not have the face for it, he knew. The dresser simply slanted him a look that spoke volumes for her opinion of men, and of him in particular, and bent over the hem again.

'Whose dresser are you?'

'Miss Penelope Maylin's.'

Lucas dropped the brush and dived under the table to retrieve it and get his face under control. The gods were on his side, obviously—not only had he found his quarry without any effort whatsoever, but she was going to be a delight to extract information from.

Not, of course, that this could go any further than a little light flirtation—if that was what it took to win her confidence. In Lucas's code of honour servants were as out of bounds as virgin gentlewomen. On the other hand, she could have been a sour-faced abigail or an old dragon.

'What is your name?' He straightened up and bent over his work again.

'Lawrence. Daisy Lawrence.'

Daisy. It did not suit her. This girl was no open-faced meadow flower. She was something altogether more subtle and cultivated. A honey-coloured rose, perhaps: scented, velvety, but with sharp thorns.

'I am—'

'I know who you are. You are Lord Danescroft's valet.' His surprise must have been evident, for she added, 'You need not be flattered. Miss Maylin remarked upon the time his lordship arrived. But you may tell me your name.'

'Lucas.' She had spirit this one. Will outranked every other guest *and* his host. That made Lucas the top dog amongst the servants, yet she did not appear to be awed by that fact. 'You may call me Mr Lucas,' he added, more to see her reaction than anything.

'Yes, Mr Lucas,' she replied meekly, confounding him by finally recognising her place. 'And thank you for showing me this brush; it has done the job perfectly.' She folded the garment over her arm and moved towards him and the door beyond. Lucas shifted round his work table as though to find a better angle and blocked her path.

'A demanding young lady, is she? Your Miss Maylin?'

'Not at all. She's as meek as meek—quite a milksop. Not like some I could mention.' There was suppressed amusement lurking in those hazel eyes, which was odd. He wondered what—or who—she was thinking of. 'Of course,' Daisy added thoughtfully, 'there is her step-mother to contend with.'

'Indeed?' Lucas lifted one leg of the breeches and frowned at the knee laces, hoping he looked as though he knew what he was doing. 'Could I trouble you to pass that small brush at the end, Miss Daisy?' Partly it was a tactic to keep her there talking, and partly because he enjoyed the sight of her moving about with a grace that must have been instilled along with her lessons with the young ladies. A family by-blow, perhaps? he specu-lated. 'Is her stepmother difficult?'

'Terrible. Ghastly, vulgar creature,' Daisy confided with some relish. 'Unfortunately Miss Maylin is devoted to her. It is the greatest good fortune, in my opinion, that she did not accompany us here—although poor Miss Maylin is almost prostrated with nerves without her support. She is hopeless in Society. I said to her, Your husband is not going to like it if you insist on your stepmama living with you when you are wed. That upset her, believe me.'

'Husband? She is betrothed, then?'

'Oh, no. But it won't be long if Lady M has anything

to do with it. Of course she's hoping for a rich man—they need it, that's for certain.'

'Really?' Lucas kept his eyes on his task, feigning only casual interest.

'Well, yes, what with the family tendency to—' She broke off. 'Listen to me gossiping! That will never do. What must you think of me, Mr Lucas?'

Schooling his features to hide his impatience with her sudden attack of discretion, Lucas put the brush down and turned with deliberation to face Daisy. She was looking somewhat chastened, an expression that did not seem to fit her confident heart-shaped face.

'Think of you? Why, that you are as charming as you look, Miss Daisy.' He leant forward. Her eyes widened but she stood her ground. 'And that you have the most kissable mouth I have yet seen in this house.'

'Oh!' She planted one hand firmly in the middle of his chest and pushed. 'Out of my way, Mr Lucas—you are an arrant flirt and I am well served for lingering to gossip.'

Amused, and too skilled to try and detain her and risk frightening her away from future conversation, Lucas stepped back. 'Miss Daisy. I look forward to seeing you this evening in the Steward's Room.'

'The—? Of course—dinner.' She swept past him, delightful nose in the air. 'But at opposite ends of the table, Mr Lucas, I am glad to say.'

Rowan shut the door behind her and leant against it for a moment to catch her breath. For a moment she had thought he was about to steal a kiss. What her father would say if he knew his only child was not only masquerading as an upper servant but was being amorously pursued by a valet, she shuddered to think. In fact she was shuddering now—or rather shivering. And it was chastening to realise that it was from excitement, not revulsion or maidenly horror.

Getting a grip on herself, she set off for the stairs and found them after only three false turns. At least running up their twisting steepness was an excuse for pink cheeks. One heard about reckless young women who threw their virtue away on handsome footmen. They always appeared to end up pregnant and in disgrace, but perhaps those were only the ones she had heard about, and the stately homes of England were rife with liaisons between upstairs and downstairs.

Well, she was not going to throw her hat over the windmill for anyone less than the man she was going to marry, so tall, dark, blue-eyed rakish valets were not going to tempt her in the slightest. *Then what, pray*, her inconvenient inner voice enquired tartly, *are you doing, getting all of a do-dad over one wink and an almost-kiss?*

Maidenly modesty, she assured her inner voice sanctimoniously, and was giggling as she let herself into Penny's bedchamber.

'You've been ages,' Penny remarked. She was sitting up in bed and looked considerably better. 'Have you been exploring?'

'I've been getting a backache trying to remove the

mud from this.' Rowan hung the pelisse in the clothes press. 'And flirting with Lord Danescroft's valet.'

'What?' Penny hopped out of bed, gaping. 'Truly? The one who winked at you?'

'Well, not the one who was his wife's lover, that's for sure. I don't know what it is about that man—he appears to employ valets of a decidedly amorous disposition. This one—*call me Mr Lucas*, if you please—crept up behind me in the brushing room and then almost kissed me, after telling me I looked delightful.'

She perched on the end of the bed and Penny sank down beside her, wide eyed. 'But I got in some telling remarks. I told him that you were devoted to your step-mother, even though she was quite frightful, and pined because she was not here and would probably expect your future husband to allow her to live with you.'

'Brilliant,' Penny said admiringly. 'That should put him off.'

'And then I implied that you were on the catch for a rich husband because the family was much in need of funds, hinted at some scandalous reason why that was so and had a sudden attack of discretion. I stopped at the most intriguing point, trust me. He must think you a family of hardened gamesters at the very least.'

'Wonderful. Much more of that and I will not need to worry about convincing Papa of Lord Danescroft's unsuitability—he will not consider proposing to me for a minute.'

'I know.' Rowan permitted herself a moment's

smugness, then caught sight of the clock. 'Goodness! Look at the time—and we both have to change.'

'Apparently she is devoted to her stepmother.' Lucas stood back and eyed Will critically, clothes brush in hand. 'What the devil have you done to that neckcloth?'

'It's a Waterfall.'

'It's a mess. Here, let me. Sit down again.' A minute passed, the silence broken only by the Earl protesting faintly that he was being strangled and Lucas's crushing remarks on the quality of the starch in the muslin. 'There.'

'Hmm. I'm not convinced, but I refuse to go through that again. Really? Devoted, you say?'

'By the sound of it she is as much a trial at home as she is in Society. Apparently Miss Penelope will want her to live with her once she is married.'

'Over my dead body. You've been very busy.'

'A pleasure, I assure you. Miss Maylin has a most superior Abigail, with a straight little nose, big hazel eyes and a crushing way with flirtation. I am, let me tell you, a libertine.'

The warmth that he had discerned in Will's eyes vanished. 'It is no doubt the general assumption that I employ such men.'

There was not a great deal to be said to that. Lucas lifted a waistcoat and held it out for Will to shrug into. 'She also let slip that her mistress is on the hunt for a wealthy match.'

'We knew that.' Will stuck a cravat pin into the folds of his neckcloth and pushed his watch into the fob pocket.

'But not why the family is in such straits—unless your grandmother dropped a hint.'

'Indeed not.' His friend paused, hairbrush in hand. 'I assumed they were simply a minor branch of the family without inherited wealth. What's the story?'

'I must confess I do not know. The charming Miss Daisy was seized with a fit of discretion at that point.'

'Daisy, eh?' Will had warmed up again. Lucas kicked himself mentally: the wounds must be raw indeed for him to take up every hint that might refer to his late wife. 'Seducing servants, are you?'

'Of course not.' Lucas shook out the midnight-blue swallowtail coat and helped Will ease into it. 'Merely getting on terms with our best source of information.' He regarded the Earl, elegant and immaculate. 'You'll do. In fact, you'll probably do only too well. I don't suppose you'd consider developing a revolting personal habit to put her off?'

'More revolting than murdering my wife?' Will lifted one eyebrow. 'I'm afraid my imagination won't stretch that far.'

Lucas stood looking at the back of the door after it closed behind his friend. The bitter words seemed to hang in the air. He gave vent to his feelings by kicking a discarded shirt across the floor, then stalked off to his own room to change. Upper servants were expected to dress for dinner and good manners would not allow him to be late—even if the lady he was to escort into dinner was the housekeeper and not a duchess. And he needed to take special care this evening: there was a certain prickly dresser to impress.

CHAPTER THREE

ROWAN entered the Steward's Room feeling much as she had on her first visit to Almack's—convinced that she would break all kinds of rules, most of them incomprehensible. On the other hand she was now twenty-four, and she had entertained the Duke of Wellington and virtually every notable at the Congress as her father's hostess. She ought to be able to manage Pug's Parlour, as irreverent lower servants everywhere referred to the rooms of the upper staff.

The evening dress she was wearing had once been hers, and had been passed to Alice, her own dresser, the year before. Now she had borrowed it back, noting that the heavy lace at neck and hem had gone—doubtless sold on as one of the dresser's perks—and had been replaced with a more modest braid. Alice had maintained the heavy moss-green silk in good order and had let in long sleeves in a fine gauze.

Worn with plain kid slippers and a simple pearl cross at her throat, the gown presented the picture of modestly respectable elegance, suitable for her position. Dressing to be inconspicuous was a new skill—one she had never had to master before, Rowan realised with an inner grin.

The Steward's Room was crowded, the guests' valets and dressers chattering away, all apparently known to each other. A tall man in a black swallowtail coat approached her. 'Good evening. I am Mr Evesham, Steward here. You will be Miss Maylin's dresser. Miss…?'

'Lawrence, Mr Evesham.' A curtsey was obviously called for. Rowan produced one graded nicely between an archdeacon and a baroness. It appeared to pass muster.

'Please come in, Miss Lawrence. Would you care to take a glass of ratafia?'

She would much prefer to drink the sherry the men appeared to be consuming, but discretion was the safer path. Glass in hand, Rowan began to make her way around the room, looking for someone to talk to. It was obviously ineligible to approach one of the men, a formidable dame who must be the housekeeper was in earnest conversation with the Steward and all the dressers were split amongst three groups, apparently graded by rank.

It was considerably more hierarchical than any Society gathering, she concluded, edging into the group she judged closest to her in the pecking order. They broke off their conversation and regarded her warily.

'Good evening. I am Miss Maylin's dresser, Daisy Lawrence.' It was enough to break the ice. She discovered that she was speaking to the dressers of Miss Lincoln, the

Honourable Miss Trent and Miss Harrington. Rowan knew none of the ladies concerned, guessing they must have come out after her departure to Vienna.

'I have not been with Miss Maylin long,' she confided. 'This is the most impressive house party she has been invited to since I have been with her.'

'Or ever, I imagine,' Miss Browne, attendant upon Miss Lavenham, remarked rather cattily. 'We have never met your predecessor, at any rate. My mistress says she's been invited for Lord Danescroft to have a look at. Is that true?'

'I believe he may be interested. It would be a very eligible connection for her, would it not?'

'Eligible?' Miss Trent's dresser enquired sharply. 'With that scandal so recent? I should shudder to think my young lady so much as *spoke* to such a man.'

'Really?' Rowan produced a look of wide-eyed surprise. 'But surely it is only some wild rumour about an accident? Leaving that aside, surely there is no cause to object to the Earl?'

Miss Browne raised an eyebrow at her colleagues. 'One does wonder,' she murmured, 'what kind of establishment his lordship presides over. They do say—' she drew in a deep breath '—that his wife was having an *affaire* with his valet.'

'Well, either he condoned such a thing, in which case there cannot be any truth in the rumour that he murdered her, or he did not. I do not see,' Rowan observed tartly, 'that you can have it both ways. Either the man is utterly dissipated or he is a murderer.'

As she spoke she glanced across the room and found she was being watched by the cynical blue eyes of the Earl's current valet. He could not possibly have heard her, but some twinge of conscience had her adding, 'Or he could be completely innocent, of course.' She held Lucas's gaze as she spoke, then realised that her own eyebrows were raised haughtily, as though to depress presumption. Only that expression would be completely out of character for Daisy Lawrence.

Hastily she lowered her eyes, feeling quite as flustered as Miss Lawrence would be. She was still trying to work out why—guilty conscience, annoyance at her lapse from her part, or the effect of that cobalt stare?—when a cool voice behind her enquired, 'Gossiping, Miss Lawrence?'

How the *devil* did he move so silently? Or so fast? She had hardly dropped her gaze from his. Rowan turned slightly, finding him all too close for comfort. 'Conversing, Mr Lucas. We were discussing reputation and how fragile it is.'

The other dressers regarded the two of them nervously, obviously in expectation of a comprehensive set-down from such a senior upper servant.

'Indeed it is.' His smile was not amiable. 'And rumour is such a dangerous thing. Sometimes, of course, it may be truth.'

He sauntered off to exchange words with an older man, leaving the four women exchanging speechless looks. Eventually Miss Gregg, dresser to Miss Trent, ventured, 'One might almost think he was trying to scare us.'

'I am quite certain he was.' Rowan narrowed her eyes at the unresponsive back clad in black superfine at least as good as that worn by most of the male guests. 'Or me, at any rate. It seems Mr Lucas does not approve of Miss Maylin as a future mistress.'

A tentative voice asked, 'Miss Lawrence?'

It was a bashful, slightly spotty youth, his Adam's apple protruding above his painstakingly tied neckcloth as he swallowed violently with nerves. He was such a contrast to Mr Lucas that Rowan was taken aback. 'Er—yes?'

'I am Mr Philpott, the Reverend Mr Makepeace's man, and I am to take you in to dinner, Miss Lawrence.' He was almost speechless with shyness, made worse by the barely suppressed sniggers of the other three dressers. His master must be as far down the scale as Penny, if not further, and Rowan's heart went out to him.

'Thank you, Mr Philpott, I am much obliged.' Rowan had encountered her share of gauche young gentlemen and had learned how to put them at their ease. She felt considerably more sympathy for this very junior valet than she had for some bumptious sprig of the nobility. She put her hand on his arm and smiled, reducing him to blushing incoherence. 'I suspect we are right at the end of the line, are we not? Never mind, you can give me some hints about how to go on.' She lowered her voice to a conspiratorial whisper. 'This is my first big house party: I am quite at sea.'

Her dresser had warned her that protocol could vary widely from house to house. In some the upper servants would dine by themselves in the Steward's Room. In others, as was apparently the case here, they would join the other servants. In that case, Alice had explained, they would probably only stay for the first half of the meal.

Then there was the vexed question of the seating plan. Once they entered the servants' hall they might split up, and the female staff occupy the table below the housekeeper with the men below the Steward.

'Me, too,' Mr Philpott whispered, dashing her hopes that he, at least, knew what was what when it came to table plans.

'Never mind,' Rowan murmured, more to reassure herself than him. 'At least we're at the back and can see what the others are doing.'

They trooped in to a scraping of chairs and a rustling of cloth as the lower servants got to their feet. There was a second table, empty and waiting for the Steward's Room party. Hanging back, Rowan watched, then nudged Mr Philpott towards the centre. 'I think that's where we go.'

She found she had another valet, a cheerful, round faced man, on her other side and opposite, Miss Browne and a man who, from his military bearing, seemed to be an ex-officer's batman.

'Do you know anyone else?' she asked, reaching for her napkin.

'No.' Philpott sent a hunted look round the table. 'Mr Makepeace has only just been appointed chaplain to Lady Hartley. Before then he was just the vicar, and never went anywhere, but her old chaplain died so she took him on. Do you know any of them?'

'Just the dressers you saw me speaking to earlier, and Mr Lucas, right up at the other end next to the housekeeper. He's Lord Danescroft's man.'

'I have heard of him.' Mr Philpott sounded as censorious as she could imagine the Reverend Makepeace might. 'My master does not approve of his presence here, you know,' he added in a whisper.

'Really? Why not?' Rowan crumbled a roll, keeping a wary eye on Lucas at the far end of the table. There was no way he could possibly hear what they were talking about, but she was beginning to develop an almost supernatural respect for his perception. 'I know about the scandal, of course.'

'Well…' Philpott seemed to wrestle with his conscience. Rowan batted her eyelashes at him shamelessly and he succumbed. 'I overheard Lady Hartley telling Mr Makepeace that she could never condone Lady Danescroft's behaviour, but she was sure Lord Danescroft had driven her to it because of his neglect. She—Lady Hartley—said that Lady Danescroft had been a sweet, pretty girl, and very lively, and then he had shut her up in that gloomy castle miles from anywhere and she had moped and pined until she was driven into indiscretion.'

Personally Rowan considered that a flaming *affaire* with one's husband's valet went somewhat beyond indiscretion, but before she could say so Mr Philpott added,

'And Lady Hartley says he has grown so cold and aloof it would send any lady mad to be locked up with him.'

Rowan struggled to be fair. Not only was it wrong to falsely accuse someone, but it was no good taking half-baked rumours back to Lord Maylin; that would do Penny no good.

'Anyone might become so after such a tragedy and the dreadful stories that were put around,' she suggested.

'Well, yes, but—' In his excitement Philpott took an over-large mouthful of hot soup, and there was a pause while he became boggle-eyed with the effort of swallowing it safely. 'Lady Hartley says he was not like that before he was married, but became so after the marriage.'

'Oh.' There was much to digest, and they could not sit huddled together whispering. Rowan turned, smiling, to the round-faced man on her other side and asked him to pass the butter.

'Paul Jenkins—man to Captain Dunkley. Miss—?'

'Lawrence. Miss Maylin's woman.'

'Well, now!' He cut some bread and passed the platter. 'There's a thing. A young lady set to rise well above her position in life, from what one hears. Next time we meet no doubt you'll be at the other end of the table, Miss Lawrence.'

Lord! Had everyone heard about the match Lady Rolesby was trying to arrange for her grandson? There was an awful inevitability about it, as though if enough people accepted it as fact then nothing would stop Penny being married off to a man who, at the very best, was an embittered, scandal-haunted semi-recluse. She wished she could get a glimpse of Lord Danescroft: she was beginning to imagine him as glowering, beetle-browed and middle-aged.

'It is by no means certain,' she said firmly. 'I can tell you—in strictest confidence, of course—that no proposal has been made. Nor has he approached her father.' Mr Jenkins merely looked more intrigued. 'Personally,' she added, beginning to wish she could have a normal dinner table conversation at a normal volume, 'I doubt she would be suitable for him. She's a nice enough young lady, but sadly scatterbrained, and nervous of children.'

Poor Penny. Her ears must be burning with all this speculation and slander. It did make Rowan wonder, as her soup plate was removed and the butler began to carve a joint, just how much the servants gossiped about all of those above stairs. She had never thought of it before, and now her cheeks grew warm at the thought of some of the indiscreet things she had let drop in front of staff.

The joint was accompanied by a good variety of side dishes and a very respectable claret. She really must ask Alice how typical that was. No wonder Papa's cellar bills were so large.

She managed the rest of the meal without glancing down the table towards Mr Lucas, or lapsing into gossip about his master. With a clatter of chair-legs on the flagged floor the most senior servants began to rise and the rest of the table followed suit. Rowan realised just in time that she was supposed to bring her table napkin and her glass with her.

In the Steward's Room his boy was waiting beside a freshly laid table set with desserts. Really, she mused, moving towards her place, she had sat down to worse dinners in some very grand houses indeed.

'That colour suits you Miss Lawrence.' That gently amused voice again!

'What colour is that, Mr Lucas?' she enquired.

'The colour in your cheeks. Have you been flirting with your two swains?'

'Flirting? Me? I think not, Mr Lucas. I suggest you look in the mirror over there if you are searching for a flirt.' His soft chuckle as she swept past him had her gritting her teeth.

'Is he bothering you, Miss Lawrence?' It was Mr Philpott, his lanky frame contorted with embarrassment. Poor young man. He probably thought she needed protecting, but was terrified at the idea of a confrontation with Lucas. Who was, if one looked at him properly, really rather a formidable figure.

He glanced up from his plate and found her staring. Coolly Rowan continued her assessment. Yes, formidably muscled under that smart suiting, broad-shouldered and with a dangerous edge to him. She lifted one eyebrow scornfully and turned to smile at the anxious youth. 'Bothering me? Not at all, Mr Philpott. I am quite capable of dealing with men like him.'

Of course she was. Probably. She might have a better idea if she had ever met a man like him before.

The meal progressed—an unsettling and distorted reflection of what was occurring upstairs. Rowan tried to work out the timing. The butler was down here, which meant that the covers must have been drawn and the ladies had retired to the drawing room, leaving the men to their port and the attentions of the footmen.

She was just trying to work out what the equivalent would be here—tea in the housekeeper's rooms?—when the Steward's boy scurried in with the information that Miss Trent's woman was required immediately as she was retiring.

'Headache again,' her dresser muttered unsympathetically, finishing her dessert with more haste than elegance before jumping to her feet and hurrying out. 'I'll have hiccups for the rest of the evening now.'

It did not surprise Rowan when the next summons was for her. At least Penny had given her enough time to finish her meal.

She found her friend roused to uncharacteristic irritation. 'So unsubtle!' she exclaimed before Rowan had the door half shut. 'I have never felt so self-conscious in my life. They placed me next to him at dinner—can you imagine? I just had to run away as soon as I could. They were all whispering about me over the teacups.'

'Pointed, indeed.' Rowan pressed Penny onto the stool in front of the dressing table and began to unpin her hair. 'What is he like?'

'Beautiful,' Penny startled her by proclaiming. 'I had no idea, only seeing him at a distance. But he is tall and dark, and has the most sensitive features.'

'Well, then,' she began, banishing her image of a beetle-browed monster. 'That's something…'

'It makes it worse! No wonder everyone was smiling behind their hands. We must have looked ridiculous together: he so handsome next to drab little me. And,' she moaned as Rowan reached for the hairbrush, 'I was positively *prattling* with nerves. What must he think of me?'

'That you are quite unsuitable, one hopes,' Rowan said. 'It is what you want, isn't it? What did you prattle about?'

'Oh, the garden at home, and the landscape, and painting, and how I found the watercolour I did of my kitten when I was nine in an old sketchbook last week.' Penny gazed at her undistinguished reflection. 'None of the things a future countess should talk about.'

'Excellent. I will reinforce that by telling everyone that you are positively bird-witted and never stop talking of utterly inconsequential things.' Penny smiled wanly. 'What do you want to do now? Sit by the fire and read?'

It was a tempting prospect. For a woman who thought nothing of dancing the night away, Rowan could not imagine why she felt so tired. And her feet ached.

'I think I'd like to have a wash and go to bed early. My head is spinning,' said Penny.

Oh, well, she could read in her own room. Rowan tugged the bell-pull and a harassed-looking chambermaid appeared eventually. 'Yes, miss?'

'Hot water, if you please. And have some sent up to my room and set by the fire.'

'Mrs Tarrant says that we're that stretched that visiting staff'll have to do for themselves, miss.'

'Thank you. That will do.' Rowan frowned at the closing door. She supposed lighting a fire could not be that hard. There had been wood and coals by the side of the hearth in the chilly little turret room, and she would have a candle, so there would be no need to strike a spark.

This experience was certainly making her appreciate Alice more, Rowan reflected as she made her way to the foot of the stairs, chamberstick in one hand, jug of hot water in the other. Going to bed had always seemed so simple—but it was not if you were the one putting the clothes away, tidying the room, securing the jewellery box and all the time answering anxious questions and soothing doubts.

She trudged upwards, one floor, then two. The handle of the jug was cutting into her fingers, but she could not use both hands and still see where she was going. The stairs unwound themselves onto a narrow landing— nothing more than a linking passage between wings, with the spiral stair to her turret curling up into the darkness on the other side.

'Ouch.' Rowan dumped the jug on the flags, splashing the cooling water, and sat down on the top step, her back to the landing while she massaged her fingers back to life.

'What's wrong?'

She jumped, stumbling to her feet. Then her heel caught in her hem and she was falling, the stone stairs beneath her and nothing to hold on to.

CHAPTER FOUR

'I'VE got you.' She was stronger than he had guessed, twisting in his grasp and using his body as a counter-weight to regain her balance. Lucas found himself with a warm armful of panting woman clutched to his chest, her hands clamped around his forearms.

'Idiot!' She might only have been wearing light indoor shoes, but the force of her kick on his shins had him stepping back abruptly, pulling her with him. Of course—he might have known. It was Miss Lawrence, not some chambermaid with a twisted ankle.

'Ouch,' he said mildly, setting her back from him. 'First my nose, now my shins. You are a dangerous woman, Daisy Lawrence.'

'You would be in no danger at all if you kept your distance from me,' she snapped.

The light was poor, and he could see little of her face, but her eyes sparked at him and he thought it a safe bet her expression was not one of simpering gratitude.

He should, of course, let go. Only he found he did

not want to, and she was clinging just as tightly, doing nothing to improve the set of his fourth-best evening coat. 'I thought you had hurt yourself.' An olive branch seemed in order. 'Twisted your ankle, perhaps.'

'Instead of which I nearly broke my neck.' There was a sudden flash of white teeth as she smiled, her irritation vanished as rapidly as it had come. 'The hot water jug was hurting my fingers. I set it down while I rubbed them.' Her voice, now she was not scolding him, was soft and held a hint of tiredness.

'Let me see.' They were still almost breast to breast. He could smell her, an unexpectedly sweet hint of gardenia and warm woman. Delicious. 'But you will have to let go of my arms.'

'Oh! I am sorry, it was the shock.'

She opened her hands as though he was hot: he rather feared he was. Very hot. Lucas took a steadying breath.

'I am not good with heights, I must confess.' She waved him away as he tried to take her hand and lead her towards the candle, walking over to hold it close to the flame herself. 'See? It is heavier than I thought.'

The sight of the whitened ridges on the smooth skin affected him strangely. He wanted to protect her, which was ridiculous; she was more than capable of standing up for herself. But those slim shoulders were not meant for lugging heavy cans of water about. She should be doing nothing more strenuous than brushing her mistress's hair. Then he recalled the sight of her, skin damp and rosy with the effort of brushing that skirt, and hefted the water jug before his imagination got any more out of control.

'I'll carry this. Where is your room?'

For a moment he thought she would refuse to tell him, then that secret smile lit up her eyes again. 'Thank you, that would be most kind. Up this turret stair. Another two flights, I'm afraid.'

She's not in the least bit sorry, Lucas thought appreciatively. *She is getting her own back.* 'You come behind me, then, and hold the candle so it lights the steps at my feet.'

The stairs were steep, twisting and ancient, worn in the centre and uneven in height. By the next landing Lucas was controlling his breathing. If he had been by himself he would have changed hands at that point, but he was damned if he was going to show any weakness in front of Daisy—and that realisation in itself was galling.

'Here we are.' There was nowhere else to go. The stairs stopped in front of a planked door. Lucas lifted the latch and walked straight in. 'Thank you, Mr Lucas, I can manage now.'

She was uncomfortable with him in the room. He should go. Lucas was very conscious that if Daisy had been a Society lady with whom he was flirting then he would let this game play out, stop and tease her a little, snatch a kiss before he left. But this was Daisy Lawrence, dresser, and it was not the action of a gentleman to take advantage of a servant.

He turned and looked at her as she set the candle down on the mantel over the empty grate. The room was cold—almost he imagined he could see his own breath in the air. 'You need the fire lit.'

'Yes. I had noticed that.'

He noticed the way she reached for the shawl that lay on the end of the bed and dragged it round her shoulders, and that flare of protectiveness surprised him again, despite her sarcasm.

'There is no need—' But he was already on his knees, reaching for the kindling that had been dumped on the hearth, building it into a neat stack and adding tiny pieces of coal from the bucket.

'Am I depriving you of a treat? Do you enjoy making fires?' he asked mildly, concentrating on the delicate edifice.

'I don't know. I have never built one.' She was kneeling beside him. Her admission almost had him dropping an over-large stick on the top of the stack.

'What? Never?' Lucas sat back on his heels and studied her face in the thin light from the candle. 'You must be a very superior lady's maid, in that case. Can you pass me the light?'

He touched the flame to the wood shavings and watched as they caught and smoke began to spiral up. Beside him, Daisy did not move, and he began to fuss a little with the fire so as to stay where he was. If her earlier career had omitted menial skills such as fire-lighting, that reinforced his suspicion that she was gently born, doubtless on the wrong side of the blanket, and had only recently had to make her own way.

Which explained why she felt to him like a woman from his world, one he could talk to on equal terms. That and the spirit that told him she would take no nonsense from him whether he was a valet or a viscount.

Rowan held out her hands to the flames, watching as the fire took hold of the wood shavings and kindling.

'You have to feed it,' Lucas said, 'or it will flare up like your temper and be gone.' She reached out for some wood but he caught her hand. 'No—too big. That will flatten it.' He released her immediately, sorting through the wood and picking out suitable pieces while Rowan sat wondering why his touch was so unsettling.

'Is Lord Danescroft a good master?' she asked abruptly.

Lucas was placing a faggot, dropped it, and swore mildly under his breath. 'A good master?'

Rowan had the impression he was stalling for time.

'Yes. He seems to be. I have not been with him long. Why do you ask?'

'I am concerned for Miss Maylin. There are the rumours, the Earl's demeanour. She is not a young woman who can cope with harshness.'

'The rumours are just that. Rumours.'

'Then there is no mystery about his wife's death?'

'It appears to have been an accident. When young women who have been drinking creep around a darkened house by the back stairs in the small hours that is not so improbable.'

'True.' She marked the underlying indignation as he spoke. 'So the rumours about the late Lady Danescroft are true, then, even if those about her husband are not?'

'That she was unfaithful and that Danescroft's valet was one of her lovers? Yes, those rumours are true. A lady with the heart of a harlot, I fear.'

'I see. How horrid. It seems worse, somehow, that the infidelity was so close, inside the household.'

Lucas nodded abruptly.

'You said *one* of her lovers—there were others?'

'Yes.' He leaned forward and began to make up the fire with bigger pieces of wood.

He spoke definitely, like a man who knew from his own knowledge, not from hearsay. The suspicion that Lucas was more than a recently employed valet began to stir.

'Then what made her do it?'

He turned and looked at her, one eyebrow raised in sardonic enquiry.

'Oh, I know what she *wanted*—but why was she not content with her husband? I've heard that she was light-hearted and gay before the marriage and that she changed afterwards.'

'She changed when she was not allowed free rein for her every whim and passion,' Lucas said grimly, as he rocked back on his heels and stood up. 'Danescroft expected fidelity and decorum from his countess—quite unreasonably, in her opinion.'

'So you do know something about this?' Daisy tipped back her head and looked up at him, standing tall and still on the hearthrug, his face unsettlingly underlit by the flames. 'Who are you, really, Lucas?'

'His valet.'

He turned and walked away from her so that his face was in shadow. She could not decide whether that was deliberate.

'I observed them both at the time of the marriage and I had heard things about her character.'

'So you must approve of your master seeking a new wife? One who will behave as befits a countess?'

'I approve of him marrying again, yes. But not to that ninny-hammer of a mistress of yours, with her vulgarian of a stepmother.'

Rowan scrambled to her feet with more energy than grace. 'Well, I *do* approve of her getting married—but not to some top-lofty, miserable recluse with a cloud hanging over him!'

'Danescroft is not top-lofty and miserable—' Lucas began, then broke off, regarding her speculatively. 'But we are agreed upon something; it is a highly un-desirable match from both sides. Does she want to marry him?'

'No, she is frightened of him—and in any case, she has no ambition for high position.' Rowan bit her lower lip and regarded her unlikely ally. 'Nor talent for it, come to that. But he wants to marry her?'

'He thinks he should marry, and Miss Maylin has

been recommended by his grandmother. He needs a mother for his daughter. I don't know that *want* is the right word.'

'What would prevent him proposing?' She had thought those dark blue eyes impertinent, alarming and intelligent by turns: now Rowan realised just how much humour they revealed as their owner narrowed them at her and grinned.

'Why, Miss Daisy, you are not suggesting meddling in the affairs of our betters, are you?'

'Yes,' she declared roundly. 'Yes, I am. And do not try and look surprised, Mr Lucas, it is exactly what you are thinking, too.'

'In that case we had better do a little plotting.' He sat down on the edge of the narrow bed and patted the coverlet beside him.

'You are sitting on my bed,' Rowan protested.

'You didn't want to go to sleep yet, did you?'

'No, and certainly not with you in the room. Get up. It is most improper.'

'Anyone would think you were expecting a chaperon to burst into the room,' he said, his eyes laughing at her again. 'You really have not been out in the world very long, have you?'

'Long enough,' Rowan observed grimly. 'Out.'

'What about our little conspiracy?' He got to his feet, all long-limbed elegance.

Rowan controlled her breathing as her singing teacher had taught her, went to the door and held it open.

'We can discuss it perfectly well in daylight with the benefit of having considered it overnight.' She was pleased with the calm way she pronounced this. No one would guess what effect Lucas's nearness was having on her.

'Very well. It is Sunday tomorrow. Will you allow me to escort you to church?' He stopped in front of her.

Rowan fixed her gaze on the cut steel buttons of his waistcoat. 'I am far too lowly for your escort, Mr Lucas.'

'No one will wonder at it. My master is courting your mistress. What could be more natural than that we should mirror that?'

Startled, she looked up. *'Courting?'*

'Merely a masquerade, Miss Daisy. There is no cause for alarm.' He bent his head and his mouth brushed hers—warm, firm. Outrageous. 'See?' And then, before she could react, he was out of the door and vanishing into the dark spiral of the stairs.

'Oh, you...!' Rowan shut the door, turned the key and stalked back to the bed in a swirl of skirts and indignation. She was no longer just being flirted with by a valet, she had been kissed by one. It was outrageous, it was shocking, it could not possibly go any further.

But. But with his help she could save Penny from Lord Danescroft. And she liked him, impertinent wretch that he was. Attractive, masculine, amusing, impertinent wretch.

'Oh, dear.' A charred piece of wood broke and fell into the hearth. Rowan went to lift it with the tongs and laid a few more pieces on the fire. Somehow she did not think she was going to get to sleep very quickly tonight.

Briskly she drew the thin cotton curtains over the window, wondering what sort of view she was going to have in the morning light. Then she hung her nightgown over the back of the upright chair in front of the fire to warm while she undressed and washed.

The water had cooled; the room was still chill. As she slipped into the nightgown she wondered if that was enough to account for the fact that she felt slightly shivery. She hoped it was. But the cold could not be blamed for the fact that her lips tingled, or that her imagination kept straying to an unknown room somewhere in the house where Lucas was perhaps undressing even now. His black coat would be hung on the back of a chair. He would be shrugging off his waistcoat, standing there in the candlelight in those tight breeches and the clinging white linen of his shirt...

With a gasp of alarm Rowan snatched up her toothbrush and scrubbed her teeth with enough energy to take off the enamel. Never in her well-regulated life had she let herself speculate on what any man of her acquaintance looked like undressing, let alone with his clothes off.

She just hoped Penny would appreciate all her efforts when she was able to escape from Tollesbury Court unattached. Because, besides aching feet, insipient chilblains and aching muscles, Rowan very much feared her moral fibre was going to be severely impaired by this experience.

December 23rd

Penelope seemed more than usually distracted when Rowan, stifling her yawns, came into the room.

'Did you sleep well, Miss Penelope?' she asked, one eye on the chambermaid who had drawn the curtains and was whisking the hearth into order before rekindling the fire.

'Yes, thank you Ro… Lawrence.' She sat up against the vast white pillows and rubbed her eyes. 'But I had such odd dreams. I cannot quite recall them, but I feel strangely flustered this morning.'

Rowan considered her friend would feel even more flustered if she so much as hinted at the nature of the dreams she herself had experienced. Unfortunately she could recall them only too well, and as they had consisted mainly of variations on being kissed by Lucas, *flustered* was a mild description of her feelings.

'Thank you,' Rowan said to the maid, who was gathering up her brushes and bucket. 'Please have Miss Maylin's hot chocolate sent up. A nice big pot and two cups. I don't care what they think downstairs,' she added once the girl had gone. 'I am not starting the day without my chocolate.'

'Have you not had any breakfast?' Penny asked sympathetically.

'I had some toast and preserves and a cup of coffee at six. Luckily they sent up a girl with hot water at half past five, or I would still be in bed asleep.'

'Oh, poor Rowan. Is this proving very horrid?'

'Very odd, certainly.' Rowan frowned, trying to work out why, despite everything, she seemed to be enjoying herself. It was very strange. 'But it will be worth it, I am certain.' Among the worries keeping her awake half the night had been whether to tell Penny about her pact with Lucas to foil the betrothal. On reflection, she thought not. Penny was certain to be shocked.

'You are not to worry about Lord Danescroft,' she added bracingly as she opened a clothes press in search of Penny's best morning dress for church. 'I am sure we can succeed in putting him off.'

'He is very attentive,' Penny observed. 'He has asked if I would like to join him in his phaeton to and from the church. Do you think I ought?'

'Why, certainly.' Rowan opened the door to admit the maid with the chocolate, and carried on carefully setting out Penny's garments while the girl was in the room. 'Quite unexceptional.' The girl went out and Rowan frowned, a pair of silk stockings screwed up in her hand. 'There will be no need for a chaperon in an open carriage like that, so you can say what you like. We must think of something shocking.' She poured the chocolate, handed Penny her cup and went to perch on the end of the bed to drink her own. 'I know—talk about how much you like to make wagers.'

'What? But I cannot even play cards without making a mull of it,' Penny wailed. 'Papa shouts at me.'

'No, not cards. Say you enjoy putting wagers on

things, and then confess you are always losing money and never have any of your allowance left. What a bad example he will think you would be for his daughter! Don't forget to look contrite and say you wish you could stop but you can't.'

'I'll try,' Penny said dubiously. 'But I am not a very good actress, and as for telling an untruth…'

'Better a white lie than a lifetime married to that man,' Rowan said forcibly. 'I am walking to church with his valet. I will tell him about your gambling habit as well.' She glanced at the clock. 'Lord! Look at the time. We must get you dressed and down to breakfast before your godmother comes in search of you.'

'Poor man,' Penny said, climbing out of bed and dragging on her wrapper.

'Who?'

'Lord Danescroft. All these people talking about him and intriguing about him. And now I have to lie to him.'

'Penny,' Rowan said firmly, 'you have a heart of butter. If you start feeling sorry for the Earl, of all people, you are lost.'

Penny still looked dubious. Rowan had a flash of inspiration prompted, she knew all too well, by her current preoccupation with Lucas.

'Has your step mother explained what happens between a man and a woman? You know—in bed?'

'Yes.' Penny blushed scarlet. 'It sounds *dreadful.*'

'Well, imagine having to do that with Lord Danescroft,' Rowan said.

Her friend's blush drained away most satisfactorily, leaving her white to the lips.

'Surely you can manage a few fibs to prevent that, can't you?'

'Oh, yes.' Penny nodded vehemently. 'Oh, yes, I am sure I can.'

CHAPTER FIVE

'Did you think of anything last night?'

Lucas's question could not have been better designed to disconcert her. Rowan gave a little gasp, pretended to slip on an icy patch, and was then thrown into even greater disorder by him taking her firmly by the arm.

'Now what have I said?' he demanded, tucking her hand into the crook of his elbow.

She should protest at the fact he was squeezing it against his side rather than letting her rest it on his forearm. But then, he was not a gentleman, however polished his speech and his manner, so perhaps he did not realise that what he was doing was improper.

Rowan shot him a sideways glance as she tried to think of something to say. His face was composed, but there was the faintest curl to the corner of his lips and a twinkle she was becoming familiar with in his eye. He knew perfectly well he was disconcerting her. She tried to ignore the warmth of his body penetrating her leather glove and the recollection of the fleeting heat of his mouth on hers.

'Nothing. It is just that I lay awake too long trying to think of ways to prevent the Earl proposing to Miss Penelope, and I'm tired and clumsy this morning.'

'Any ideas?'

'I told her to confess to him about her fatal addiction to wagering and how she is always outrunning her allowance as a result.'

Lucas grinned appreciatively. 'That's a good one. I don't suppose she can have a fatal addiction to card play or dice as well?'

'Miss Penelope? Goodness, no, she can hardly remember the basic rules, let alone put on a convincing show as a hardened gamester.'

'That's what you were trying to hint about when we met in the brushing room, wasn't it? You thought you could drop hints to me and I would run back to Danescroft with the tittle-tattle.'

'Well? Did you? I can see that you did.'

'Your remarks about Miss Maylin's stepmother wrought most effectively upon him.'

'Excellent! What did he say to the idea of her living with them after the wedding?'

'"*Over my dead body,*"' Lucas quoted with some relish.

'Oh. I suppose he is more than capable of enforcing that sort of decision,' Rowan brooded as they neared the edge of the coppice that filled one corner of the park and separated the church, graveyard and vicarage from the estate.

In front of them the upper servants walked in pairs, Sunday best muffled under shawls and scarves. Behind them the lower servants straggled, a less disciplined crocodile, with the pair of giggling boot boys bringing up the rear.

'Why did he not put his foot down with his late wife?' she asked.

'Because the sense of betrayal was so great, I imagine. She broke his heart: dragging her away and locking her in was not going to bring back the woman he had thought he loved, was it?'

'No. I suppose not.' Rowan was shaken by the force of feeling in Lucas's words. 'Would you do the same thing? Turn a blind eye if it were your wife?'

'No. In his shoes I would kill her lover and lock her up on my most dreary and remote estate,' he said, with a smile that was pure ice.

There was not a great deal one could say to that. Rowan wondered just how a vengefully inclined valet would go about disposing of a rival. A gentleman would demand a duel, but Lucas was not a gentleman. Where, exactly, had he been when the late Lady Danescroft met her end? Lucas might have only become Lord Danescroft's valet after the murder, but he seemed strangely partisan for such a short acquaintance. She gave herself a little shake for giving way to such lurid Gothic imaginings. But there was a mystery here.

The group in front of them had slowed to pass through the gate that led into the coppice.

'Oh, look,' Lucas murmured. 'A kissing gate.' And so it was. A small gate hinged to move within a vee-shaped enclosure so that only one person at a time could squeeze through and stock or deer would not be able to move through it. The Steward was holding it for the housekeeper to pass, standing well back. But, as Rowan knew perfectly well, if the person holding it stood close enough they could snatch a kiss with ease.

'There has been all the kissing there is going to be,' she murmured back. 'If it were not that I need your help for Miss Penelope I would not be walking with you now, believe me.'

'I said a kissing *gate*.' Lucas managed to look convincingly shocked. 'I said nothing about intending to kiss you, Miss Daisy.'

'Good,' she retorted, furious with herself for betraying what she had been thinking about.

'Not in front of the entire Upper and Lower Halls, at any rate,' he added, freeing her arm and slipping through the gate to hold it open.

The presence of a gaggle of housemaids at her heels prevented Rowan from verbal or, more temptingly, physical retaliation. She ignored his proffered arm and continued on her way, both hands clasped with pious poise around her prayer book.

There was no possibility of further plotting, flirtation or quarrelling once the churchyard was reached. The housekeeper, Mrs Tarrant, gathered the female staff around her, reminding Rowan irresistibly of a mother hen with a large brood. After running a gimlet eye over them she led the way into the church and up the left-

hand set of stairs into the gallery. The male staff trooped
in, following the Steward, and took the right-hand flight.

It had never occurred to Rowan before to think what
a perfect bird's-eye view the servants up aloft had of the
pews below. There, in the box pews that seemed so
private and enclosed to the occupants, the family and
guests of the Tollesbury Court were taking their seats,
while the village notables filed into their places.

And Christmas was coming. In the bustle of life
below stairs she had lost sight of the reason for the
house party. Now, seeing the nave decked with evergreen boughs, and trailing ivy and holly bunches hung
on every pew door, she realised that this would be her
first English Christmas for two years. What would it be
like in the servants' hall? Would there be plum pudding
and a Yule log? Hot punch and merrymaking?

Her attention was caught by Penny's entrance on the
arm of Lord Danescroft. A short woman in a fashionable
bonnet was with them; it must be Penny's godmother,
his grandmother Lady Rolesby, who was promoting the
match. The Earl held open the pew door and ushered the
ladies in, assisting them to find their hassocks and
prayer books. Heads turned to watch until they were
seated and only the tops of their heads showed above
the panelled walls. But from high above Rowan could
see the occupants of the other pews leaning together to
hiss a few words of gossip about the sight of plain little
Miss Maylin and her scandalous catch.

She leaned in her turn, craning to catch a better

glimpse of Lord Danescroft. *Beautiful*, Penny had called him. *Sensitive*. All she could see was his height and the top of a well-barbered dark head. If she could not manage to get a better look at him when they left church then she would have to find another way to view him. It ought to be possible to tell *something* from studying his face—the way he looked when he spoke to Penny, the way he comported himself with other people.

Mrs Tarrant was frowning at her. Returning an apologetic smile, Rowan straightened up, but not before she caught Lucas's eye. *What is he staring at?* she thought, already flustered at being caught out behaving inappropriately by the housekeeper. He winked, upsetting her precarious decorum, and she bit her lip hard in an effort not to dissolve into giggles.

Mortified, she opened her prayer book and made herself concentrate. She, Lady Rowan Chilcourt, behaving like a kitchen maid in church! The hassock was hard and lumpy under her knees: a just penance for her frivolity, she told herself sternly.

Her deportment for the duration of the service was perfect. Descending the staircase afterwards, Rowan determined to maintain her ladylike poise, whatever Lucas's provocation might be. Unfortunately for this worthy ambition the first thing she saw when she walked out into the snow-covered churchyard was Lucas, and the second Penny standing talking to Lord Danescroft.

'Bother it,' she muttered under her breath.

'What?' Lucas was at her side.

'Him. Lord Danescroft. Penny was right. He is *beautiful*.'

'Well enough,' his loyal valet said, with a grin. 'He owes it all to the way I dress him, of course.'

'Really? That produces his height and the width of his shoulders and the muscles in his thighs does it? And that perfectly straight nose and the firm jaw and those very fine dark eyes?'

'Miss Lawrence, I am shocked! *Thighs?* A young lady should not acknowledge that gentlemen have such things, let alone assess them.' He clapped his tall hat on his head and looked sanctimonious.

'We can see them, Mr Lucas, not being blind. Naturally most of us are also not blind to the defects of character the possessors of such features may have. Miss Maylin, I regret to say, seems willing to be dazzled, despite her apprehension about his lordship.'

'And you, Miss Daisy, are you capable of seeing past handsome features to the character within?' He took her arm again and began to make his way down the path to the gate, not waiting for the Steward and the house-keeper to assemble their flock.

'Well, certainly.' Rowan watched her step, sparing him just one flickering sideways glance as they stepped through the gateway. 'When I find myself in the company of someone so endowed.'

'Ouch,' Lucas said, a laugh in his voice.

'You should not fish for compliments, Mr Lucas.'

'I am justly reproved. But we are not much further forward in our quest for ideas. What a pity Miss Maylin was not accompanied by her stepmama. Half an hour of that dame would send Danescroft fleeing without his bags packed.'

'Sir Gregory Maylin did not require Lady Rolesby's warnings about that, you may be sure. Apparently he was heard to say that some game birds come better to a lure than they do if flushed out by beaters.'

Lucas gave a smothered snort of amusement. 'I can just see her, purple toque on her head, frightening every pheasant in the Home Counties, let alone every eligible bachelor.'

He opened a wicket gate and Rowan followed, still smiling at the image he'd conjured up. They were several yards down a path before she noticed their surroundings.

'This is not the path to the house.' It was a winding route cut through shrubbery to form a wilderness walk, she guessed. The overarching trees had sheltered it from the snow, and the trodden earth beneath her stout boots was almost dry.

'It will get us there almost as quickly—it comes out in the orchard behind the kitchen gardens—and we can talk without fear of being overheard. Now, can we rely upon Miss Maylin refusing Danescroft if she is sufficiently wary of him?'

'No.' Rowan shook her head, quite certain. 'She is very timid, and has never refused to do anything her papa has told her to before. Oh, dear, if he is *not* a murderer, and she comes to like him, perhaps the best thing would be to let things run their course.'

'Does she need someone to love her?' Lucas asked. 'Or would the title and the status be enough for her if she could overcome her fear of him?'

'She would shrivel without love and gentleness, and she would be terrified of having to be a countess with all that implies. Why?' They emerged from the wilderness in front of a stile in the orchard fence. 'Do you think he really will propose, even if she gives him no encouragement?'

'If she does not actively repel him, yes.' Lucas eyed the stile. 'Let me climb this first, make sure it is stable.'

He stepped onto the cross-plank, brushed the snow off the top rail and swung one leg over, then the other—allowing Rowan, if she was so inclined, a fine opportunity to admire their length and strong musculature. Regrettably, considering that it was a Sunday and she should have had her mind on matters spiritual, she found herself quite unable to avert her gaze.

'Quite safe. Up you come.'

'Turn around, then.' Obediently he turned his back, then swung round again when she had both feet safely on the orchard side of the cross piece. 'Give me your hand.'

'I am perfectly capable of jumping down eighteen inches.'

He did not budge, standing in front of her with his hand held out.

'Oh, very well, if you insist on treating me as though

I was feeble. I am used to long walks every day, I will have you know. And I am more than capable of negotiating a few stiles.'

'Really?' Lucas took her hand while she jumped down, then released it. They began to walk up the slope towards the high red brick wall of the kitchen garden.

'Er, yes…my last mistress was a very active lady and always required me to accompany her.' Rowan turned around before he could ask her anything else about her fictitious past and began to walk backwards. 'Look at our footprints. I do love the snow when it is fine and crisp and pure like this.'

'And look at this view.' Lucas had stopped under one of the gnarled old apple trees and gestured across to the south. The great ornamental lake stretched out before them in the distance, the tree-dotted parkland was shrouded in snow, and the only movement came from the herd of fallow deer that had just emerged from the woodland edge.

'Oh, lovely! It reminds me of ho—'.

'Of?'

Home. 'Homebury Park, where my last employer often stayed,' Rowan improvised airily, leaning back against the trunk of the tree, which acted as a welcome windbreak. 'Never mind the view—what about Lord Danescroft? We are agreed that Miss Penelope is too timid to refuse him, so we must concentrate on putting him off her.'

'And he is not going to believe her tarradiddles about

losing her allowance on wagers. Not unless she is an exceptional actress.'

Rowan shook her head.

'So it is unlikely that she wagered on how many red-headed choirboys there were before they entered the church?'

'Highly unlikely! So what *would* put him off?'

'Lying, immorality, unkindness to children.'

'Oh. That's a daunting list. Nothing minor, then?'

'I doubt it. I have recounted all your hints and gossip. He just shrugs it off.'

'This is much harder than I thought it would be. Is there nothing I can tell her about him that is so bad her father would refuse the match?'

'No.' Lucas's brows drew together sharply. 'There is not. And I am not going to make something up, either. If Sir Gregory is not baulking at the current scandal anything that would put him off *would* have to be appalling. What about you? Can I tell him she is spiteful and deceitful, or has a clandestine lover?'

'No! She is none of those things, and I am certainly not going to risk her reputation. You will just have to keep pointing out to him the disadvantages and inequalities of the match, and I will try to persuade her that the world will not end if she stands up to her father.'

Lucas watched Daisy's face as she leaned back against the rough bark of the tree and looked out across the valley, her eyes narrowed either in worried thought or against the snow dazzle. She intrigued him. More than intrigued, if truth be told. Her upbringing was that of a lady, yet here she was, waiting on a little dab of a nobody. Her need for employment must be serious. He liked her fierce loyalty towards Penelope Maylin, the way she stood up to him, the humour that was always lurking in those big hazel eyes—and he liked looking at her.

He had liked the feel of her mouth under his in that fleeting kiss last night. Warm, full, trembling between outrage and response. A bird began to sing above their heads, sweet and clear on the cold air. Lucas glanced up and smiled. It was so very tempting to indulge in a little dalliance. Just a very little. He did not think he could disturb Miss Lawrence's heart too much, and he had every confidence that she would send him on his way with a clip around the ear if she found his actions unwelcome.

'Look up, Daisy.'

'Hmm?' She tipped back her head and stared up through the bare branches. 'Oh, a robin—how lovely. Look at the way his throat is working with the force of his singing. You would never believe such a tiny scrap could make so much noise.'

'Look just above it.'

She refocused, and he saw the tiniest twitch at the corner of her mouth when she saw what he was referring to. Then it was gone, and she was saying repressively, 'Mistletoe?'

But it had been there, that spark of mischief. He moved in front of her, put both gloved hands on the tree trunk either side of her head and leaned in. 'Mistletoe. And we will bring down the wrath of Druids everywhere if we do not do the proper thing when beneath it—especially at this time of year.'

'Wrathful Druids will be the very least of your problems if you try and ki…'

It was everything he had guessed it would be, kissing Daisy Lawrence. Softness, the fragrance of warm femininity, and the dangerous spark of her temper as she decided whether to kiss him back or box his ears.

She tasted very faintly of peppermint. He slipped his tongue between her lips, urging them to part for him, wary that he would find her teeth, not the sweet heat inside. She was still braced against the tree, her hands by her sides.

She lifted them suddenly, and as suddenly moved away, just enough to gasp, 'Oh, you *wretch*,' before clasping her hands in his hair and pulling his head down to hers again.

CHAPTER SIX

SHE was angry with him, but she shouldn't be—she was kissing him just as much as he was kissing her. Although it was patently obvious that Lucas had far more experience than she had. Either that or he had startling natural talent.

His mouth was hot and hard and flexible enough to drive her distracted, and his tongue was quite blatantly impertinent in its exploration. No one had ever kissed Rowan with anything like this sensual impact. And she should not be kissing him. She knew she should not.

Her fingers bumped against the underside of his hat and she felt it tip and fall off, giving her unrestricted access to his hair. It was springy between her fingers, like a live thing. At her back the tree was solid, hard and uncomfortable. At her front she was pressed against his body—almost as hard, certainly as solid, but far from uncomfortable.

Her insides were feeling very strange indeed: tense, hot, aching with an almost-pain that ran from her belly down the inside of her thighs. This must stop…now. Or in a minute or two…

Just a few moments more. *Now*.

Rowan opened her eyes and pulled back with enough force to bump her head against the tree trunk a few inches behind. She found she was panting slightly, and that Lucas was, too. He did not move back. He was so close she could see where his beard was already beginning to show, despite a severe morning shave, so close she could see that there was a ring of darker blue around the indigo of his eyes. So close that the mist of their breath mingling in the cold air hung between them.

'I—' She should reprimand him. Or she should just walk away. Or say something dignified about it being both their faults and it must not happen again: for of course it must not. Instead she looked him straight in the eye and said, 'That was very nice.'

'I thought so,' Lucas said gravely. 'I suspect my hat may be ruined, but that is a small price to pay.'

'Hadn't you better look, before it gets too wet?'

'Yes.'

He did not move. It was really very pleasant, standing so close. Warm, intimate, friendly. Only her toes were becoming very cold and her inner voice was demanding to be heard. Her behaviour could be excused, *just*, it reminded her sternly, if the man concerned was betrothed to her. Under no circumstances could she ever have such a relationship with a valet, so she had acted purely for the pleasure of kissing him. Which was scandalously wanton and she should be ashamed of herself. But she wasn't, which was even more shameful. Her conscience nagged on, relentless.

'Oh, do be quiet,' she muttered, earning a startled look from Lucas. 'Sorry—just thinking aloud. My feet are cold.'

'Then we must go in.' This time he acted on his words, turning to pick up his tall hat and brushing the snow off it as they walked towards the kitchen garden gate. 'Where were you last employed?' he asked, abruptly changing the subject.

'With a middle-aged person—more as a companion than anything,' Rowan said, with perfect truth. 'Abroad, mostly.'

'In which country?' Lucas opened the gate onto the practical formality of the kitchen garden. Within the sheltering walls the snow lay only patchily. Men were working around the glass frames, shifting covers. One lad was picking the tight button heads of borecole off the robust stalks that leaned drunkenly in the cold earth, and a man Rowan guessed was the head gardener was supervising a delivery of coals by the stovehouse door.

'Austria.' There was no point in lying about it. If he knew she had been out of the country he was not going to ask questions about English families or houses, and she was not going to have to risk an error.

'The Congress?' he asked, and she nodded in reply. 'Interesting.'

'It certainly greatly entertained my employer.' It had

entertained her as well. The endless round of balls and receptions, picnics and parties, political gossip and scandalous *on dits* were a world away from the careful formality of the servants' hall at dinner time. 'It seems a different world,' she added, stamping her feet on the brick path to get rid of the snow.

In Vienna now she could be going on expeditions into the forest in a horse-drawn sledge, or shopping in the luxurious stores and emporia that lined the streets. But Papa was coming home early in the New Year, and she had agreed with him that it would be best if she came on ahead and got the town house opened up.

If she had not come then she would not have known about Penny's predicament until the deed was done and her friend irrevocably married. And she would not be having this insight into the parallel world of the servants, or the freedom to indulge in her scandalous flirtation.

'I'm not sorry to be back.'

'No. Neither am I. Although I suspect I will never get warm again. I had forgotten how cold this country can be.'

'You have been abroad, too? For how long?'

'Five years. I got back a few weeks ago.'

Thank goodness. He could have had nothing to do with Lady Danescroft's death.

'I have been in the West Indies.' That explained the faint colour his skin held, as though he had been brushed lightly by the sun.

'As a valet?' The sound of the other servants arriving

back met them as they rounded the edge of the stableblock and the yard behind the kitchen door came into sight.

'No. More as an estates manager. I had not expected to take this job when I returned, but it was…expedient.'

An estates manager sounded considerably more respectable than a valet. Younger sons of quite good family became estates managers. Rowan realised she was pleased by this discovery, and then, a moment later, why she was. *For goodness' sake. Slightly better breeding does not excuse flirtation! Valet or younger son of a gentry family, it does not matter. I am the only child of Roland Chilcourt, third Earl of Lavenham, and I know what is due to my name.* The scandal would be resounding if anyone ever found out. Acting as Penny's dresser might be excused as a prank; kissing a valet would put her beyond the pale.

Then don't get found out. She was shocking herself. She glanced at Lucas as they mingled with the other returning churchgoers, all shedding hats and wraps and stamping the snow off their feet as they trooped back into the warmth. There had been other men in her life— attractive, eligible men whom she had liked very well. Several had proposed, and with two of them she had thought long and hard before refusing. But never had she been tempted to kiss one of them. She had not felt oddly breathless with either of them, and they had certainly not disturbed her dreams in the way this man had last night.

'What are you daydreaming about, Miss Lawrence?'

Miss Mather's dresser enquired acidly. 'I would have thought Miss Maylin required all your attention.'

'What? Oh, Lord—they'll be back, of course.' Rowan gathered up her outer things and hurried to the foot of the stairs. Time to do what she could to ring the changes with Penny's limited selection of afternoon gowns—and to find out what had happened in the big box pew.

She fled up the spiral stairs to her tower room, pausing to gasp for air on one of the cramped little landings. There was a stone window ledge at just the right height to rest her elbows on while she caught her breath. The view, once she had scrubbed cobwebs off the glass, was the same as they had had just now, looking out from the orchard over to the lake.

And there was their apple tree. As she watched a tall figure appeared, hung his coat over a low branch and stood for a moment, hat in hand, as though wondering what to do with it. Then, with a shrug, he tossed it over his shoulder into the snow and swung up into the tree.

Lucas. What on earth was he doing? Then she realised: he was picking mistletoe. 'Going to work his way round all the female staff, I'll be bound,' Rowan said severely. But with a small glow inside she knew it was only for her. It took only a few seconds and then he swung down again, as lithe as a lad scrumping apples, and pushed something small into his pocket.

Penny was looking somewhat pale when Rowan hurried in, trying to keep the grin off her face. She was more composed than Rowan would have expected after having been singled out by Lord Danescroft quite so conspicuously.

'Well?' Rowan demanded, whisking round her, untying bonnet strings and shaking out her cloak. 'Were you able to put him off?'

'Put him—? Oh, the tale about wagering. I tried, and he laughed and said he would wager on how many times Godmama dropped her prayer book, if I liked.'

'He laughed?' That was bad news. 'I thought you said he never smiled?'

'I know.' Penny bit her lip. 'I don't think he has been put off me.'

'Oh dear. Well, do not despair. Mr Lucas, his valet, and I are trying to think of things, but it is very hard without inventing something so frightful about you that no one would believe it, or that would ruin you utterly if it was true.'

'It is very good of you to associate with him just to help me,' Penny said, standing meekly while Rowan unbuttoned her morning dress and lifted it over her head.

Rowan paused, dress in hand, and regarded her friend through narrowed eyes. 'Penelope Maylin, are you teasing me?'

'A bit,' Penny admitted with the ghost of a smile. 'Mr Lucas is very good-looking.'

'Well, that makes two of you who think so,' Rowan said tartly. 'And for goodness' sake, Penny—as if I'd flirt with a valet!'

'I expect you would for my sake,' Penny said loyally.

'He has been in the West Indies as some kind of estates manager.' Rowan took out all three afternoon dresses and scrutinised them. 'I don't think he is really a valet at all.'

'What about the amber one?' Penny asked. 'I can wear it with the kid slippers and the paisley shawl Stepmama lent me.' They lifted it over her head and she emerged, shaking out her hair. 'Perhaps Lucas is a Bow Street Runner, employed to discover the real murderer?'

'At a house party?' Rowan asked sceptically, wondering distractedly if it was better or worse to be attracted to a Runner rather than a valet.

Penny looked downcast at this reception of her theory, and they brooded silently while Rowan found the slippers and Penny sat at the dressing table and began to brush her hair. 'Do you think it looks better down?' she asked after a few minutes, twisting ringlets round her fingers.

Rowan studied the reflection in the mirror. 'It does, actually. In fact it suits you very well. But we cannot do it that way—the last thing you want is for him to find you attractive.'

'No, I suppose not.'

Rowan took over the brush and concentrated on piling Penny's hair up into her usual arrangement.

'I might wear it like that at the ball, though. How will you dress your hair?'

'I'm not going to any ball, silly.'

'There's the Servants' Ball. Miranda Fortescue says

they always have one at Tollesbury Court. Lord
Fortescue lights the great Yule log in the hall on
Christmas morning, then the family all go over to Lady
Fortescue's family at Deddington Manor a few miles
away, to spend the whole of Christmas Day, and the
servants have a proper ball in the evening. Lord
Fortescue even hires in waiters, so the footmen and
butler can join in. And then on the twenty-sixth the
Fortescues have a St Stephen's Day Ball here and invite
all the neighbouring families.'

'Well, I haven't got a thing with me, and you haven't
got a second-best ball gown I can borrow.' Just for a
second Rowan had seen an image of herself dancing
with Lucas, the expression on his face when he saw her
in all her finery…

'But your things are just down at the inn in the
village, aren't they?' Penny demanded. 'Along with
Alice and Kate.'

'Of course!' Rowan pushed in the last hair pin. 'How
on earth could I have forgotten? And there I was
fretting about how to get that red wine stain out of the
cuff of your white organza while all the time we have
our own highly accomplished dressers just down the
road. It is very remiss of me. I do hope they are comfortable there.'

'Well, it seemed a good inn when we dropped them
off with your luggage,' Penny said, slipping a plain gold
bangle over her hand. 'And Dorritt and the carriage
have gone back there—he would be sure to come and

let us know if it was not respectable. It would be good
if they can do something about that stain.'

'I'll walk down tomorrow, taking a basket, and see
what they can do with it. If I take a big basket I can bring
something back to wear at the Servants' Ball.'

'A very big basket,' Penny observed, pinching her
cheeks to get some colour up. 'There's the gown and
your petticoats, and silk stockings and slippers, and a
shawl and some hair ornaments and jewellery…'

'Nothing too fancy—and not jewellery,' Rowan said.
'This is the Servants' Ball, don't forget.'

'You will look lovely, and your Bow Street Runner
will lose his heart to you.'

'Don't joke about it,' Rowan said, with more force
than she'd intended. Penny blinked in surprise at her
tone. 'Sorry. But really it is too ridiculous. Now,
remember this afternoon to be as insipid as you possibly
can. If we cannot think of anything to shock him at least
let's try and bore him into thinking again.'

'What the hell have you done to that hat?'

Lucas looked at it. It was sodden and the brim was
beginning to buckle. 'Thrown it in a snowdrift a
couple of times.'

'And the state of your trousers and waistcoat! If I
didn't know better I'd think you'd been climbing a tree.'
Will reached for the clothes brush and attacked the
streaks of lichen and bark on his valet's legs.

'I have been. Ow! Give me that.' He finished the job

off himself, only too aware that he was doing it in order to avert his face from his friend's bemused scrutiny.

'Why?' Will demanded, not unreasonably. He went back to paring his nails and looking as relaxed as only a blameless morning in church listening to a soporific sermon could make a man.

'Picking mistletoe.'

'You don't need to pick it. You simply manoeuvre the young lady underneath it.'

'I'm damned if I'm going to freeze in the orchard every time I want a kiss.'

'You'll leave the entire female half of the servants' hall in blind despair when you leave,' his friend remarked.

'Just Miss Daisy. And I doubt if she ever gets into blind despair about anything. She is far too determined.'

'You should not, you know,' Will said reprovingly. 'This is not like you—to get into a serious flirtation with a servant girl.'

'This one's different. She was brought up in a gentleman's household—family by-blow, I've no doubt. It's like being with a girl of our own class, but one with spirit and independence.'

'Makes it worse.' Will tossed aside his knife and put his prayer book in a drawer. 'You'll forget the rules and she'll not know whether you're serious or not. Unless you are going to offer her a *carte blanche*? You haven't got a mistress in keeping at the moment, have you?'

'No.' Lucas felt decidedly snappy. Of course he was not going to offer Daisy a *carte blanche*. Of course he was not going to get any deeper into this than he already was. But there was the sprig of mistletoe in his pocket, and the memory of her curves and warmth and sweetness to make his body ache and his groin tight.

He bent and picked up Will's discarded boots. 'Do you need anything else?'

'No. Thank you. Go and get some luncheon while you can. But, Lucas—what are you going to do about the Servants' Ball?'

'They have one here?'

Will nodded.

'When?'

'Christmas Day. You need to pull back, Lucas, let her down lightly. If the pair of you spend all evening dancing and making sheep's eyes at each other there'll be hell to pay in the morning.'

'I won't hurt her,' he said tightly, wondering if it was himself who was going to get hurt. His mind seemed all too full of Daisy Lawrence for comfort. 'She thinks me an amusing rogue, I believe. She's too bright to fall for my blue eyes, Will.'

And Daisy certainly did not appear to be inclined to pay him much attention when he reached the kitchens. She was patiently helping one of the lads unravel a skein of Cook's knitting wool the stableyard cat had knotted into a tangle while the kitchen maids bustled about them laying the table for the upper staff to eat their luncheon.

'Get along out of here.' It was the under-butler, his arms full of bottles, arguing with someone unseen at the back door. 'There's nothing we want here.' The person outside must have been persuasive, for eventually he turned and called, 'The potter's here with a cartload of stuff if anyone's interested.'

The young women, apparently uninterested in any hawker not selling ribbons and furbelows, turned back to their tasks by the warm fire, but Cook, arms floury to the elbow, and several of the men braved the cold to look.

The potter had a flatbed cart laden with baskets and pulled by a skinny nag. 'Presents for your loves,' he wheedled. 'Fine serving dishes for your table.'

'I want a good big ashet, and nothing that'll chip and crack at the first hot thing that goes on it, either,' Cook said, peering into the biggest basket.

The men went to dig amongst the mugs and bowls, gaily painted with mottoes and flowers.

Idle, Lucas looked over their shoulders, smiling at the naive vigour of some of the decoration. There was a little brownish-green mug, almost the colour of Daisy's eyes. Lucas stretched a long arm and hooked it out, twisting it in his fingers to read the slipware motto. 'I'll take this.' He handed over a few coins, starting a flurry of buying, and went back indoors, asking himself what had possessed him to buy something like this.

'Is there anything interesting?' It was Daisy, right by his side.

'No, just kitchen wares and crude stuff.' The little mug was small enough to slip into his pocket, where it made an inelegant bump.

'Oh.' She turned away to admire Cook's new ashet, and he took the opportunity to slip away to his room to hide it.

Like a lovesick ploughboy with a fairing for his girl, Lucas sneered at himself as he set it on the dresser. On impulse he found the battered sprig of mistletoe in his pocket and dropped it in, then, shaking his head at his own foolishness, ran back downstairs to eat.

CHAPTER SEVEN

December 24th

MONDAY, Christmas Eve, dawned clear and dry, and, with the wind dropped, felt slightly warmer. Rowan left Penny to the tender mercies of Lady Rolesby and went to get dressed for a walk. Penny's godmother had decided that all that was required to convince Lord Danescroft of Penny's eligibility was to hear her play the piano and sing and, with only one day to practise, had borne her off to the music room.

There was nothing Rowan could do to help—Penny played well enough, if rather stiffly, and her singing voice was sweet, but never raised above a terrified whisper in company. She normally made herself highly popular by volunteering as an accompanist to more confident singers or by playing at small dancing parties. A recital by her would only captivate Lord Danescroft if she was sitting on his lap so he might hear it.

Smiling at that improbable image, Rowan picked her way down the rutted lane to the hamlet of Tollesbury Parva, where the biggest building was the Lion and Unicorn, a coaching inn on the toll road. Many of the guests had left their carriages, horses and grooms there, to relieve the pressure on the big house. When they had set out on the journey Penny had left with her dresser, Kate Jessop, in the family carriage. A few miles along the road, well clear of her stepmother's beady gaze, they had been joined by Rowan in her hired chaise with Alice Loveday and all her trunks.

The dressers, the Maylins' coachman and the groom were now ensconced in three rooms in the inn with Rowan's luggage, looking forward to several days' holiday from their usual duties with all the activity of the inn for entertainment.

The four were sitting in the bigger chamber, playing cards with a pile of broken spills for stakes, when Rowan walked in. The men effaced themselves while Kate and Alice swept the cards off the table and pulled the bell for tea.

In answer to Rowan's concerned questions they were adamant that they were comfortable and happy, but were much more eager to talk about Penny and Rowan than their own situation.

'How are you getting on, my lady?'

'Well enough, Alice. I haven't disgraced your teaching yet I don't think, and Miss Penelope is very patient. But I've brought you this—Miss Penelope's organza. I can't seem to get the wine stain out—and I need something to wear for the Servants' Ball tomorrow.'

Kate tutted over the mark and bustled off downstairs to borrow something from the kitchens that she swore was a sovereign remedy, while Alice dragged out trunks and threw back the lids.

'How about your second-best cream silk?'

'Too fancy, don't you think?' Rowan eyed the thick lace trimming doubtfully.

'Probably. And there isn't time to get a plainer lace to fit this deep vee neck.' Alice folded it back and dug deeper. 'Here! There's the bronze-green silk that has that stain near the hem we can't identify and nothing will shift. It isn't terribly obvious, and it could well be the sort of thing a mistress would pass on to a dresser.'

'Excellent. And the brown kid slippers, because I wouldn't be able to afford the ones we had made to match it, and the cream kid gloves that have been cleaned a lot. Miss Penelope can help with my hair.'

Alice began to sort out the linen needed to go under the gown while Rowan rummaged in the box containing her simpler jewellery. 'This comb, the amber ear drops and this lace-trimmed handkerchief. Perfect.'

Warmed by the tea, and the knowledge that their staff were happily settled, Rowan pulled her scarf up over her nose and trudged off, basket over her arm.

'Hello. Have you sneaked out for a mug of huckle my buff?'

Rowan jumped, dropped the basket and made a

wild grab at the handle before the contents fell out on the ground. 'A *what?* Look what you have made me do, Lucas.'

'Hot beer, egg and brandy,' he explained, removing the basket from her grasp and hooking it over his arm.

'Certainly not. It sounds disgusting. Although I assume that is why *you* are here. Miss Maylin's groom and carriage are at the inn and I came down to get some things that had been left by mistake.'

'I haven't touched a drop. Smell my breath.' He leaned invitingly close. Rowan pursed her lips and resisted the temptation to meet his. 'See—no spirits. I came to check on my...on Lord Danescroft's horses and grooms and to get some fresh air.'

'I can manage the basket.' Rowan eyed him uneasily. She had half convinced herself in the course of a decidedly restless night that it was only the novelty of such unchaperoned freedom that was making her light-headed enough to flirt with Lucas, and that if she avoided him she would soon feel her old self again.

'I am going back. It is too heavy for you.' He set off up the lane, leaving Rowan glaring at his retreating back. She picked up her skirts and ran to catch him up.

'You are bossy.'

'So are you.'

For some reason this made her smile. They walked on in amicable silence, Lucas swinging the basket, Rowan hopping over frozen puddles. The lane went down a slight slope, then levelled out. Heavy, wide-wheeled farm carts had cut deep ruts that had filled with water and now made long, parallel ribbons of ice, perhaps eighteen inches wide apiece.

Lucas set the basket down on a tree stump, took a run, and slid down one shining length of ice, arms flailing to keep his balance. When he got to the end he turned, took another run and did the same thing, arriving back, grinning, in front of her. 'Sorry—couldn't resist that. It has been a long time since I have seen ice.'

One thing two winters in Vienna had done for Rowan was to teach her how to skate. She held out her gloved right hand to him. 'One, two, three!'

It was a ragged start: she tried to lengthen her stride to match him; he shortened his. They were already laughing when their feet hit the ice, and Rowan was screaming with a mixture of delight and terror as they skidded down the icy ruts. There was no room to move their feet. The only way to balance was by waving their arms about, and they staggered off at the end, breathless and whooping with laughter.

Lucas pulled Rowan into his arms and they clung together, shoulders shaking, as their mirth subsided. It left them standing there, locked together, tears glistening in their eyes and suddenly in no mood to laugh, only to stare. She seemed to be drowning in the blue of his eyes; he seemed no more willing to unlock his gaze from hers. Something was happening. No, something *had* happened. Something wonderful…and dreadful.

Slowly she raised her hand, clumsy in its thick

woollen glove, and stroked it down his cheek. He turned his face into it, the strong jawbone rubbing along her fingers, then he caught the tips in his teeth and dragged the glove off. The air was cold, but his mouth, as he pressed it into her palm, was hot.

His hat had fallen off again. She stared down at the dark head, bent so intently over her hand. The exposed nape, the vulnerable softness of the skin at the base of his skull, the virile curl of the hair there, the strength of the muscle. So male, so strong, so gentle. Something inside was hurting, as though pressure was building in her chest.

'Lucas?' She hadn't meant to whisper, but that was how it came out. But he heard it and looked up, and she wondered that the word *gentle* had occurred to her for a moment. The blue eyes blazed, his face was hard with something that reflected the baffling pain inside her, and his mouth when he pulled her hard into his arms and kissed her was savage.

She needed it. Gentleness would have made her cry. Rowan kissed him back without inhibition and the pain dissolved into something dark and urgent and—

'Come on, bor! You going to stand there all day, rutting with that there wench?' The thickly accented bellow brought them apart as effectively as a bucket of cold water thrown over fighting cats. Rowan caught a glimpse of a red-faced yokel perched up on the box of a wide farm wagon, two shaggy horses steaming patiently in the shafts.

With a gasp of mortification she turned her back. Lucas

stepped onto the verge, drawing her with him, feet crunch-
ing in the snow. 'Sorry to keep you waiting, friend.'

'Ah, well, bor, you needs be doing your courting
inside this weather. Fine wench like that'll soon warm
you up,' the carter advised cheerfully as the wagon
trundled past, shattering the ice on their impromptu
skating rink.

'Oh!' Rowan emerged red-faced and flustered from
the shelter of Lucas's shoulder.

He looked at her for a long moment, then went back
for the basket. 'This won't do, will it?' he observed as he
rejoined her and they began to walk on to Tollesbury Court.

'No,' Rowan agreed bleakly.

'Tomorrow is Christmas Day and the Servants' Ball.
We will talk after that.'

'Not now?' They had reached the gates; soon there
would be precious little privacy.

'Do you believe in magic, Daisy?' Lucas was looking
away from her, out across the frigidly still parkland.

'No.' She shook her head.

'Neither do I. But let's pretend, until tomorrow at
midnight, that magic does exist—for us.'

Common sense said *End it now*. The warning voice
inside her agreed. *You'll get hurt*. Rowan listened to
them, to the voices of duty and reality. *But I am going
to be hurt anyway—better tomorrow than today*, she
thought defiantly. *I love him and it is quite impossible.*

'Until the stroke of midnight on Christmas night,
then I believe in magic.'

'Give me your arm. No one can object with this slippery surface.'

They walked in silence. What Lucas's thoughts were she could not guess, but her own, circling, came up with a bump against a mystery.

I know it is hopeless, because I'm not really a dresser and I could not possibly marry a valet. But why does he think it won't do? Oh my God—he is married.

'Are you married?' Rowan demanded, stopping dead outside the kitchen door.

'No!'

'All right. I just wanted to be sure.' She took the basket from his grip while he was still staring at her and went inside, exchanging greetings with the kitchen maids and Cook as she hurried past.

I know this won't do. The Viscount Stoneley cannot marry a servant—even one with illegitimate blue blood in her veins, even one raised gently. But how does she know? Lucas was frowning over the conundrum as he let himself into Will's bedchamber. His friend was sitting in the window seat, gazing out idly, a book in his lap.

'Not downstairs socializing, Will?'

'Thinking. I can't get a moment to myself down there. If I'm talking to Miss Maylin, Grandmother is hovering, hanging on every word. If I'm not, she's at my elbow trying to get me back.'

'Maddening. Still, you are seeing enough of the girl to convince yourself she won't do, I imagine?'

'She is terrified of me.' Will dropped the book on the floor and swung both feet up onto the window seat, leaning forward to rest his folded arms on his knees and presenting Lucas with the uncommunicative barrier of his shoulders.

'You see—impossible for a countess. The girl's a mouse.'

'A very sweet mouse, and a very kind one. She would be wonderful with Louisa.'

'Do you want a woman who is frightened of you? Of the life you must lead?'

'No. But—'

'I'm sure she would make a wonderful governess, but that is not what you need. You need a Society hostess and an exciting woman in your bed to give you sons.'

'God! Do you not think I have had enough of exciting women? One was enough.'

'You need one who loves you.' Lucas stayed where he was, wondering, with a flash of pain, who he was arguing with.

'I loved Belle. You have no idea what it is like to love and to lose, Lucas. None.'

'Oh, yes, I have.' But he said it too quietly for Will to hear, turning his back to begin laying out his evening clothes.

'How did the music go?' Rowan asked.

Penny shrugged. 'As usual. I played adequately.'

'And the singing?'

'I whispered—as usual.' She fidgeted with her reticule, finally tipping it out on the bed and sorting through the spill of trifles. Rowan tried to study her expression, but Penny would not meet her eyes. 'How are Alice and Kate? And Dorritt and Charles, of course.'

'Very comfortable, and enjoying their holiday. See—your organza is clean again.' It had taken three more rinses, and then careful pressing with warm irons, but now it was perfect again. The manual work had allowed her to think in rather more tranquillity about Lucas. Because of the mystery surrounding Lady Danescroft it was easy to see mysteries everywhere. Lucas simply did not want to become entangled with a woman. He could tell she was falling…no, *becoming attached*. That was all he could see, surely? He could see this, and was acting to let her know it was going no further than a flirtation.

As Penny admired the dress Rowan let her mind wander back to him. It was her duty to marry well. Sooner or later she was going to find a man, a suitable gentleman, of whom Papa approved and whom she could respect enough to marry. She did not have to love him. Many people would say it was desirable that she did not. And in her heart she would hold the image of the man she did love. So impossibly.

'Did you say something?' Penny looked up.

'What? No. A hiccup, that was all.'

She would go to the ball and have her magical evening with Lucas. And then, like Cinderella, it would all vanish at midnight. Only she would leave her heart behind with him, not her slipper.

'Rowan?' Penny was watching her, frowning. 'You look sad. What is wrong?'

'Nothing.' She forced a smile.

'You are tired, and bored with this, I am sure. I do appreciate you being here, you know.'

'How is it with Lord Danescroft? Honestly?'

'I wish I was not so shy.' Penny looked down at her hands, clasped tightly together. 'I wish I had the courage to speak out about what I truly want.'

'It's the rest of your life, Penny. You must tell the truth about how you feel. I can't help you. I realise that now. There is nothing about Lord Danescroft that your father could possibly object to, and I truly believe he is innocent of everything except making a very poor choice of first wife.'

'Yes.' Penny drew in a deep breath. 'I will do my best. Now, what are you going to wear tomorrow night?'

CHAPTER EIGHT

December 25th

'LADIES and gentlemen, Miss Daisy Lawrence!'

Rowan paused at the top of the ballroom stairs and blinked. The room was thronged with the indoor staff of the big house, the outdoor staff, estate workers and the tradespeople and professional men who serviced Tollesbury Court. Those who were married had brought their spouses and their adult children. It was almost as hectic a crush as a Society ball: the noise level was certainly as great.

But the guests were decidedly different, she realised as she began to descend. There were the upper servants, dressed as she was in the good-quality discards of their masters and mistresses, well groomed, assured in their setting. There were the lower indoor staff, more plainly dressed, awkwardly on their best behaviour, but comfortable in a room they knew.

Then there were the outdoor staff, red of face and decidedly weather-beaten, stiff and proud in their Sunday best. Mingling with them were the tradesmen and their families, the doctor and the curate, the banker's agent and the shopkeepers, their respective prosperity and standing accurately reflected in the gloss of the ladies' dress fabrics and the cut of the men's coats.

Lord Fortescue had done them proud. A string band was playing on the rostrum, hired footmen circulated with laden trays of wines and cordials, and the hot-houses had yielded up some of their precious blooms to make the evergreen arrangements glow in the candle-light. On her visits to the kitchen, nervously checking to make sure she did not bump into Lucas, Rowan had seen Cook ordering about a battalion of hired staff to produce a lavish supper.

Now Cook herself, magnificent in deep green bombazine and a turban, was holding court halfway down the room. The prevailing fashion for high waists and low-cut necklines could hardly be said to be flattering to her, but Rowan considered that she had seen less impressive dowager duchesses.

'Miss Daisy?' It was Mr Philpott, nervous in high collar and slightly shiny suit. 'I expect all your dances are taken already.'

'Why, no—none are. I have just come down.' Rowan opened her dance card and showed its clean pages.

She circulated, chatting, her card filling slowly but surely. Where was Lucas? Had he decided after all that this was a mistake? It was becoming hard to maintain her poise and her smile and to focus on whoever she was speaking to, not look over their shoulder for a glimpse of a dark head and elegant back.

She was exchanging polite, if barbed compliments with some of the other dressers, whose sharp eyes had seen the mark on her hem and were smug as a result of it, when she felt a touch at the nape of her neck—as tangible as though he had laid his fingers there. Lucas was watching her.

'Miss Lawrence. May I hope your card is not filled?'

'Mr Lucas.' Her curtsey was shallow, the graceful acknowledgement of a gentleman who was her equal. She was aware of Miss Browne's raised eyebrows, but ignored it. Another few days and she would never see these women again. Provided she did nothing to bring opprobrium upon Penny, she did not care what they thought. She lifted her wrist so he could write in the card against whichever of the four remaining sets he chose. When she looked down she saw the bold 'L' against every one—including the supper dances.

It was shocking—or it would be if this was a London Society ball, or Almack's, or anywhere else Lady Rowan Chilcourt frequented. But this was a ball out of place and out of time. A magic ball: the rules did not apply to her. She let the little card drop on its wrist cord and smiled. 'The second set, then Mr Lucas. I look forward to it.'

With a bow he was gone, leaving her to the mercy of Miss Browne and her colleagues. 'You *have* made an impression there, Miss Lawrence. Are you looking ahead to when your mistress and his master are married?'

Rowan laughed lightly. 'Goodness, no. But he is the best-looking man in the room, don't you agree?'

They bridled, scandalised by her boldness, but then Miss Pratt giggled. 'He is indeed. Why, we are all jealous.'

Rowan smiled and passed on to meet the head gardener's wife and pretty daughter, both of whom were looking very handsome, with hair well dressed. She felt a pang, wishing she could emulate them.

Lucas's dark looks suited the severity of evening black tailoring and crisp white linen. He was as well groomed and dressed as many gentlemen, whereas she had had to be very wary about her appearance.

Her heart wanted her to look as beautiful as she could for him—to style her hair in the most becoming way, to dress in the silks that best showed off her colouring, to wear her pearls to gleam against her skin. But it was not safe. Soon she was going to have to go back into Society: she had to preserve a distance between Daisy Lawrence, even in her prettiest gown, and Lady Rowan.

She feared she would disappoint him, but the look in his eyes when he came to claim her for the first dance of the set put her mind at rest. A series of vigorous country dances with Mr Philpott had put colour in her cheeks, but she could still blush when he took her hand for the quadrille, murmuring, 'Magic, my lovely.'

The formality of the dance steadied her, and the need to watch out for the less able dancers on the floor distracted her from retreating into a world that held only Lucas. By the end of the set she was composed, confident that she was showing a decorous face to the company.

He yielded her hand to the curate for another set of country dances and strolled away. She managed to follow him with her eyes under the pretext of paying close attention to the figures of the dance, while all the time maintaining a sprightly conversation with the curate. He was young, cheerful, much given to sporting pursuits and proved a boisterous dance partner. By the time Lucas found her for the first of the set preceding supper she was panting slightly and fanning herself.

'My, it is warm in here! And you look as cool as a cucumber—have you been sitting out?'

'Strolling around and flirting wildly,' he said with a chuckle, taking her hand and sweeping her onto the floor. 'What is it? Did you not realise this was a waltz?'

'No. How very dashing of the Steward to permit it!' She had not expected it. Not expected to have to be in Lucas's arms in front of everyone. Not expected to have to guard her expression and her gestures so very carefully.

'I suggested it would be intolerable provincial of him not to,' Lucas drawled, placing his hand lightly at her waist.

Rowan managed not to draw in her breath, reminding herself she had waltzed with the Duke of Wellington without a qualm.

'After that he obviously felt that the honour of the house was at stake.'

The floor was less crowded than it had been. Many of the lower staff and the men did not know how to perform this dashing and fashionable dance, but all were interested. Rowan felt she was on stage. 'They are staring,' she whispered. 'It is most disconcerting.'

'It is because you are so beautiful,' he replied, not troubling to lower his voice.

Mercifully the band struck up to save her blushes and habit took over. Smiling serenely, as though there was nothing in the slightest unsettling about being held close to a man and swept around the floor in his control, their bodies swooping and gliding, Rowan let her feet follow the steps without conscious thought.

Every instinct, every sense, was focused on the man who held her. He was a good dancer—she had expected it from the way he moved. He led with authority, but without force. And he was close, so very close, and intent on nothing but her. Rowan drowned in his eyes, surrendered to his strength and lived only in that moment.

When the set finished and he led her off the floor she knew she was trembling with desire, dazzled with enchantment and quite hopelessly in love.

'Daisy? Are you all right?' He bent over her as they reached the edge of the floor.

'No,' she answered, meeting his gaze frankly. 'I am not all right. Not at all.'

He knew she was not referring to the heat, nor to any possible over-exertion on the dance floor. 'Would champagne help?'

'It can hardly make it any worse,' she murmured, half joking.

The supper room had been set with small tables, many already filling up with family groups or pairs of friends. Lucas sat her at an empty one, removed all but one other chair, and vanished into the throng. When he returned with two plates, a waiter at his heels with a whole bottle of champagne and glasses, she had emerged from her daze and was uncomfortably aware that her solitary state was attracting attention.

'They are *still* staring.'

'The women are jealous of your looks, the men are hating me.' He shrugged. 'I have acquired the very last lobster patties: please tell me you like them. I had to run the gauntlet of the doctor's wife to get them from under her nose.'

'I love lobster, thank you.' It was a welcome distraction.

'Really? You eat it much?'

Lord! Dressers were hardly likely to acquire a taste for such delicacies. 'Vienna,' she said airily. 'They were two a penny.' He looked sceptical. 'The Congress— such a demand for them, you see.'

'Why is it that you do not trust me, Daisy?'

'I...' He was regarding her steadily over the rim of his glass. She focused on the spiralling bubbles in the straw-coloured liquid. So he knew she was lying about her past. 'I cannot... It is too complicated. It is not all my secret.'

'Is Daisy your real name?'

'No.' She wondered why he smiled and counter-attacked. 'Why do you not trust me? And is Lucas *your* real name?'

'Because it is too complicated, and not all my own secret. And, yes, it is my name.' He picked up a lobster patty and paused with it halfway to his mouth. 'Has the magic gone now we have stopped pretending?'

'No.' She took a morsel and chewed, her brain spinning. What to do? Lucas sat, apparently content to watch her in silence while she swallowed and took a sip of the champagne. She loved him and there was no future for it, whatever he felt—whether he was a valet, an estate manager or a Bow Street Runner. That was clear.

It was almost a relief how clear it was. There was no possibility of agonising about how to get around it, wondering if there was some way to make a miracle happen. They didn't happen. Not even at Christmas. She knew what she had to do.

'I love you,' she said, holding his gaze so that she saw the way his pupils widened until his eyes were almost black, heard the sharp intake of his breath.

'I love you, too.' He said it as clearly and as calmly as she had, and the very simplicity convinced her.

'I cannot marry you,' she added, as though they had been discussing going for a walk.

'Nor I you.'

There was pain there, behind the three simple words. Pain he was not letting show on his face—just as she would not betray the realisation that something inside was cracking open into a scar that would last a lifetime.

'Make love to me.' Rowan was not sure whether it was a question, a plea or a demand. It was only when she had said it that she saw from his face just how shocking her words were.

He leant forward to refill her glass, the action bringing his head close to hers. 'You are a virgin, are you not?' His voice was husky. Desire? Regret? Horror at her suggestion? 'I cannot do it.'

'Yes, I am.' She wondered just how she could hint at her thoughts, and discovered that with Lucas she could simply say the words. 'I have no experience, but it is possible, is it not, to make love without…that?'

As he struggled with the shock Lucas wondered if she knew just what she was asking of him. She was watching his face intently, and although he did not think he had betrayed himself, she read his expression.

'It wasn't fair of me to ask that, was it? It is asking you to exercise a great deal of self-control at a time when you will want to simply follow your instincts.'

'For you, to be with you, a little self-control is nothing.' With a woman he did not love it would be everything. This would be heaven—and hell. 'Even without…that—' her mouth quirked in amusement as he used her own euphemism '—it is very intimate, very intense. Are you sure you want that? Are you sure you will not regret it afterwards?'

'I will not regret it.'

Daisy—he dared not ask her real name—was maintaining a bright, social smile, even nodding and waving to people at other tables.

'All I regret are the things that are keeping us apart.'

They sat in silence for a while, sipping their wine, spinning out the minutes into a memory.

'Do you want to…to go now?' Daisy asked when her glass was empty.

'Yes. But we will dance again.' He wanted to be with her in public, as though she was his for all to acknowledge. He wanted to weave the measures of the dances with her, savouring the fleeting touch of her hand, the little smile as they managed a complex step safely, the aching thrill of the scent of her, warm and feminine, as she brushed against him.

'But you said until midnight,' she protested as they rose.

'I did not know then that you would let me love you,' he said, low against her ear, pretending to free a wisp of hair from her simple earring. 'We have all night, Daisy. All night to make magic.'

He must have danced with hundreds of women in his lifetime, Lucas thought, watching Daisy laughing as she linked hands with the Steward and let herself be spun around as the clock struck twelve. He could recall the faces of none of them. He had fancied himself in love more than once, but he could not remember their names now. He had believed himself strong and above emotional pain, and now he knew he was wrong.

Daisy was still laughing when he took her hands again and swung her out of the set, through into the hallway and up the stairs.

'Lucas,' she protested. 'The front stairs!'

'Only the best for you, my lady,' he teased as they ran up to the first landing and along the corridor to the back stairs, and he wondered why she blushed.

CHAPTER NINE

THE room was in darkness save for the hot glow of the banked fire. Inside the door Lucas released her hand and went to kneel by the hearth to kindle a spill for the candles.

I should be afraid, she thought. *I should be shy and apprehensive. Or at the very least ashamed of myself. But I am not. I love him. I do not know how to pleasure him, but he will show me and I will do it.* Lucas turned his head and looked at her, a long, serious look that turned her bones to water.

'I must sit down. My knees…' She sat on the edge of the narrow bed. Was there room enough for both of them? Yes, if he held her tight. Rowan closed her eyes.

'I have a Christmas present for you.' She opened them and found he was standing there with a small lumpy parcel in his hands. 'It is a trifling thing. Foolish. But when I saw it…'

Rowan reached out and took it. It was surprisingly heavy for its size. She spread back the paper and found a small mug inside, made of glazed earthenware with an uneven verse trailed in cream slip around its curving belly. Smiling at the feel of it in her hands, she tilted it to the light and read:

To Forget and Forgive is a Maxim of Old
Tho I've learnt but one Half of it yet
The Theft of my Heart I can freely Forgive
But the Thief I can Never Forget.

'Oh, Lucas.' It was ridiculous doggerel. Why, then, did it bring a lump to her throat and a shimmer of tears to her eyes? 'Thank you. I might have given it to you and the words would be just as true.' She placed it carefully on the trunk beside the bed and looked at him. 'Come and kiss me. I thought sitting down would stop my knees knocking together, but I am still foolishly nervous.'

'Only because this is important.' He tugged his neckcloth loose and shrugged out of coat and waistcoat together, then came and knelt in front of her. 'At any time if you want to stop, to leave, you have only to say.'

Rowan nodded. She might be innocent of a man's embraces, but she had picked up much about what actually happened, and she knew that for a man, once launched on this particular activity, stopping suddenly was not an easy or pleasant thing.

Then he kissed her, and she ceased to worry about whether he could or should stop—or about anything at all. There was only Lucas and his heat and his strength, and the edge of fear and the knowledge of safety and the scent of aroused man in her nostrils.

It was not a particularly easy dress to unfasten, but he had managed it without her realizing. His big hand was cupping her right breast, warm through the thin shift, and the silk was pooling around her hips. She moaned as his other hand slid down, under her, lifting so that he could tug the gown free, and she was clinging to him, only her undergarments and his shirt between her breast and his chest.

He had not stopped kissing her, his mouth hot and excitingly moist and arrogantly demanding. She thought hazily that if she wanted to stop she would have to box his ears to gain his attention, for he seemed intent on nothing more than reducing her to a quivering puddle on the bed.

Rowan found she could squeeze a hand between their bodies and found buttons, dragging his shirt open until her hand could slide inside against skin that was silk over muscle. She explored, fascinated, aroused, until with a growl he brought her down onto the bed beneath his weight, his fingers teasing her nipples until she gasped for mercy against his mouth.

'Too much?' Lucas raised his head and looked down at her.

'Yes… No. I just need to touch you.' He shrugged out of his shirt and she lay and looked at the firelight on his skin. It seemed to hold the remnants of the golden tan it must have had a few months ago—or perhaps her love gilded her sight. 'Take everything off,' she asked, greedy for him.

'I had planned to be more discreet,' he said, getting to his feet, his hands at the fastening of his silk evening breeches. He stripped without bravado and without any apparent shyness, standing there as though waiting for her reaction before touching her again.

'Oh.' *He is beautiful. And frightening.* Part of her wanted him inside her. Part was grateful he would not be. She had not realised that men were quite so…so… At least he seemed to find her arousing. To hide her confusion Rowan tugged her petticoat and shift over her head, then bent up her knees and wrapped her arms around them. That felt…safe. She was not sure what to do about her stockings.

'You are a lovely woman,' Lucas said slowly. 'But that is not what I love about you. I love you and your courage and your grace and your fierce loyalty and your humour. And your eyes and your skin, and how I imagine it will feel when I loose your hair, and your scent.'

He was sitting on the end of the bed now, and it was apparent he knew exactly what to do about her stockings. They were rolled down, snagging now and again against the skin of his strong rider's hands, then they were off and those hands were smoothing down the curve of her calves, up to her knees. 'Lie back, sweetheart.'

She swallowed hard, but obeyed, almost soothed by his gentling hands, still quivering in anticipation. She knew where this was leading, but Lucas did not seem to be in any hurry to get there. Up the outside of her thighs to the curve of her hip, down to the soft skin behind her knees, up again, until she relaxed and her legs became limp. The next smooth stroke brought his palm to cup the hot, moist triangle of hair and his fingers slid in to touch her, stroke her.

Rowan arched against the pressure, gasped, and one finger slid deeper, just where she was aching the most, just inside, and she cried out as the world spun and shattered.

She came to, to find herself full-length against him, cradled so that she could hear his heart under her cheek. 'I'm sorry.'

'Sorry? Have you any idea how flattering it is that I touch you and it has that effect?' His voice rumbled in her ear and his breath stirred her hair.

'No.' She felt bonelessly heavy, and yet something was stirring again where he had touched her. Her breasts were aching and she wanted to move against him.

'Believe me.' Lucas's hand was moving again, down over her flank.

Bold, she moved her own hand from his chest, her fingertips riffling through the crisp hair down to his navel, finding an intriguing trail of coarser hair to follow.

'Ah.' He sighed as she found the hard, unsatisfied length of him, her fingertips tentative as she stroked the unexpectedly soft skin.

'Show me how.'

He did not speak, simply took her hand and wrapped

it firmly around, moving it within his own until she found a rhythm. It was powerfully erotic, feeling a man react to her touch, feeling the elemental sexuality of him, the heat, the shifting of their bodies together, the tantalising caress of his hands as they shifted their position so that he could pleasure her, too.

The power of his climax, his gasp of release, her own shuddering pleasure swept her away utterly. She had no idea where she was, only with whom, only that they loved. Only, finally, that they slept.

December 26th

'Sweetheart, wake up.' Lucas's mouth was close to her ear, his breath warm.

'No.' Rowan snuggled closer, denying his efforts to pull the covers down. He was warm and comfortable and all hers, and she was *not* going to be dislodged from this blissful dream.

She heard a muffled snort of laughter, then he slid out of bed. There was a brief tug of war while she lay there, bedding gripped in her fists, eyes tight closed, then he seemed to give up.

'Come back to bed,' she mumbled. He was moving about. Rowan cracked open one lid and found the room almost dark. Lucas, in his shirt, had lit one candle and was pulling on his breeches. 'It is too early yet.'

'It is four o'clock. You must get back to bed.' Rowan dragged the sheets over her head, then yelped in protest as he picked her up, bedding and all, her clothes tangled on top. 'My love, all the magic has run out. It is the morning.'

'I love you.' She lay still in his arms as he shouldered the door wide and carried her out.

'I know. I know, my love.'

He carried her along the corridors, up the steep, winding stairs to her turret, and laid her on her own bed. 'Sweetheart, this is goodbye. I will not see you again.'

'You are leaving?' She struggled up in the nest of bedding until she was sitting, trying to see him in the faint light.

'After the ball—after Lord Danescroft has retired for the night.'

'Then there is all of today, tonight—'

'Do you think I am made of iron?' he asked harshly. 'Are you? Can you do this again? I thought I could. I thought I could spend a day and a night with you, knowing it was the end. But I find I do not have the courage for a lingering death. Let us make it a clean break. Goodbye, my love. Be happy.' He bent and kissed her—swiftly, hard, with an anger she knew was for himself.

The door closed with a click. She heard his heels clattering briefly on the stone steps, then silence. Rowan turned her face into the pillow and lay, dry-eyed, waiting for morning and the rest of her life.

'Was the ball lovely?' Penny's smile was over-bright, her movements lacking her usual slightly dreamy grace.

'The… Oh, yes. Delightful. Most entertaining, and really surprisingly lavish and sophisticated.' Rowan managed to inject creditable enthusiasm into her tone as she bustled around her friend, helping her out of her travelling clothes.

'Only you look rather strained.' Penny tossed her muff onto the chest of drawers and sat down at the dressing table to whisk a hare's foot over her nose and cheeks.

'It was a late night. And then I was too excited to sleep.'

The pain had to ease, surely? In a day or two it would settle down into a perfectly manageable misery, and in the meantime all she had to do was act. Not that that was easy. She had found the little mug outside her door later that morning and had had to go back inside for ten minutes to regain her composure before coming down. It was sitting on her dresser now, waiting for her.

'How was the visit?'

'My singing was every bit as painful as you might expect, but once that was over the rest was very pleasant. The dowager had her grandchildren to stay and they were delightful.'

'Was the singing so very bad? Did your godmother insist you perform in front of everyone?'

'Of course. But Lord Danescroft said he wanted to sing, too, so we sang a duet and he quite drowned me out. Thank goodness.'

'How rude of him.'

'Oh, no, he meant it nicely, for he could see I was

nervous, and he confided that he was sure to be asked so we could get it over with together.'

'I see. So you are thinking more kindly of him now?' Rowan spread out Penny's afternoon dress, even though it seemed tiresome to change, given that she would be retiring for a lie-down at four o'clock in anticipation of the ball.

Penny set down the hare's foot with a snap. 'I am quite decided about Lord Danescroft,' she said, with surprising crispness.

'Well…good.'

Penny got up and tossed aside her wrapper for Rowan to lift the afternoon gown over her head. 'I have made up my mind that you are right,' she announced as her head emerged from the floss-trimmed neck. 'I must speak up and say what I really want, what I feel, and to…*hell* with the consequences.' She went quite pink and looked terrified at her own boldness.

'Excellent,' Rowan said with emphasis. She only hoped that Penny felt better tomorrow than she did. No, it was wrong to think she felt *bad*, exactly: she felt…confused and sad, and her body felt wonderful, and her heart… *Oh, Lucas*.

'So you will?' Penny had obviously been talking for several minutes. She had pinned up her hair without Rowan's help and was putting on her slippers.

'What? Sorry, I was air-dreaming.'

'Come to the ball tonight.' There was a knock at the door. 'Come in!'

Two footmen staggered in, a large trunk between them.

'But that's my—'

'That's the trunk we did not think we would need,' Penny said smoothly, so the men could hear. 'I had it brought up from the inn. Thank you—that will be all.'

'I cannot come to the ball! I'm your dresser.'

'Yes, you can.' Penny threw back the top of the trunk. 'I had the idea yesterday afternoon. When they brought the mail over I pretended I had received a letter from you—the real you—saying you were staying in Tollesbury Magna. Of course everyone made much of the coincidence, and Lady Fortescue said I must write and invite you. So I sent the groom to Alice and Kate instead, and pretended again that you had accepted with delight.'

'But how on earth am I going to get to the ballroom?'

'There's a side staircase—I think left over from the old house before this wing was added. If you go down it there is a passage, and you can slip out into the stable-yard. The carriage will be there for you at ten. You get in, it drives round to the front door, and down you get.'

'Penelope Maylin—what a pack of lies and deception! I had no idea you had it in you.'

'I know. I must say, being wicked is quite refreshing, don't you think? No one will recognise you—not with your hair dressed and all your jewellery and your best gown. Who would expect to?'

Rowan turned and looked at her reflection in the mirror. No, once her hair was freed from this tight, sleek style, and she was wearing her diamonds and her new cream silk gown, quite unlike anything she had been seen in before, no one would recognise that Lady Rowan Chilcourt was Miss Maylin's humble dresser.

Lucas would, of course, but then he would not see her. The valets did not appear downstairs during such events—not like the ladies' maids, who were on hand to deal with fainting misses, torn hems and wilting coiffures. She must take care to avoid the retiring rooms.

'I will do it.' Last night had been an enchanted dream. It was time to stop being Daisy and become Rowan again. Time to forget she was in love and to think of Papa and of finding a suitable alliance with an eligible man. Time to do her duty.

CHAPTER TEN

'LADY ROWAN CHILCOURT!'

It was last night all over again—only now the ballroom glittered not just with silverware and glass, candlelight and crystal, but with the unmistakable gleam and glow of gemstones, silks and satins and silver buttons.

Rowan descended the stairs to the receiving line with grace, her fan held just so, her chin up, her smile perfect.

'My dear Lady Rowan, such a pleasure you could join us.'

'Lady Fortescue, I am so grateful for your invitation. My wretched carriage broke a pole, fortunately not far from a most respectable inn—but I am sure Miss Maylin explained all that. And of course I have my woman with me, and my groom and so forth. But to be stranded over Christmas is dreary indeed—now I feel I have been transported back to London!'

'Your friend Miss Maylin is somewhere here. She will soon introduce you to everyone you do not know.'

Rowan passed down the line, greeting the Fortescue

family, making small talk, until she was able to emerge at the other end and mingle with the throng. The dancing had not yet started, and people were strolling back and forth. Rowan recognised some young women of her own age she had met during her first Season, before Papa had whisked her off to Vienna, and went to reintroduce herself.

'I owe my invitation to Penelope Maylin,' she explained to Miss Anstruther, when that excited damsel had finished recounting the riveting tale of how she had become betrothed to Lord Martinhoe and thought to enquire how Rowan had popped up in the middle of the snowbound countryside. 'I haven't seen her yet.'

'She's here somewhere. I saw her earlier. The poor girl seems to be trying to avoid Lord Danescroft, but then she has been all week,' Lady Fiona Davidson chipped in. 'Have you heard the scandal?'

'Yes, dreadful,' Rowan agreed, wondering if she should find Penny and stick like glue to forestall any approach by his lordship. He might have the idea of making a declaration during the evening. On the other hand Penny seemed very determined to be firm, so perhaps it would be better to get it over with while her resolution held.

A footman—James, the one with a stammer who was sweet on Edith the kitchen maid—came past with a tray of cordials. Rowan took one with an unsmiling inclination of her head and he walked on, oblivious to the fact that he had just served a woman who had teased him about his smartly powdered wig only the day before. She let out a pent-up breath and relaxed a little.

A gentleman joined them, and then another. The group began to ask her questions about Vienna and the Congress, and she relaxed even more. She could do this. She could pretend to be charming and social and gracious, and no one would guess that she was in love and pining for a man she could not have.

'Well, the shops are nothing *but* temptation,' she was saying to Lady Furness. 'My allowance would vanish like snow in sunshine within days of me receiving it! The tailoring is not as good as in London, of course. I still sent home for my riding habits—'

The room shifted and blurred as a dark-headed man passed across her line of sight over her ladyship's shoulder.

'Lady Rowan?'

'I am sorry—a moment's dizziness.' Of course it was not Lucas. Goodness, if she was going to have palpitations every time she saw a tall man with dark hair she would be in a decline within a week.

'Might I have the honour of a dance, Lady Rowan?' Now, which young man was this? Oh, yes—Mr Maxwell. She smiled and nodded, and agreed to the second set, while behind her Lord Furness could be heard greeting someone in his rather over-loud bray.

'Stoneley! They told me you were back from those far-flung estates of yours. Come and be introduced to my daughter and some of the other pretty young ladies and tell us all about your adventures.'

'Unless you count a hurricane, very little that would serve as an adventure I'm afraid, Furness. Not a pirate to be seen.'

The voice was deep, dark and amused. The guard stick of Rowan's fan snapped in her gloved fingers. *I am losing my mind…*

'Now, then—you remember my wife, I'm sure, but you won't have met my daughter Annabelle. And this is Miss Anstruther, and—ah, yes—Lady Rowan, may I present Viscount Stoneley? Stoneley—Lady Rowan Chilcourt.'

She turned, slowly, to confront the man with Lucas's voice, a social smile fixed on her lips. She had heard people say that blood drained from their faces with shock, but she had never believed it until now. It was a physical sensation, an unpleasant one, accompanied by a rushing sound in the head and—

'Wake up. Hell and damnation, Daisy—Lady Rowan—whoever you are, open your eyes.' By sheer force of will he had made them give way to his assertion that he would carry her out to a retiring room and have her dresser summoned immediately. Lady Furness had helped him, shooing the others back, telling them Lady Rowan needed air, that she had seemed faint earlier.

What she would say now, if she could see him with the unconscious woman on a sofa, no chaperon and the door locked, he could scarcely imagine. But he could not risk whatever Daisy said when she came round.

This was insane. Yet he was not delusional, as he had feared for a moment he was. Hating the noise, the social chitchat, the need to remember the tale Will had drummed into him about mistaking the evening and calling to take his friend off to a party, he had acted his way through embarrassed apologies to the Fortescues and finally a graceful acceptance of their pressing invitation to spend the evening.

'Why sit upstairs twiddling your thumbs?' Will had demanded. 'You look thoroughly blue-devilled. Come to the ball. No one will recognise you.'

And, of course, no one did. Well-trained servants did not stare at guests, let alone allow their imaginations to run riot over a passing resemblance between a viscount and a valet. He had thought it was a good idea—that it would stop him thinking about Daisy. But of course all it did was to conjure up visions of last night, of her warm and responsive as they waltzed, hot and passionate as they loved.

And then a slender society lady had turned slowly to face him and he'd thought he had lost his mind. He still did. Perhaps he was feverish and this was all his delirium…

'Lucas?' No, that *was* Daisy.

'Yes.' He knelt by the sofa and took her hand in his. Under his thumb her pulse was beating wildly. 'Yes, it is me. What in heaven's name do you think you are doing? How do you expect to get away with this?'

She opened her eyes, wide and green on his. 'Me?

How do *you* imagine… No. You really are Lord Stoneley, aren't you? Lord Furness knew you.'

'Yes. I really am Lucas Dacre, Viscount Stoneley.' Surely now she would realise why they could not be together? Why his duty demanded he break both their hearts?

But she was smiling—not bravely, but joyously. 'And I really am Lady Rowan Chilcourt. Lucas—why on earth have you been pretending to be Lord Danescroft's valet?'

'To try and persuade him not to marry Miss Maylin. And you?'

'To support her in refusing him, of course.'

Lucas sat back on his heels, trying to accept this miracle, afraid to believe it. 'You understand why I could not—'

'Of course—and why I could not. Oh, Lucas, we've been making ourselves miserable because of honour and duty and what we owe to our families, and all the time we are each other's perfect eligible match!'

'Is that a proposal Lady Rowan?'

'It most certainly is, my lord!'

Yes, it was true. No, he was not hallucinating. His irrepressible, wonderful love was smiling at him from the sofa, her hair half down and her gown disarrayed, and an expression compounded of mischief, love and desire on her face.

'Well,' he drawled, 'I suppose as I have compromised you I had better make an honest woman of you.'

'Could we, do you think, make quite sure of that?'

Rowan reached out to bring his head down to hers. 'Could you perhaps completely ruin me?'

'With pleasure. But not—'

'Lord Stoneley!' The rattle of the door handle had him on his feet and six foot away from the sofa in seconds. 'Are you in there?'

'Hell! Lady Rolesby!' He ran a hand over his hair and went to unlatch the door. 'Ma'am, the door seems to have swung to and the lock engaged. Lady Rowan is much improved. I was just about to ring again for her woman. I cannot imagine what—'

'Penelope is not here?' Lady Rolesby, ignoring Rowan's attempts to straighten her hair and her gown, swept the room with her lorgnette.

'Miss Maylin? No, ma'am, I have not seen Miss Maylin all evening.' Behind him, he heard Rowan getting to her feet.

'I have not seen her at all, Lady Rolesby. Is there some problem?'

'No.' Her ladyship frowned. 'I assumed she would have come to assist you. It is just that I cannot find her.'

'Has Lord Danescroft seen her?' Rowan queried.

'I cannot find my grandson, either. Oh, I wash my hands of them! There is no helping young people these days. And you, young man—you run along at once. Doors shutting by themselves, indeed—do you think I was born yesterday?'

'No, ma'am,' Lucas said with a meekness which earned him a painful rap over the knuckles with her lorgnette.

'Humbug. Go and make yourself useful and find Danescroft. You, too, Lady Rowan. See if you can find Penelope while you are about it.'

'Yes, ma'am,' Rowan said.

She had managed to pin her hair back up with that dexterity that always amazed him in women, and now came to stand by his side, looking, he was amused to see, as if butter would not melt in her mouth.

'I shall expect to see the announcement of your nuptials very soon,' Lady Rolesby said abruptly, making them both jump. 'And if I do not I will have a word with your father, young lady. He is back in Town—without, apparently, any notion of where *you* are. Now, off with you both.'

'Old witch,' Rowan said with a chuckle. 'I nearly expired with embarrassment when she rattled the door handle.' Papa was back! Was it possible to be any happier? He was going to love his son-in-law.

Beside her, Lucas snorted with amusement. 'You'd have done more than that if I'd yielded to your blandishments and joined you on the sofa.'

'I suppose you are going to become tiresomely honourable and not lay a finger on me until we are married?' Rowan sighed. It was torture not being able to touch him. She just wanted to stroke him, reassure herself that he was real.

'Of course. I will be a pattern book of respectability. But then, I do not intend having to wait very long. If I go up to Town tomorrow to speak to your father and get a licence, what do you say to a Twelfth Night wedding?'

'Oh, yes!' Rowan tried to realise that this was truly happening—that her utterly unsuitable love was about to become her completely suitable husband. 'Where?'

'Is your Town house open?'

'It can be. St George's Hanover Square, then—?' Rowan broke off. 'Lady Smithers? Yes, thank you, I feel much better now. Something I ate, I think. Quite. Have you by any chance seen Miss Maylin? No?'

They passed on, scanning the room.

'Oh. Lord, where can she have got to?'

Lucas was nodding and chatting, his eyes running over the crowd crammed around the walls now the dancing had begun.

'Where's Will? Never mind your pea-brained friend.'

'She is not pea-brained!' They passed a door leading to the conservatory. 'Let's look in here. She might have escaped for some peace and quiet.'

'May as well. At least I can kiss you in here,' Lucas observed, making cold shivers run deliciously up and down her spine by kissing the nape of her neck as she dodged around a potted palm.

'Shh, there is someone in here already.' She tiptoed forward, conscious of Lucas on her heels, and parted the fronds of a large fern.

A tall, dark man had a young woman locked in his arms, kissing her ruthlessly. She had no chance of escape but hung, tiny and fragile in his arms, as he ravished her mouth. There was no mistaking that gown of blonde lace and pale amber silk. She had fastened it herself that evening.

'Stop it at once, you brute!' Furious, Rowan launched herself out of the shelter of the fern, tugging on Lord Danescroft's sleeve.

'Madam!'

'Rowan!'

'Lucas!' Lord Danescroft pulled himself together first. 'I do not know who you are, ma'am, but my fiancée and I—'

'*Fiancée?* Penny, you do not have to do this—'

'Will, for heaven's sake *think*! This is the rest of your life you are—'

'Stop it—all of you.'

Rowan blinked at her friend. Penny was flushed, but her small round chin was firm and her head was up. Indignation flashed in her eyes.

'I am marrying Lord Danescroft. I love Lord Danescroft. And if anyone else tries to stop me I shall—'

'Penny, my love,' Danescroft said tenderly, 'it is quite all right. Lucas and his friend—I am afraid I do not know her name—have your best interests at heart. They just do not know yet that we love each other.'

'Lucas?' Penny glared at him. 'Your valet? That libertine?'

'Yes, that one. Lucas Dacre, Viscount Stoneley, at your service ma'am,' Lucas said with a bow. 'Will, may I introduce Lady Rowan Chilcourt? Sometime dresser to Miss Maylin under the soubriquet of Daisy Lawrence. And shortly to be my wife.'

'Really? Oh, Rowan!' Penny hurled herself into her friend's arms, knocking her back several paces. 'I love him, you see, and I was determined to tell him, and say that I didn't want to marry him just to be a mother to his daughter and a good, conformable wife, and that if he didn't want a love match then I didn't want him. But he loves me! And is that truly Lord Stoneley?'

Over Penny's shoulder, as she patted her on the back while she shed happy tears into her cream silk, Rowan watched the men gripping hands. Then Will pulled Lucas into an embrace and she saw his face: pure happiness. It was going to be all right. For all of them. But she had to be sure, for Penny's sake.

'Lord Danescroft?'

'Lady Rowan?'

'What is the truth about your wife? It will go no further, I swear.'

'I loved her—she, I discovered, loved many.' His voice was harsh, and Penny pulled out of Rowan's arms and went to wrap her arms around him. he looked down at her, stroking his hand over her mousy hair. 'Lucas had tried to warn me, but I was besotted. Once I discovered that she was happily cuckolding me with a number of gentlemen, I sent her off to my country estate. I thought there would be no temptation: I had not realised she would simply start working her way through the male staff.' He paused, his face stark.

'And she began drinking—gin, mostly. I went away for a couple of days and came home unexpectedly, in the early hours. They were not expecting me, so the front door was bolted. I knew where the back door key was and went round through the kitchens, intending to go up the service stairs. I met her coming down— drunk, fresh from her lover's bed. She saw me, screamed, turned to run and fell. There was nothing I could do.'

'I am so sorry,' Rowan said, drawing a deep breath. They could go on picking over the past, or—

'Penny?'

'Yes?'

'Stop crying, dear. Shall we get married together? St George's Hanover Square on Twelfth Night?'

Lucas and Will came over. Will was holding Penny gently against his shoulder, his other hand on Lucas's shoulder as he grinned at his friend. 'Be my best man?'

'Of course. If you'll be mine.'

'And what is going on in here, might I ask?' It was Lady Rolesby, with what appeared to be half the guests at her heels.

Lord Danescroft looked sheepish, Penny quailed, but Lucas's arm came around Rowan's shoulders and he stepped forward. 'Madam, I have an announcement. We are all going to get married. For Christmas.'

In the ensuing uproar Rowan tipped her head back to smile up at him, and he added in a whisper only she could hear, 'For Christmas. For life. For ever, my love.'